COLT

Joseph Williams

Aidric Publishing

ISBN: 9780692657997

1

It began in darkness. A holo-projector sighed to life on a platform overlooking a deep, shimmering pool.

The Great Colt.

She was more imposing than he'd imagined. Indifferent. Hands crossed behind her back, shallow mouth barely moving even as she began to speak. Her stare burned through his skull as though she were truly standing in front of him rather than a universe away, ready to pass judgment or lend a helping hand.

Like God.

Like Colt.

An indistinct form. A voice. A shadow.

"You are surrounded by microscopic, poisonous creatures. The human body cannot withstand more than twenty-seven seconds among them, sixteen in a cloud of this concentration. You've already inhaled their toxic breath. A *human* will be dead within ten seconds." Her eyebrows rose slightly. They showed neither malice nor benevolence. They were simply elevated. "You, therefore, must not be human."

He couldn't find the voice to respond. His senses were awash in the emergent spectacle: gaseous shadows illuminated by the wavering twinkle of the hologram over the pool, searing pain as the creatures bit into his esophagus and lungs. The end. Staring down death through a long, lonely corridor. A kaleidoscope of colorful pain reflected in her eyes, and she withdrawn to clinical observation as though she didn't care whether he lived or died. Perhaps she didn't.

I am not human, he thought, scrambling to remember his training. Regulating his breaths the way the Duri Master had taught him high in the mountains on a dark, rainy day that had seemed to last forever.

"You will die because you do not know God."

It was not the accusation he'd expected, but the sacred manual had warned him to be prepared for improvisation. One out of every five Called warriors was dealt a change in the ritual, and evidently, he was that one. He wondered if the designation should be a source of pride or concern.

Pride dwells in the tongue of the dead man.

A nonsensical saying, perhaps, but one which had been sufficiently drilled into his head between the manual and the Duri teachings to be sacred in its own perverse way. It stuck to the roof of his brain like *solta* butter and wouldn't budge no matter how hard he tried to drive it out through meditative exercises.

This is nothing like I expected, he thought futilely, praying that the Great Colt hadn't spotted the hopelessness creeping over his face. *I will die before reaching the end.*

"You will die either way."

Again, she probed his thoughts. Reaching in with hooked fingernails and peeling apart his insecurities to examine on her throne at the end of all realities.

Time was running out.

"There's no such thing as time," she countered.

Another seemingly nonsensical saying that boasted profundity while never quite achieving it. Part of the test. Part of seeing what he was made of and whether he had the intellect to wade through the illusions and archaic chants of his religion to find a greater truth than any living creature had ever known.

I can do this, he reminded himself.

He was one of the Called, after all, a solemn charge awarded to precious few. If he succeeded in the trials, he would inherit the mantle of the most revered warriors in the universe, the enlightened purveyors of Justice and Truth who served the Great Colt in her infinite wisdom.

He would become Hidria.

But for now, he was going to die.

"You must not die," Colt told him. "You must not be human."

Steeling himself, he breathed deeply of the toxins and surrendered his body to helplessness despite the searing pain. Pain, after all, was human, and he could not allow it to take hold of him in this strange new world.

I cannot show weakness.

His blood boiled as the creatures wormed through his veins. A gasp escaped his lips before he could draw it back into his lungs. Yet Colt did not appear behind him with her fiery sword, nor did she stab him through the heart and spit on his corpse as the manual had said she might at the first sign of unworthiness, so he assumed he was still in the running. Still malleable in her estimation.

I am not human, he reminded himself. *I am Hidria.*

The moment the thought entered his mind, the sense of poison in his body faded and ecstasy consumed him as completely as death. The contrast was too overwhelming to effectively process. His brain began to overload.

"You are not human," Colt said firmly. The platform disappeared and he was suddenly kneeling in a thick jungle before a thundering waterfall. The sky was a psychedelic swirl of purples, blues, and greens. The wind blew hair softly across his forehead. "You are Hidria."

Reborn at the hands of the Great Colt.

"Not by *my* hands," she corrected him, "but by your own. By your own, and by God's. Nothing can be done without God."

But I don't know God.

"If you survive, you will. Humans cannot know God, but you are Hidria. You are the Called."

This was entirely different. The landscape shifted beneath him and he was suddenly in deep space with no visible planets or stars and no spacesuit for life-support.

"You will know God or you will die."

The Great Colt appeared before him once again, but her face was now a rotting skull with maggots squirming through her eyes and mouth.

This is how we all must appear, he thought, not knowing why.

A whole new universe had opened to his mind and he needed only to endure this peculiar cosmic suffering to attain it. A trial more terrible than any battlefield or enemy dungeon imagined in the most corrupt minds of the troubled galaxies. A sonic prayer culled from his cries of agony, and the hope that the God of the universe would not turn a blind eye to him in his time of need.

I do not know God.

Eyes bulging. Heart stopping. Skin freezing and sloughing off. Or maybe that was just his imagination. Maybe it was all a trick, an effect of the sacred drugs he'd ingested prior to the Calling. It *felt* real, though. It felt like his soul had been ripped from his body and stuffed into an insidious celestial womb that would inevitably strangle him stillborn.

He would be cleansed. He would be Hidria or he would die.

I cannot die. Hidria do not die.

Suddenly, he was seated before a long stone hallway with a laser sword in his right hand and the severed head of the Evil One in his left. There was no way in or out as far as he could see, only forward.

The trials begin, he thought.

Already, he could hear the murmur of some wretched beast deep within the winding corridors. Already, he felt his constitution shifting within him as though his body were tearing itself apart and rebuilding for a nobler occupation.

To know God and thereby know the universe.

To die and be re-born as the most feared and revered warrior across the galaxies.

To be Hidria.

You must not be human.

He inhaled deeply and allowed his mind to settle into the transformation.

2

The first Watchman appeared before he'd taken ten steps down the hall, and that was sooner than they usually arrived. He already sensed how the stakes had been raised for his trials, and once again, he didn't know whether to feel pride or despair.

Shadows rippled off the turquoise walls, hinting at a liquid luminescence nearby that was otherwise hidden. Another subtle illusion designed to distract him from the truth.

I am not human, he reminded himself. *Distraction is human.*

He clenched his jaw and tried to regulate his breaths, but the sight of the Watchman disturbed him. He supposed that was to be expected. After all, Watchmen were gatekeepers to the afterlife, wraiths who either stole your soul for Tscharia or granted you passage into the Great Unending. Every man and woman feared the Watchman's arrival and prayed for mercy when it came. It was the oldest fear among humans. A fear of death. A fear of eternity.

I am not human.

He held the laser blade in front of him and calmly tossed the severed head of the Evil One down the hallway toward the apparition.

"An offering," he said.

The Duri Masters frowned upon open confrontation with the Watchmen as they were extraordinarily powerful in the dark arts and quick to anger, but he was not afraid. He could not afford to be. Fear was the great death.

Fear cannot exist within the Hidria, Colt's voice assured him. *The Hidria are above fear because they are above death. They are death, as they are life. You cannot fear what already exists within you.*

Circular thought, it seemed to him. Circular teaching. But what was the real message and what was merely the design of the Evil One to distract him?

"A bargain," he continued, forcing his legs to remain steady as he crossed the stones toward the hooded figure. There would be a red mask beneath that hood, he knew. A representation of evil pervading the universe despite the presence of Hidria. In direct enmity to them, in fact. The Hidria existed to oppose the Watchmen and it was likewise said that the Watchmen existed because of the Hidria. The Duri taught that they were one in the same, but the declaration befuddled the warrior. Once he'd told his Duri Master as much, how it was like saying that his weapon and his enemy's weapon were one when they sparked against each other on the battlefield. He'd expected a maddeningly vague response from the Duri Master about how all things are one with each other and eternally angling towards communion, which was the sort of extravagant refuse the Zarlytes fed to the hapless masses, but the answer had surprised him.

"It is more like saying ice is solid, liquid, and gas at once."

Because they were all different states of the same being. Good, evil, and apathetic: the three states of existence according to the Duri.

"Where will you take me?" he asked the Watchman.

Slowly, the hooded figure bent and retrieved the head of the Evil One from the floor, carefully brushing blood and dust from the dead thing's horns. "By the end of this day, you will know the face of the Devil," the Watchman growled deeply. "Not tricks. Not illusions. You will know what it means to have your soul ripped from your body before your eyes. You will see the agony of Tscharia."

The warrior continued forward unabated, flexing his fingers over the hilt of the laser sword and preparing to attack if necessary. "I will know God," he said, drawing the glowing blade over his shoulder for a strike. "I am Hidria."

The Watchman stood to his full, imposing height and roared. Baring his teeth and digging his boots into the cracks between stones for purchase, the warrior drove forward until he skirted striking distance, then leapt into the air and slammed the blade down at the hooded creature.

The Watchman was one step ahead of him, though. Before the laser blade found its target, the abomination fell to the ground and kicked out his right leg with lethal grace.

Should have seen that coming.

The warrior braced for impact.

The blow connected heavily with his sternum, hurling him headfirst to the ceiling before he crashed to the stone floor in a heap. His breath left him again, just as it had when Colt transported him through deep space.

I am not human, he reminded himself as he gasped. *Humans need to breathe, but I am not human.*

He sensed the Watchman's heavy, curled fist bearing down on him before it was visible and spun to his right, driving upward with the laser blade at the same time. Neither blow landed—his nor the Watchman's—but that was all right. If there was one thing the Called approached confidently during the trials, it was combat. The most difficult aspect of the vision-quest involved finding God amid a never-ending labyrinth of illusion, false prophets, and temptation. In comparison, combat was simple and automatic.

As if on cue, a jolt of reflexive, manufactured tranquility shot through his body with such fierce determination that he could hardly move. It was the battle calm, a numbness drilled into each of the Called from the outset of training so they could stare Death in the eye without blinking. This time, however, the shocking serenity that instantly settled his soul far exceeded his considerable combat experience. Exceeded, even, all the Duri Master had taught him on the windswept mountaintop before he'd known his true self.

This was Hidria. This was Colt.

The Watchman roared and lunged forward, clutching at the warrior's throat, but he easily evaded the attack and recovered well enough to jab the end of the sword through the Watchman's stomach. It happened so quickly that the demon set his feet and prepared to strike again before realizing he had been gutted. He growled at the warrior defiantly.

"Tonight, I will see you in Tscharia."

The warrior withdrew his glowing blade and sliced through the demon's neck in one deft motion. Its head fell noisily to the floor, bouncing once off the stone tiles before rolling to a rest against the wall.

"You will never see me in Tscharia," he told the corpse, "because you aren't real."

The words were true—at least, he *believed* they were—but unsatisfying nonetheless, as was the creature's death. The fact remained that he had killed another being, no matter the form it had taken to manifest in the trials, and he was still no closer to knowing God.

"Patience," Colt's voice drifted to him from a shadowed corridor jutting off to the right. "To rebuild, you will need to tear down every aspect of yourself." A wisp of smoke twirled over his shoulder and swept down the hallway, beckoning him onward with sweet-smelling memory. "You are still human."

If he succeeded, he wouldn't be for long.

Hidria, he thought.

As he understood the term, it was a state of being paradoxically superior to humans through its subservience to humanity. A position of no power which necessitated great power. Access to anything and everything one's heart could desire, yet lacking the capacity for desire. An executioner who eschewed violence.

Hidria. God's great paradox.

Not human, he told himself. *I am not human.* He couldn't imagine the words ever being true.

Pressing the switch to retract his blade, the warrior followed Colt's essence down the hall. Distractions enticed him from every wooden doorway they passed; castle chambers lit with blue flames where monsters and abominations dwelled, marble fountains of exquisite beauty overflowing with spiced wine and glacial cascades of honey, patients awaiting appointments with physicians, accountants, or politicians.

All distractions. Irrelevant. Human.

"You still have a long way to go," Colt repeated.

So he followed her without looking back.

3

The warrior had once been a boy named Nurisarma who lived on a planet called Dublokee. Before his extraction, he'd had hazel eyes, black hair shaved to stubble, and arms and legs as thin as the straw he fed blue-maned Trulup horses in his family's stables. The hazel eyes had remained, but his hair and beard had both grown wild while his arms and legs filled out to accommodate the heavy weaponry carried by the Called. After years of Duri training, the boy was unrecognizable even to himself.

For a time, Nuri lived an idyllic childhood in the lush paradise of colorful forests, wide prairies, and rolling mountains surrounding his home. His parents had made a living by caring for indigenous wildlife in the world-spanning animal preserve and they enjoyed the work. Dublokee, after all, was every bit a pleasure planet. It was often referred to as True Eden in advertisements, and given the natural beauty of the landscape, the designation wasn't much of a stretch. In some ways, that made the world an ideal place to set down roots, but it also meant that its people relied heavily on galactic tourism from wealthy politicians and entrepreneurs to survive.

Out of necessity, therefore, it was more than just exotic fauna that gave Dublokee its reputation as a utopian pleasure planet, and it was those 'seedier' elements which eventually drew the eye—and the ire—of the Duri Masters from their seats atop the Blessed Mountain. By the transitive property, Nuri figured, those same elements had led to his abduction. Having caught wind of the gambling and idol worship among the tourists, the Duri Masters journeyed to the planet in the clay colored, cross-shaped vessels of their order and deemed it a corrupted hellhole rife with sin and distraction. A few among them indulged in the nuances of the culture but they quickly left Dublokee and warned the natives—Nuri's parents included—to repent their evil ways or the wrath of God would soon descend upon them.

But the concept of God and damnation wasn't the same on Dublokee as it was in Duri-occupied space. Nuri had never heard of one supreme, omnipotent being that controlled the lives of every creature in every universe for all time. His parents shrugged aside the threats of the Duri Masters and persisted with their daily chores just as they had for as long as Nuri could remember, and, he imagined, long before his arrival.

Months later, however, the Duri Masters made good on their threat. The cross-shaped vessels returned to Dublokee, and once the clergy determined that the people were unrepentant and shamelessly persisted in sin and debauchery, they enlisted the army of Called soldiers at their disposal to cleanse the planet. Lacking a suitable doomsday weapon and at least realizing it was a waste to completely decimate the natural beauty on Dublokee which had no equal, the Called swept through the cities and countryside like a noxious wind. No man, woman, or child was left alive.

Until they found Nurisarma, that is. The moment the Called warriors laid eyes on Nuri, they decided he was different from the other natives. They sensed the presence of the Divine Infinite within him. A *knowing*. Whether he had been raised in sin or not, they knew he was one of the Called like them. When they took him from his home and sent the rest of his family to rot with the Evil One, they called him kin. A few of the Duri Masters who were franker than the rest routinely joked in low mutterings that he'd only been spared for his haunted, lonesome eyes which made him seem much more spiritually engaged than he truly was.

But in the trials, that was inconsequential.

He was one of the Called now, and passing this test meant he would not be condemned to the fate of Justice-Bearing as a failed Hidria recruit. Instead, he would be one of the Chosen. A man who knew God.

Hidria.

Is that what you've always wanted? Colt's voice drifted to him as he followed deeper and deeper into the labyrinthine temple on the edge of eternity.

"It doesn't matter what I want," Nuri recited, recalling the words of the Duri Masters and their denial of free will. "It is my calling. It's why I was spared the corruption of my home world."

Colt said nothing, but that was to be expected. She was not meant to provide definitive answers. She merely forced the Called to question everything in his or her life and then left it to the subject to decide where among those myriad distractions and convoluted histories lay the true seeds of God's calling.

Assuming there actually *was* a Calling, of course. The consensus among the Duri Masters was that if you failed the trials, you had never been truly Called in the first place. You were an impostor, a manifestation of the Evil One among men, and every bit as reviled as the Watchmen. The only true redemption from such disgrace was to serve the Duri Masters in the Called army as Failed Hidria and continue to carry out their will, just like the warriors who had taken Nuri and flown him across the galaxy in a stuffy cargo hold to the Duris' mountaintop monastery. Failure in the trials meant a lifetime enforcing penance on wicked outer colonies. There was no graduation from recruit status.

I'm not like them, he assured himself as Colt led him deeper into the darkness. Already, the luminescent, turquoise ripples lapping against the bottom of the walls had faded behind him. Everywhere he looked, the walls shifted with new life, yet it was still fundamental darkness. A separation from light. The wrong direction, in other words.

Where there is light, there is God, the Duri Masters always said. They never dealt much with darkness other than to condemn it.

"Your thoughts are human thoughts," Colt told him. "Weak. Distracted. If you are human, you will not survive."

I am Hidria, he recited, and as the twists and turns of the corridor began to disorient him and he felt inexplicable panic arise in his chest, he realized he'd never felt further from being Hidria in his life.

"That does not mean you are further from God," Colt said.

"You're wrong," Nuri countered. "The Duri profess that there is no greater distance from God than darkness. It is the utter absence of His presence. God is light. Therefore, darkness is not God. Darkness is the Evil One."

Colt's ethereal mist continued through hallways as they pressed tightly in around him. She maintained a dutiful silence.

For a while, they walked the winding corridors in the same fashion, and the warrior's anxiety grew as the walls narrowed. He could no longer see his feet as he walked. The only light in the stone building was the dim trail cast by Colt's spirit. Every so often, he glimpsed a wooden door beside him again and even sensed movement nearby on more than one occasion, but it was clear by Colt's unfaltering pace that he was meant to follow wherever she led, and that she had no intention of investigating the ancient doorways to other worlds. He wondered idly when they'd last been explored by humans, assuming they'd been explored at all through the millennia in which the trials had been practiced.

At last, the corridor halted at another wooden door and Colt abruptly turned to face him.

"Here," she whispered. "Survive."

"Survival is not the supreme goal of a godly life," Nuri regurgitated. Even his voice mimicked the subtle nuances of his Duri Master's. It was in the monotonous glottal fry that emerged from his throat as dry as any desert on the forsaken worlds. It was the barely concealed threats that resided within any recitation of Duri doctrine.

This is why He made us, Nuri pictured the Duri Master saying. *We are all meant to suffer. We are all meant to reside in His Light. We are not meant to survive.*

Nuri wasn't sure how or why but that particular teaching always made him shudder. It wasn't necessarily the idea that all humans were mortal, but that mortality was a malevolent, calculated suffering which Supreme God held over the heads of each and every sentient creature. The knowledge that they would someday perish in their human bodies while He endured.

Perish?

"Go," Colt told him forcefully. She had assumed full physical form and now glared at him from above. "Evil awaits."

This was something altogether new, as well. Colt was not supposed to warn him of dangers ahead. She wasn't even supposed to guide him along the stone corridors. In his estimation, he wasn't truly supposed to be alive.

Am I special, he wondered, *or a failure?*

He supposed that, in a way, the question resided in the hearts of most spiritualists. They all shared the desire to be recognized as something more than human, and yet only a dozen Hidria were Called from each generation, perhaps less. The Book told him so, though the contradictions therein frequently astounded him.

Nuri approached the door, stepped around Colt's dissipating form, and frowned.

It cannot possibly be me, then, he thought. *I am not holy like the others. I am not Hidria. I am human.*

"If that is what you believe, then you have already failed," Colt told him mournfully.

She disappeared and he was left to contemplate the door ahead.

I haven't failed yet, he thought, *or she would have cut my throat. It's too late now, either way. If I failed right in the beginning, I would have simply become a Justice-Bearer, but once the Called survives the trials as long as I have, he cannot return to an earthly existence. The mind cannot handle the transition. He either dies or lives forever as Hidria.*

But was it a literal death or another kind of death, he wondered? And where did Colt factor into that equation? All he knew of her was legend. Duri texts referred to her alternately as the Hand of God and the Executioner depending on the context. The purveyor of knowledge and discovery, and simultaneously, the oppressor who negotiated the path to Tscharia where the Evil One lived and fed on the damned. Many among the Duri also said that Colt was all things because she was part of the Living God.

Only God Himself is all things.

He pressed his hand softly against the door and stepped through the light onto a snow-capped mountain.

4

Nuri sat on the banks of a mountain river with his legs folded and his sword laid out on the grass beside him. He'd crept away from the cottage that morning as his Duri Master slept, hoping for a short respite from training before the old man sought him out. He would undoubtedly be punished for stealing away without permission and likely end up training well into the night because of it, but in the moment, it seemed an acceptable loss. He rarely got the chance to enjoy the mountain's natural beauty in the daytime.

He skipped rocks until he ran out of suitably flat specimens, then pulled up blades of purple grass and watched the wind blow them from his palm. His mind was blank and that was the way he preferred it to be at the river, where other adolescent boys and girls played once they'd completed their daily chores. In place of the usual work allotted to a boy of seventeen, however, Nuri spent his days not only learning how to decapitate enemy soldiers, but also memorizing the scripture passages explaining why the Divine Infinite would not suffer a heretic to live. Never was the contrast more conspicuous than when he dipped his toes in the river and felt the overwhelming urge to forego his responsibilities for the rest of the day and simply float in the current with his peers.

It's all lies, he thought, frowning, as his hand reached for the hilt of his sword. It was a reflex so ingrained in him that he didn't realize his hand had wandered at all, or that he'd instinctively grabbed for the blade because another presence had emerged along the riverbank.

"It's early in the day for a disciple to dirty his hands," a girl's voice called to him.

Nuri's head shot up, startled. He searched the opposite shore for the source of the sound and spotted a light-haired, fair-skinned girl standing directly in the splintered rays of the rising sun. Her complexion was so pale she appeared almost white in the glare. Nuri had to cover his eyes and squint just to get a good look at her, and even then, her form seemed indistinct, as though she'd been projected onto the riverbank rather than standing there herself. More hologram than real girl.

"It's never too early for silent prayer and reflection on the Divine," he recited, though his thoughts had been occupied by anything but the Divine before she arrived. At least, not directly.

"I hear more of your Duri Master than yourself in those words," she said, cocking an eyebrow.

Nuri didn't respond. He watched her stoop in the cold shallows to draw water from a receptacle which appeared nearly modern in comparison to the rustic aesthetic the Duri had carefully crafted in the village.

"You're not supposed to be on that side of the river," Nuri called to her. When she looked back at him, he nodded toward the rising slopes at her back. "That mountain is forbidden. I thought all villagers knew that."

She grinned and went back to emptying her pail in the hovering, black crate she evidently used to transport the water. "Who says I'm a villager?" She lowered the device into the river, waited for the *ding* alerting her that it was full, then glanced back at him again. "Not everyone in the universe falls under Duri jurisdiction, no matter how arrogant they become."

"It's not *Duri* jurisdiction," he pointed out. "It's God's."

The girl dumped her pail into the black crate again and waded into the river. "Is it?" she asked incredulously. "The

Duri act more like corrupt men than servants of the Peacekeeper."

"Who is the Peacekeeper?" Nuri asked. He'd never heard of such a creature in his studies of scripture or any other religious text.

"God," the girl said. "Omega. Whatever you choose to call Him." She dropped her pail on the riverbank and placed her hands on her hips. "He is a Peacekeeper first and foremost, therefore the aim of all religions that honor God should be peace, as well. Any act of violence against another living creature is destruction of God's creation."

"By that logic," Nuri argued, "we shouldn't raise our hands against our enemies even for survival. Even if they attack us."

"The Duri definition of an attack and the true definition of an attack are two entirely different things. Verbal attacks and dissension do not necessitate a violent response."

Nuri felt himself being drawn into an argument against his will and was stunned by how quickly a stranger had riled him up. He pressed on anyway without knowing why. "Heresy *is* an attack on God. Believers must defend the Divine Infinite from such an attack."

"By destroying the Divine Infinite's creation? That's the absurdity of man. Always driven by rage and testosterone, seeking out wars for ridiculous causes where none should exist."

"Ridiculous causes?" Nuri clenched his fists. "How can you call the Creator of All Things a ridiculous cause?"

She folded her arms across her chest. "The Creator is *not* the reason you kill the innocent. The Duri claim that is the case, but even a cursory assessment of their orders should tell you otherwise. For example, what justification did they give for the last colonial massacre by their Called soldiers?"

Nuri jogged his memory with a furrowed brow. It had been a full two weeks since the last cleansing mission, but they were still frequent enough that it was difficult to keep them straight. "The chairman of the colony had referred to God as 'She' in the daily prayers and refused to acknowledge that it was heresy."

"That *what* was heresy?"

Nuri scoffed. "Calling God a woman, of course."

The girl raised her eyebrows. "*How* is that heresy?"

If Nuri hadn't finally adopted a measure of the composure drilled into him by his Duri Master, his jaw surely would have dropped at the sheer audacity of the question. *Everyone* in Duri-occupied space knew that God was a man. How could she be so foolish? Did she truly not know?

It's the voice of the Evil One, his conscience insisted.

Still, he was intrigued by her apparent dismissal of the obvious heresy, which had been unanimously denounced by the Duri Masters and therefore led to the swiftest cleansing verdict in decades.

"Everyone knows that God is a man," he told her.

The girl shook her head emphatically. "No. He *became* Man when he condescended into this primitive form," she corrected, stretching out her arms to draw attention to her body. Nuri couldn't help noticing the scars revealed on her biceps in the glare of the morning sun but was too outraged by her declaration to comment on them in the moment. "What makes you think the Supreme Creator of the Universe would be confined to one gender? How would one even *identify* God's gender from where we stand in our mortal reality? Does God have genitals dangling between His legs? If so, for what purpose? Urination? Reproduction? Decoration?"

Nuri fumed in silence. He didn't know how to argue the girl's logic because he'd never thought to ask such ridiculous questions and wasn't prepared to debate the issue. He didn't have any theological ammunition from the Duri Masters at his disposal to go on the offensive, and that was the only way he knew how to argue. Defense was a foreign concept to the Duri and the Called. She should have just *known* God was a man and that would have been the end of it. That was the way it had been written in the Old Book *and* the New Book, after all. That was the way it had always been.

The girl wasn't finished, though. "The most powerful entity in the universe, the Beginning and End, the font from which all creation flows, cannot be confined to one gender or even one species. God is All. All creatures. All places. All things. All time."

"Then why did He become a *man* on Earth?" Nuri demanded.

She'll have no response for that, he thought to himself, but a noxious weight continued to spread through his stomach. *Will she?*

"Any fool could answer that," she replied with a sardonic grin. "Because we have free will, and the social constructs of that time would have simply dismissed a woman, if not worse. As oppressed as the gender is now beneath Duri rule, women had even less political influence at the time and place of His coming. If He'd taken feminine form in those days, He would have been stoned as a heretical witch before He had a chance to preach no matter how many miracles He performed. The Divine knows all and therefore does not leave room for accidents. The masculine form was the most obvious and convenient choice, but it does not reflect a preference on His part. We are all His creation from the moment the soul enters the body. Do you truly believe he loves one gender more than the other? And aren't we all a piece of Him?"

"Creator God can do anything. If He truly wished to take female form, He would have done so and simply transformed the culture to accommodate His choice."

"Yet He allows free will, and therefore, though He *could* have changed an entire cultural infrastructure to prove a point, He would not have done so for they are merely human constructs. They do not have any impact on the Divine Realm. And because we have free will. To take female form, it would have been necessary to soften a considerably higher volume of stubborn hearts than was practical." She paused and her stare narrowed. "And, still, that is an oversimplification. There was more to the decision than we can ever know as humans. Or do you believe that man can guess the intentions of the Divine Infinite?"

Again, he found himself biting back a poorly formed response which he knew would only weaken his position. Luckily, or perhaps unluckily, the girl wasn't finished yet.

"Besides, you are focusing on the wrong aspect of the Divine Incarnate's First Coming. By taking male form, you inherently assume that He preferred men to women even if you haven't acknowledged it. That belief is the basis for the political hierarchies within millions of governments and religious institutions. Yet to whom did He entrust His development and birth? To whom did He announce His arrival? Who was the only human creature to physically contain the grace of the Divine inside her womb?" She grinned slyly and drew another step closer, gaining momentum and volume in her speech with each new idea she expressed. "If God can be said to be any gender, would it not be the one that mimics the nurturance and creation of life? Does pregnancy not represent the ultimate sacrifice of giving one's body for the sake of another?" She glared at Nuri. "Tell me, boy, what does *man* do for the Divine but seek power and corporeal satisfaction? Why are there no women among the Duri clergy? Because God abhors women, or because the men empowered by the false teachings of your faith abhor women? Because they resent the weaknesses that women expose in their own commitment?"

Nuri held his breath with considerable effort. He was afraid to speak but knew he had to provide some form of refutation for the sake of his own sanity. The girl had gone too far for her radical heresy to go unchecked, even if he couldn't bring himself to call for help. He swallowed hard and forced a rebuttal, hoping to buy himself some time and traction while awaiting divine inspiration. "Yet, for all your belief that women are the sacred sex and men are nothing but savage beasts obsessed with war and corporeal pleasure, you still refer to God as a 'He' when you speak of His designs."

"True. When dealing with the prejudices of the human faith, one must pander to those predilections or risk complete denial out of shock alone." She smirked at his obvious agitation and softened her tone. "Relax, boy," she chuckled. "I'm not claiming that men and women are anything but equal in our sins. I'm merely pointing out that men fight to put themselves in a position where they sin through a desire to control, and that it is this obsession with the seemingly masculine traits of the Divine like rage, wrath, and a desire for conquest, that has driven generations of religious zealots to unnecessary genocide. If the clergy adopted more traditionally feminine aspects of the Divine and allowed the female voice a place within their dogma, the religious institution would become more balanced. The marriage of feminine and masculine into one body would lead to a dramatic transformation of the Duri faith from a church of the Old Book to a church of the New Book. The union would represent the perfect fulfillment of the Divine Sacrifice.

"But that is only a discussion of politics and religious institutions, not God. God is not the figurehead of a governing body. God is not man or woman. God is God. It makes little difference how you refer to Him. Words offend men and women, not God. But since your people insist on assigning one pronoun or another to the Creation Presence, 'He' works just as well as 'She' or even 'It,' and since God *did* become Man to redeem creation, it is acceptable to refer to Him as such."

"Then why argue at all? Why forfeit your life to prove a point to me?"

The humor vacated her eyes at once and she locked stares with him across the water. The river had never seemed so wide nor so suffocating. "Because you have your doubts, and because you are not yet beyond saving."

Nuri glanced over his shoulder reflexively, searching for any signs of villagers who might have overheard the girl. "You should watch your tongue," he said flatly. "If the Duri or their people hear you, they might cut it out to keep you silent." He added an edge to his voice he didn't truly feel just in case they had an audience. The whole conversation could have been staged, he knew. The Duri often tested Called soldiers to make certain they were pure of faith and ready to defend the order at all costs. Even when the dissenter was a girl the same age as he. Even one who didn't know any better.

"I'm not worried about the Duri," she replied, turning away and tapping the crate so it would follow her back into the forest on the forbidden mountain. "The only being you need to worry about is God, and He doesn't fault those who point out injustice when they see it. It might not hurt for you to do the same." She stopped walking and looked back at him, one eyebrow cocked playfully. Her words belied her lighthearted expression. "After all you've done, it may be the only way to save your soul."

Before Nuri could argue the worthiness of the Duri cause, she disappeared behind the thick line of trees at the foot of the mountain, leaving him to stew over her perceived insults and questions about his faith.

I should report her, he thought, fuming. *I should go straight to my Duri Master and make sure she's punished for the heresy she's spoken out in the open.* Anyone *could have heard her. She's inciting rebellion.*

Her voice followed in his head without skipping a beat. *Are you worried that someone heard me speak it, or that they might have seen you considering my so-called 'heresy?'*

He frowned and craned his neck to spot her through the trees as she returned to whatever nearby—and unknown—settlement she called home. He told himself that it was just so he could give his Duri Master a closer approximation of where she'd hidden to aid in the pursuit and inevitable punishment of the girl for speaking out against God's Holy Order, but deep down, he knew he was only curious because the girl intrigued him in just about every meaningful way a person could be intrigued.

Maybe you're worried because you already know everything I've told you is true, or at least suspect it. If you're not careful, they'll drown the goodness and compassion from you with demands for murder and the tautological arguments of texts they've adapted to suit their needs. If you're strong, you might one day allow yourself to know the truth of Omega and the end of the universe, where all things are made new.

Grabbing his sword, he rose wordlessly from the riverbank and set out for the cottage. He had to give the village a wide berth to avoid being seen before the Duri Master rose, but he didn't mind going the long way this time. It gave him an opportunity to reflect on what the girl had said and the doubts that had crept into his heart. He was worried he'd dismiss the unease in time as he grew more comfortable with the Duri lifestyle and his identity became so entwined with being a Called soldier that he forgot Duri treachery.

Your family was killed by these men, the girl's voice told him. *They kidnapped you and brought you here. They've forced you into a life of servitude. They may pretend you are an esteemed warrior, but you are little more than a cog in the great machine of their Ego.*

Nuri bit his lip and fought the urge to turn and pursue her through the wilderness. He could kill her himself, he thought, and no one would know. The best part was that the killing would be justified. No Duri Master would have listened to her heresy without ordering her public execution. He would truly be doing God's work if he hunted her down and cut off her head.

Instead, he picked his way through the heavy underbrush beyond the village and hiked around to the cottage on the mountainside. His Duri Master was still asleep when he arrived—it had been a long night of spirits and leafing through his forbidden copy of *The Divine Incendiary*—but Nuri knew he would be awake before long.

Still, he wandered into the Duri Master's room with his sword drawn and stood over the scarred, middle-aged man as he snored. He stayed there for a while, contemplating the advantages and disadvantages to killing the Duri Master and then attempting to escape the planet to begin his life anew. To take back what the Duri had stolen from him in the name of a god he'd never heard of prior to his family's slaughter on Dublokee.

If you kill him, you may escape, but you will be doing exactly what he's trained you to do. Remember that the true nature of God is Peacemaker, not Sword-Wielder. Never forget that and you will do His work. Never hesitate to spare a life when it can be spared, and never allow yourself into a situation where a life cannot be spared. Let God alone pass judgment as He sees fit.

The Duri Master finally stirred.

Nuri sighed. His grip on the sword relaxed by degrees. He backed quietly away to his room and closed the door behind him. It wasn't until he collapsed onto his bed that he realized he'd been sweating profusely and his hands were shaking. It wasn't until the Duri Master awoke and yelled for him to fetch eggs and water that he realized just how close he'd come to killing the man.

After that, the girl never left his thoughts entirely, even while the Duri broke his spirit into submission.

5

Nuri knew the cold desolation on the other side of the door immediately, even if it was a planet rarely visited by humans or any other species.

Shehoora, he thought, preparing his laser sword and his blaster rifle for the enemies he knew he would find among the tall trees and rocky cliffs.

Shehoora was a planet of special import to the Evil One. The icy planet was the site of his original temple, which had been constructed long before his banishment from the realm of humans by God and, therefore, long before his captivity in Tscharia. This was where he had forged his legacy through the blood of billions led to torture and slaughter beneath the mountains, where evil creatures older than time lurked in chasms that dropped off into deepest unreality.

This is different, Nuri thought, shivering in the cold. *No trial on record has ever taken place on Shehoora.*

He trudged through the deep snow, grateful at least that he still wore his ceremonial armor save for his helmet, which was forbidden during the trials, anyway. Scanners and projected images were an affront to God's Holy Presence, or so the Duri Masters taught. Nuri wondered how much they'd experienced in the trials themselves or whether the entirety of their knowledge originated in the Divine Revelations of Colt. He further wondered whether any of them had seen Shehoora.

Likely not. It is a bad place.

That much was certain. In fact, he could feel the fundamental derangement of the planet radiating through the snow. The Duri claimed the endless white curtain before him represented God's great purge of the Evil One's stain from the planet. Unspeakable horrors still dwelled beneath the surface in places where the Creator's light could not reach, but the visual effect was impressive enough. Sufficiently fear-inducing and awe-inspiring. All the aims of the Duri Masters, in other words.

Fear is the gateway to human spirituality, his Duri Master had once told him. *Humans can only be made to know God through the catharsis of fear and suffering.*

Nuri shivered.

It was impossible to survive Shehoora for long without a breather. By all rights, he should have been dead already. The frigidity of the planet's surface should have frozen him instantly with so much skin exposed.

I am not human, he reminded himself. *I am Hidria.*

He could think of no greater proof than surviving the frozen wasteland.

We are not meant to survive.

Forcing the contradictory doctrine from his mind, Nuri continued aimlessly through the thigh-high snow. If he were meant to discover a new doorway or to face evil incarnate, it would find him eventually. The natural, guided path of his steps would bring him exactly where he was supposed to be.

That's not always how it works, the voice of his Duri Master reminded him. *Sometimes, you must bring about God's Will for events to occur as pre-ordained.*

It was yet another nonsensical teaching—at least, in Nuri's mind—that he suspected had been designed specifically to muddle his thoughts, but there was no point in pondering the merits of the Duri teachings now that he was committed to their trials. He'd already made his choice and wagered his life upon it. The faith of the Duri was now *his* faith. It was the only true path to God in existence, and that made it the only thing that mattered. The issue of whether free will could ever truly be free as long as God had a plan and knew every choice before it was made was one that had bothered Nuri immensely, primarily because he could not imagine such a glaring oversight from an omnipotent being. More likely, the Divine existed outside of the human conception of space and time. In that sense, he supposed Colt's seemingly ludicrous assertion that there was no such thing as time held some merit for the faithful. Since Nuri existed within those constructs, however, and everything around him was likewise stuck on a linear progression, he was incapable of imagining anything different.

Focus, he told himself, *or nothing will matter one way or the other. You'll be dead. Rotting in Tscharia.*

Indeed, the cold had already worked its way into his blood. He could barely move his legs, and not just because the snow drifts were so tall that he could not properly discern his proximity to the surface of the mountain. Hidria or no, *trials* or no, he sensed hypothermia licking its chops, ready to devour him.

Why am I here? he wondered, hoping Colt would catch his train of thought and provide some form of response. But, of course, Colt's role was not to provide answers. She was there to challenge him, to question his faith, his humanity, his dedication. His worthiness, in other words. If he needed assistance during the trials, he could only look within for a solution. Wasn't that the whole point, after all?

Evil awaits, she had told him. Perhaps he would be better served focusing on her premonitions—or rather, prophecies, as the Duri would have called them, although Nuri wasn't sure the term applied. She was in complete control over where she led him and which doors he opened.

The question, then, was what evil still dwelled on Shehoora? Should he be searching for the ancient temple of the Evil One where the root of all treachery had spawned, or was there a more immediate and obvious threat he would encounter beforehand?

If I don't find out soon, I'll die anyway.

A human *will die*, Colt corrected him. *Humans do not know God. You must be Hidria.*

Clenching his teeth to keep them from chattering as well as to stave his tongue from directing blasphemy toward the Hand of God for her redundancy, Nuri stopped walking and took a deep, frigid breath. He covered his eyes with his forearm and searched the landscape stretching beneath him.

Shehoora was beautiful in its own way. Majestic, really, if viewed from orbit or on a holo-display. Experiencing it was another thing altogether, yet if he just separated himself from worldly concerns—or bodily concerns, as it were—he assumed he could successfully appreciate the aesthetic beauty.

What is the lesson here, then? he wondered, allowing his gaze to wander over the forests and mountains and snowbanks. *Is it that even evil has its beauty? That evil can be alluring if we dwell on it for too long? That true Hidria don't feel the elements but instead appreciate the world around them, regardless of circumstance?*

An endless veil of confusion and overwrought theology, and Nuri in the center of it all attempting to see the truth.

Before he could contemplate the issue any further, however, a howl echoed off the foot of the mountain. It was so loud that the snow shook beneath him and he worried the movement would trigger an avalanche. For the time being, at least, it didn't, but the resounding chorus of howls that followed shook a heavy layer of snow from the mountain.

Jhrupa, he thought.

They were the fabled snow beasts of Shehoora. The existence of the giant primates had never been reliably verified, but Duri texts referred to them often.

They say they cannot be killed.

More and more beasts assembled at the foot of the mountain to contribute their cries of rage and hunger to the chorus. Each accompanying voice made the snow shudder more violently until he was convinced a catastrophic avalanche was imminent.

Better start running, he thought. Yet staring down the teeth of two-dozen snow monsters was no more appealing than being buried beneath them.

Inaction will kill you, Colt warned. *You must keep moving.*

Before his brain devised a more appropriate strategy, his combat instincts took control. He descended towards the Jhrupa in a series of bounding leaps as the mountain quaked beneath his feet, then ignited his laser sword and hacked through the midsection of the first white-coated primate. He barely caught his balance quickly enough to duck below the swinging fist of the second. A frantic roll avoided the initial strike, but the same creature reached out its other arm and clawed into his armor just below the ribs.

The pain was blinding.

I am Hidria. I am Death, he told himself.

The sudden warmth in his stomach stole his breath, but as a warrior, he knew better than to seek solace in surrender. Before the creature's claws withdrew from the depths of his armor and skin, Nuri spun and jabbed the glowing blade through the Jhrupa's chest, tearing upwards with all his might until he saw the full illuminated beam sticking out the other side. The snow monster split in two from stomach to throat before dropping alongside Nuri's first victim. The sight of two fallen kin was enough to spur the other monsters to charge in a rising cacophony of screams and howls.

Glancing over his shoulder to gauge the developing avalanche, Nuri planted his feet and retracted the laser blade in favor of the blaster rifle holstered to his back. He couldn't risk close combat given the sheer numbers of the Jhrupa, but if he could pick off a fair amount before they reached him, he might just make it through the lot of them alive.

And bring down the mountain in the process.

It was a sobering reminder that one stray shot could be enough to trigger the white curtain. He had to be careful.

I will not be afraid, he told himself, calmly training his rifle on one Jhrupa, blasting it through the right eye, and moving on to the next. *Fear is human.*

He clenched his jaw and fired again.

And again.

And again.

I am not human.

One by one, they fell, each shot more efficient than the last as his nerves shook off the battle adrenaline and his hands grew steady.

I am Hidria.

He fired until his weapon beeped for a recharge, then gracefully re-holstered the rifle and ignited his blade just in time to decapitate a charging Jhrupa from beneath its massive, outstretched arms. The headless body lurched forward while black blood and gristle sprang from its neck. It collapsed at Nuri's feet over the bodies of its fallen brethren.

I am Hidria.

The mountain's shudder reached all the way to Nuri's chest. He knew he didn't have much time, but a half-dozen angry Jhrupa still stood between him and the remote hope of finding refuge. Assuming the ancient texts were correct, miles upon miles of tunnels had been built into the mountains back when the Evil One called Shehoora home. If he could locate an entrance to the labyrinth somewhere, he might be able to stumble his way out the other side and avoid the destruction altogether. There *had* to be a solution, after all. It was a trial and a very difficult one at that, but there had to be a way out. Otherwise, Colt never would have led him there in the first place.

Or would she?

He had never heard anything about the Called visiting Shehoora. Nuri's trials *were* something entirely different. Whoever controlled the ritual (presumably God, although it could just as easily have been Colt or the Duri Masters themselves) had gone far off the beaten path when plotting Nuri's journey.

We each forge our own path, Colt's voice boomed into his head. *As everyone has for all time.*

Snow toppled over the mountain in a tidal wave. The sight was startlingly beautiful and momentarily locked Nuri in place. But while he stood there, gaping at the thundering blanket of snow, a Jhrupa tackled him from behind and smashed his face into a hidden rock.

You are always in the crosshairs of the Evil One, his Duri Master's voice reproached as Nuri gasped for breath ten inches deep in snow. He was already losing feeling in his cheeks and nose. What little sensation remained in them was overwhelmed by the shudder of the mountain against his exposed skin.

"I will not be afraid!" he cried out, thrashing wildly with the laser blade. "Fear is human!" The longer it took for the weapon to find purchase, the more his panic intensified.

At last, the blade buried itself in flesh, although whether it was the flesh of the Jhrupa drowning him beneath the snow or another monster altogether, Nuri wasn't certain. Either way, an agonized howl reached his ears through the thick layer of accumulation. Then, the pressure on the back of his neck momentarily lessened and he didn't hesitate. Hesitation was human.

I am not human.

He kicked backward as hard as he could and immediately rolled to his left, slashing with the glowing blade in case another Jhrupa was about to pounce as he landed sideways. He managed to slice through the claws of the nearest snow monster but nothing else was near enough for him to damage. A Jhrupa continued to howl in pain, presumably the one he'd wounded while his head was buried. The other four struggled to maintain their footing while evidently deciding whether the prospect of a fresh, warm meal was worth braving an avalanche.

Nuri left them to work it out on their own, gracelessly staggering down the mountain toward the giant stone doors of the main temple. A lone Jhrupa charged after him, kicking up absurd amounts of loose snow in its wake, but Nuri managed to drop it with a quick trio of shots from his sidearm. The other Jhrupa eventually retreated the way they'd come—the opposite end of the valley from Nuri's destination—and he never saw them again.

I am Hidria.

The mountain rumbled so loudly that, for a moment, Nuri was convinced it wasn't a mountain at all but a colossal creature waking from an eons' long slumber to swallow the planet whole. He felt its long, white tongue follow him down the slope toward the valley where he would certainly be buried alive, not only failing the trials but condemning himself to an icy, unmarked grave on an abandoned planet.

I am Hidria, he reminded himself as he ran. *I am Death.*

The roar of the approaching snow was deafening, and unnerving enough in its promise of total annihilation that he nearly ran straight past the narrow passageway on the mountainside.

Steady, he thought, planting his feet and leaping back toward the opening as the wall of snow bore down on him from twenty yards away. *Stay calm.*

It was a difficult charge back to the doorway with deep mounds of snow sucking at his legs. He managed to roll through the cave opening and slam his palm into the glowing blue button on the wall beside the door just in time to seal the hole before snow filled the corridor and suffocated him.

For a moment, he stood facing the opening with his hand still pressed against the controls, panting, waiting to see whether the snow would burst through the door, heedless of his efforts. It had to be tens of thousands of years old, after all, and the avalanche was bigger than any he'd witnessed among the Duri.

It wasn't until the rumble of the mountain began to subside that he at last turned to face the darkness, unsure what he would find in the shadows or if he'd even wound up where he was supposed to be. Where Colt had designed for him to go.

I'll find out soon enough, he thought.

And so he did.

6

"The world around you is an illusion. Everything and everyone in the universe is a distraction designed to draw you away from God. The trees, the water, the air you breathe, it is all distraction. The true essence of God can only be discovered through a life of service to Him, forsaking all human bonds of wonder and the pursuit of corporeal satisfaction."

Nuri was seventeen years old, kneeling on the wooden floor of his Duri Master's cottage with the cool, midday breeze whistling through cracks in the walls. His stomach was in knots, but he'd recently mastered the calm exterior which all Duri disciples adopted during training. Although the scolding had only just begun, he wasn't concerned with how long it would last. He had decided to willingly accept his punishment and continue his training as though nothing had happened. It was easier that way. In the end, each of his transgressions was forgiven regardless of the Duri Master's judgment. That particular dogma didn't make Nuri any less devout or mindful of morality, but it did make the punishments at the hands of the Duri Masters easier to bear. Physical pain was an illusion, after all, so if he could endure his mind's trickery while he received his lashings, his soul would be purified and he would achieve paranormal communion with God once more.

"Women are an illusion, just as men are an illusion" his Duri Master continued. "Lust. Impure thoughts. Sins of the flesh. They are all agents of the Evil One and they will enslave you if you are not careful."

Nuri kept his head bowed dutifully, focusing on the swirled intricacies of the wooden floor so his eyes would not be drawn to the scarred face of his Duri Master. He was searching for any distraction he could find because looking upon those scars for too long was a sin. It sparked curiosity and made him perceive his teacher as a mortal creature capable of being damaged, and those were both horrible sins. Perhaps unforgivable, even with the aid of the purging whips on the Duri Master's cane.

When he reached the window to look out upon the wooded valley, the Duri Master sighed and tapped his fingers against the glass. "That girl," he said, pausing thoughtfully as though something had caught his attention within the windowpane. Perhaps a memory from long ago, back before he'd achieved perfection in the eyes of God. Back when he had still been susceptible to entrapment by feminine wiles. "She is impure."

"She's done nothing wrong," Nuri protested. He regretted the words the moment they left his tongue. The Called were not to speak while a Duri Master imparted wisdom. The Called were not to speak in the presence of clergy at all unless it was their direct Master. Nuri braced himself for the inevitable backlash, gripping the hem of his pants tightly and swallowing hard.

Thankfully, the Duri Master did not seem to notice his transgression or did not view it as particularly egregious. "Her actions are not impure," the Duri Master said, "but what her body *symbolizes* is impure. Women were the Evil One's first distraction. In the Garden of Eden, the Evil One used the woman to redirect the First Man's mind to matters of the flesh and worldly concerns when his eyes should have been fixed on the Ultimate Reality of God."

Nuri nodded dutifully and bit his tongue.

We were all born of this sin, then, he thought. *This impurity.*

It was all convoluted. He didn't see logic in any of it, but the Duri Master's confidence was jarring. It made him reconsider his own feelings and—according to the Duri Master—that was a good thing. Boys weren't made to dwell on thoughts and emotions. Only God. Their eyes were to be ever upward, as the Good Book said, never heeding the serpent at their heel. That was the way of sin. That was the way of corporeal concern and the Great Death.

The Duri Master turned back to him, casually flicking a glance to Nuri's sword at the far end of the hut. It was a foreign object to the Duri Masters, who forsook all matters of the flesh including the blood culling (although they had no qualms ordering it), but Nuri knew the command when he saw it.

"In the end," his scarred and hideous Duri Master continued. "We must all be purged of our iniquities. We must all face the cleansing blade of eternity."

No, Nuri thought frantically. *Please.*

But to deny the culling order from a Duri Master was to spit in the face of God, as the Good Book said. So, he rose wordlessly from his knees with his head still bowed and retrieved the sword with deliberate slowness. The blade was too heavy for his adolescent arms to wield for long even after years of physical and spiritual training on the holy mountain, but he lifted it over his head anyway because that was what the Duri Master expected.

"You know what you must do, boy," the Duri Master said firmly. "Go, then, and do it."

Hands shaking beneath the weight of the blade forged within the mountain itself, Nuri bowed and left the cottage without further complaint. His mind raced as he stepped onto the garden path leading to the valley.

This has all been a test, he thought. *A test of my faithfulness and devotion.*

The Duri Masters never allowed any woman or girl into the quiet village who was deemed too enticing for adolescent eyes, and certainly never someone as close in age to the apprentice as the river girl.

They brought her here purposely. He hacked angrily at the underbrush once he was certain he'd passed beneath the eye-line of the Duri Master. *Did she know she was going to her death? Did he know that he would wind up forcing me to kill her to prove my faith?*

Not to him, a voice reminded. *To God.*

The sun glinted off his blade so stunningly that it momentarily washed away his anger, but it was also a sin to behold the beauty in things and so he quickly averted his eyes. In a universe vast beyond human comprehension, there was only room for the wonder of God Himself and not the fruits of His creation.

We must exist beyond the corporeal, his Duri Master always said.

And, therefore, she must die.

He grimaced and picked his way stealthily down the mountain. He'd been trained well enough not to make noise when navigating wilderness. He was a soldier in the holy army, after all, and though the Duri Masters' religious doctrine was paramount to the order, combat training was a close second. The Called carried out the will of God, spilling the blood of sinners as tribute for the Holy One, and therefore had to be prepared for any martial situation. The skill had hardly benefited him to that point in his young life, but now he was grateful for the ability to avoid detection by the other clergymen who dwelled on the mountain. He wove between branches, rocks, leaves, and twigs soundlessly, affording ample time for quiet reflection. His mind was elsewhere and well occupied.

All those seen to be impure must be purged by blood to remind them of the Ultimate Sacrifice, which Creator God humbled

Himself to endure. It is only through blood that we are saved. It is only through the tribute of suffering from all peoples.

After a time, he gave into impulse and leapt down the mountain in an undisciplined sprint, barely noting his footfalls and not frightened in the least that one false step might send him hurtling to his death in the valley before carrying out God's will as relayed by his Duri Master.

A test, he thought bitterly. *Only a test.*

He had never killed someone he knew. He didn't think he had the stomach for it, especially considering that he'd never really had the stomach for killing in the first place.

This one was unique, too. She made him feel different than anyone ever had. He wouldn't dare say that he was in *love* with her even within the sanctuary of his own thoughts, but he was more than just physically attracted to her the way an adolescent boy is attracted to an adolescent girl. She was light-years' different than anyone he'd met since being taken from Dublokee. A poignantly startling contrast to the rest of the Duri villagers along the mountain. Come to think of it, he wasn't sure how he hadn't realized she was a test from the outset. No one who stood out so brilliantly from her peers was to be trusted, his Duri Master had told him, because that meant she was tainted by the Evil One. Women strove for vanity, he'd said, and if there was one thing the Duri Masters hated, it was vanity.

She is evil, then, he tried to convince himself. *If the Duri Master says that she's evil, then she is evil.*

He chewed over the idea as he neared the valley, but it still didn't taste quite right. The girl was intelligent and strong-willed. Nuri didn't know how those qualities made her an enemy to God or a servant of the Evil One. She was rarely in a bad mood and always made an effort to greet anyone she passed in the village.

The Master is wrong, then, he decided.

Except the Duri Master *couldn't* be wrong. It was impossible. Everything Nuri had learned since he'd been taken to the holy mountain assured him that the Duri Master was *always* right. He spoke the very will of God.

And the will of God, the Master's voice spoke into his head, *is for you to kill that girl. To purify her and yourself before the poison of the Evil One weakens you.*

Grinding his teeth, Nuri passed through the city gates, unmarked and unbidden. He had urgent business now, grim though it was. If he didn't complete his mission in a timely manner, his Duri Master would starve him for three days in confined, prayerful solitude. Worst of all, the girl would die whether he delivered the killing stroke or not. All because he'd taken an interest in her beyond a stern hand of rebuke and forced repentance. How the Duri Master had detected his feelings, he would never know. He told himself he would do all he could to find out discreetly, but he couldn't imagine having enough resources to succeed when the townsfolk considered the Duri the mouthpieces of God. No villager who lived safely on the mountain would dare speak against them. For one thing, it was considered heresy, and heresy was (of course) punishable by death. So, too, was attracting the gaze of a member of the Called.

Which was precisely why the girl had to die.

Because I am weak.

Nuri could see her filling a pail by the river as he approached, a menial task among dozens of others designed to keep the villagers honest even though the Duri provided for them in every way. Her back was turned so he was unable to look her in the eye, but it felt as though he could. It felt like she was staring back at him already. Even then, he pictured the shining reflection of water on her cheeks, the way it lit her eyes and brightened her hair, and that was why he'd been sent to kill her. Because he could picture it, and because it was all he ever wanted to do.

Lust is the fundamental weakness of man.

What Nuri felt wasn't lust, though. He would never find the words to articulate what exactly 'it' was, but it was near enough, he supposed, to make him ashamed. Spiteful. Confused. All sorts of emotions he didn't understand in the least because he'd never been given the opportunity to explore them.

The life of the Called is lonesome because that is God's will. Asceticism is the only true path to knowing Him. It is the only way you will ever reach Prime.

A filthy, stooped old man cut in front of him with a trio of pigs in tow. He cursed them quietly so the Duri Masters would not overhear him, but Nuri was near enough to catch his words. They stunned him. Enough to distract him from the task at hand, and that was no small feat. He'd never heard a public curse in his life that he could remember. At the very least, not since he'd been taken from his home. The other villagers deliberately ignored him so as not to draw his attention or wrath, but the pig farmer's disinterest was another animal altogether. Nuri had grown used to being ignored by the Duri Masters and their servants (he preferred it, in fact), and he was likewise accustomed to being ignored by the villagers, who were paid to act out the illusion that it was a simple village at the base of the mountain where the equally simple, godly pleasures of a rural life free of technology played out to the satisfaction of the Duri Masters. This man was different, though. His dismissal wasn't polite deference to his status, nor was it a lack of awareness for Nuri's proximity. The pig farmer saw him and deliberately cut him off, then had the nerve to curse in front of him on top of it.

Heathen, Nuri scowled.

He'd heard the Duri Master use that word often when referring to a condemned city or species, and it was about as close as any of the Duri Masters came to swearing in his presence.

Incensed, Nuri stopped in his tracks and stared at the back of the old, stooped man as he sauntered away.

Distraction, a voice spoke in his head.

The recognition was buried beneath layers upon layers of misplaced anger.

"Farmer," Nuri called after the man, barely suppressing his rage.

The villagers could no longer pretend they hadn't noticed the Called warrior in their midst. They continued to play at their monotonous chores, but their eyes and ears were fixed on the two men at the center of the village: one young and one not so young anymore.

"Old man!" Nuri shouted when the pig farmer didn't turn to face him. "Come back here!"

He tried to convince himself that it was the audacity of the pig farmer that spurred his anger and not his own feelings of helplessness, which were greater than any he'd experienced in his life even accounting for the time he'd watched his parents being murdered before his eyes as an uncomprehending child, but the villagers watched him now. So, too, did the girl fetching water from the river.

Still, the old man did not turn.

Nuri passed his breaking point. "Heathen!" he shouted, starting towards the farmer with his sword held out menacingly in front of him.

The villagers stiffened, some doing their damnedest to suppress gasps. They no longer pretended to do their jobs. They all watched Nuri and slowly backed away from the lethal weapon gripped by God's Right Hand. They were terrified, and with good reason. From the time he'd been brought to the mountain, Nuri had been indoctrinated with the teachings of the Duri Masters, but he'd also been bred to be a part of the foremost group of warriors in the galaxy.

The Called. The Hidria.

God's Justice.

He still had years of training left before he would undergo the trials, but the villagers knew he was no stranger to a blade or to killing. Especially for one condemned as a heathen.

This is distraction, his Duri Master's voice told him. *A willing distraction to forsake your duty. Distractions are evil. You will learn to be strong in the face of the Evil One's wiles.*

But he couldn't back down now with all the villagers watching him so closely. His Duri Master wouldn't stand for it, and he was already assured punishment for the incident before the day was out, anyway.

I have no choice, he thought as he bounded toward the old man with his steel glinting in the afternoon sun. Each step further removed him from the overwhelming rage he'd felt in the pivotal moment, but it was too late to change anything. *It's either him or her. This is the only way that she can live.*

At last, the pig farmer ceased his hunched shuffle through the village and turned toward Nuri.

Quickly. Mercifully. Before you have to look him in the eye.

Avoiding the death stare was considered wrong by the Duri Masters, of course. The Hand of God was guiltless, inhuman. Hidria were not disturbed by staring into the very souls of the heathens they condemned to Tscharia.

Humans are weak and prone to sentimentality.

You must not be human.

You must be Hidria.

The old man was halfway turned.

Do it now.

For a moment, he felt the collective, dawning realization of the villagers and the bloodcurdling screams they quickly buried in their tongue-less obedience. The air around him grew so heavy as he drew back the blade that he was later convinced the mountain itself tried to stop him from going through with the kill. This was murder, after all, and for no greater slight than cursing in the presence of the Called. A minor offense, indeed. Certainly not punishable by death and often ignored altogether even by the strictest of Duri Masters.

It's either him or her, he reminded himself.

The thought gave him just enough nerve to bring the devastating blade crashing through the old man's shoulder, dragging violently downward until it stuck in his ribs and wrenched from his grip.

Done.

It was an ugly kill. The pig farmer—old and useless as he was—would suffer through the night and all the way into the next afternoon before someone finally put him out of his misery. But Nuri wasn't there for that. Instead, he was hung upside down in the Duri Master's purging chamber, only prevented from dropping into a fire-pit by steel hooks that buried deep in his skin. A reminder of how suffering for God was the only thing that kept him, and all peoples across the galaxy, from Tscharia.

"Heathen," he whispered, tapping the blade and stepping back as blood sprayed his armor. The old man collapsed with wide eyes. Gasping. Demanding an explanation.

Why? he could hear the old man's soul cry out to him.

Because you are not her, and because God demands tribute. Blood for blood.

The village fell utterly silent. The people were unsure whether they should rush to the old man's aid (someone's family member, surely) or leave him there to die alone rather than risk a similar fate.

Nuri fell to his knees before the old man, certain he was about to vomit but fighting it back with every ounce of his being lest the villagers think him weak. They would report any show of guilt or indecision to the Duri Masters and the Duri Masters would make him pay dearly for it if they caught him.

Slowly, the sharp thudding in his head slowed to a manageable drone. The farmer finally screamed. A few brave villagers broke their paralysis and rushed to the old man's side to tend his fatal wound as best they could, though anyone with eyes could tell he had no hope for survival.

Nuri didn't notice them. His ears rang and he suddenly felt on the verge of fainting.

Distraction.

He glanced once towards the river and locked eyes with the girl. It was only a moment, but it was enough for her to understand his meaning and make herself scarce before the Duri Masters descended the mountain.

I did this for you, he thought in her direction as she sprinted up the opposite slope, which was forbidden to all but the most revered Duri. *It was him or you.*

Distraction, a female voice whispered in his head.

He rose on unsteady legs and stumbled back toward the Duri Master's hut, purposely leaving the blade lodged in the old man's chest. It was going to be an ugly, arduous job prying it free, and it wasn't right for the villagers to see one of the Called sweat in such a way. It gave them the impression that he was weak as they were weak, and that was simply unacceptable.

The people cannot respect someone who is weak. Therefore, they will not follow the law of one they perceive as weak. This is why God orders the destruction of Heathens, to remind them that He is not weak. He is Death and Suffering itself, even as He is Life and Joy. To be God-like, we must be both brutal and kind. You can only manage these dual natures by making just judgments and remaining aloof from human indignities. Sweat. Blood. Love. Tears. Emotion of any kind. To be like God, you cannot be like humans.

Humans are weak.

You will be Hidria.

The teaching provided little—if any—consolation, but at least it occupied his mind as he ascended the mountain to accept his punishment at the Just Hand of God.

Distraction.

It kept him from thinking about the girl, and from wondering what would become of her among the bloodthirsty monsters on the Forbidden Mountain.

Maybe someday, he would find out for himself.

7

Distraction, **Colt's voice echoed** before Nuri had a chance to orient himself within the new darkness.

The rumble of the avalanche had finally ceased after several anxious moments of wondering whether the barrier would hold. Now that he was certain the way behind him was completely blocked off, he shrugged snow from his shoulders and drew his laser blade to illuminate the mountain passage. He could only see two meters ahead of him at a time, but that was more than enough to recognize the corridor's similarities to the winding tunnels in the sacred temple. Perhaps, he thought, it had been built in mock tribute once upon a time. Such extravagant, sardonic homage was not beyond the capabilities of the Evil One's disciples, though it was impossible to know which of the two had been constructed first. The only glaring difference between the hallways was the lack of aquatic luminescence that had conveniently guided his footsteps back in the temple. For the time being, his blade provided the only light.

He didn't take long weighing his options before deciding there were virtually none aside from venturing deeper into the mountain. He figured moving forward was his safest bet for progressing in the trials, anyway, even accounting for his certainty that unspeakable horrors lingered from the Evil One's reign over Shehoora. Likewise, he had no doubt that those same terrors eagerly anticipated his arrival.

That doesn't change anything.

To hesitate was to admit fear and fear was a human preoccupation. Hidria bore no fear—as both his Duri Master

51

and Colt had repeatedly pointed out to him—and the trials were designed to discern whether he truly *was* Hidria, or at least had the capacity to be. Allowing the prospect of peril to dissuade him would only prove his unworthiness.

Besides, he had to focus to survive. He had to stretch his senses to the limit and accurately process the slightest movement in the shadows around him. He knew well that there was more to fear in the trials than God and demons.

Insanity, he thought with a frown.

Nuri wasn't sure if the legends were true, but many among the Duri claimed the longer it took the Called to complete the trials, the less of his or her sanity remained. Assuming, of course, that he didn't perish in the extraction process first, which was hardly a certainty. He supposed that was why it was rumored that all Hidria were insane, though he'd never met one himself to prove or disprove the claim. As far as he knew, no one had ever met a Hidria after its transformation. They were not meant to be seen while they purged the galaxy, and especially not to interact with creatures of a weaker constitution.

You, too, must remain unseen, Colt's voice materialized just beyond the arc of light from his blade. *It won't matter what awaits in the darkness so long as it doesn't see you coming.*

Nuri frowned and dabbed absently at his chest wound. His suspicion was piqued. The way he understood her, Colt had just suggested he sheathe his laser blade and proceed blindly through the darkness, an action which would leave him utterly exposed to any foul creature that happened upon him. His first instinct was to dismiss the idea offhand, but upon further reflection, he had to admit there was a certain logic to it. He might not see danger as it approached without the light of his blade, but neither would his enemies see him as he moved along the corridor, or so he hoped. He could imagine that the eyes of whatever dwelled in the mountain were now accustomed to the darkness, or that their other senses compensated for the absence of light.

It would at least be safer to shut off my blade than broadcast my location, he thought.

The only question then was whether his enemies—Watchmen, Jhrupa, or the infamous ice-wraiths—already knew he was coming. If they did, their heightened senses would mark his approach long before betraying their own presence. He'd been trained to walk in almost complete silence with footsteps discernible only to the most careful ear, but lacking other noises in the hollow mountain as distractions, the Watchmen would surely hear him. And if they did not, they would sense him, nonetheless.

Then there's no point in tiptoeing, he decided, pushing his blade even further from his body to illuminate the passage another half-meter. *Might as well make it really bright while I'm at it.*

He continued with the beam held out for a while until a new idea struck him. Without breaking stride, he sheathed the blade and drew his rifle from its holster.

One shot will light this place up all the way to the far wall, he thought.

The flash would only last a moment but that would be enough time to survey his surroundings with the added benefit of saving the charge on his blade. Not by much, but every little bit counted when it came to conserving the energy store of his favorite weapon. Besides, blasts from a pulse rifle would provide more cover than a blade. His enemies might be able to see him for a split-second during the flash, but then they'd be plunged into just as much darkness as he and hopefully blinded by the sudden glare. They would know his general location, but it would level the playing field. They'd have a harder time pinpointing a strike if he knew what areas to avoid.

Here goes nothing, he thought.

He aimed a blaster bolt into the corridor ahead, fighting to keep his eyes focused despite their instinct to close against the poignant beam.

Nuri's stomach lurched when he saw the crude assembly of creatures shrinking from the light, but his combat training quickly took control. He rolled forward and pivoted toward the wall, then came to rest on one knee with the rifle braced against his body for another round.

Lord of All be my blade and my resolve, he prayed silently.

There were at least ten hostiles by his reckoning, but he'd only managed a brief glimpse of them. They were crouched along a series of broken doorframes before the corridor curved to the right on a downward slope. Neither Jhrupa nor Watchmen as it turned out, though there was a distant resemblance between them and the unholy, red-masked mages.

They must be ice-wraiths, he realized. Like the Jhrupa, he'd read about the foul creatures in the *Mantra of the Unholy Other*, which was the Good Book for disciples of the Evil One. Also, like the Jhrupa, he'd never heard of anyone seeing them in person, least of all one of the Called during the trials.

Is their presence a sign that I've already failed? he wondered. *That I shouldn't be here at all?*

The idea made his skin prickle ominously. Perhaps this was his consequence for failure. If he was unworthy of knowing the True God, it seemed oddly appropriate that he should encounter increasingly difficult obstacles until he succumbed. Yet he was still alive for the time being, and there were enemies ahead. He couldn't afford to dwell on morbid possibilities.

Each doubt is merely a distraction, Colt reminded him. *An attempt to muddle your thoughts and undermine your resolve. Uncertainty is the weapon of the Evil One. Hidria are decisive and authoritative. They do not require introspection or self-doubt because they know that all impulses living within them are a representation of the Holy One.*

That's a contradiction, he argued. *True Hidria are servants of both God and the Duri Masters. They rely on instruction. Hidria are ascetics and death-bringers. They deny themselves to purify their actions. Listening to one's own urges and impulses is the opposite of asceticism. It is the causeway to the Evil One.*

He could hear the enraged ice-wraiths hissing as he crept along the corridor and prepared to unload the rifle on the lot of them, but now Colt's debate clouded his mind as well. He found himself hesitating to gather his thoughts before proceeding again.

Distraction, Colt mocked.

Nuri was about to argue that if *all* distractions were servants of the Evil One and Colt was herself distracting him, then surely she was an agent of the Evil One. By that logic, he shouldn't suffer her to live whatever arcane existence she'd carved out beyond the influence of the jealous Duri Masters, who could never achieve her proximity to God no matter how strictly they followed their own doctrines or how many affronts to the Creator they neutralized through the reckoning blades of the Called.

That's precisely what she's doing to me, he realized. *She's drawing me away from the road ahead just long enough to lower my guard so the Watchmen can strike. I'll either be dead, exiled, or stationed at a failed Called installation until I die. At best, I'll be an errand boy.*

He might have pondered the issue further (he was known for considering the world around him altogether too carefully, much to the chagrin of his Duri Master), but the ice-wraiths were so enraged by his presence and the blinding light of the rifle blast that they could wait no longer and attacked as one writhing mass of shadow.

Here they come, Colt warned. *Your hands must be swift and steady.*

He felt the charge more than saw it. The sound of their eager, starved snarls threatened to break his resolve. Their collective footsteps shook the corridor.

As the calm surety of battle covered his doubts, Nuri planted his feet shoulder-width apart and aimed his rifle toward the heaviest concentration of gargled curses at the far end of the hallway.

I am not human, he reminded himself as he pulled the trigger and locked his knees against the sputtering recoil. *I am Hidria.*

The angry screams that followed were so piercing that he barely registered the rifle blasts over the raging cacophony, but neither sound fazed him. He simply held his finger against the trigger and arced shots across the corridor, unable to see how much damage he inflicted. The light from the rifle was too bright to make sense of the moving shadows. He did, however, catch brief glimpses of the creatures with each new series of reports. They were horrible things. Pale, diseased faces. Razor-blade incisors. Glowing, pupil-less eyes. It wasn't until they were two meters from him that he realized a few were climbing the walls and ceiling.

More distractions, Colt reminded him. *Focus on the greatest threats. The ones on the ceiling will drop eventually. If you play it right, they could become obstacles for the others.*

He would have been wary of her advice if he'd had the time to consider it closely, but the battle calm was upon him and he wasn't processing in any conscious way. His training had beaten out most of the irrational thoughts that distracted during battle. He had been wholly transformed into a series of finely tuned reactions, his instinctual warrior-self calculating each move before he had a moment to digest what was happening around him.

One by one, the ice-wraiths dropped, then two by two, then they all bunched together and tripped over their dead.

But the swarm kept on coming without an end in sight.

They are strong, Colt told him. *You cannot match their numbers nor their blind hatred. You must be smarter than them if you want to survive.*

Nuri eased off the trigger for a moment and edged back toward the doorway. He couldn't see the ammunition indicator that predicted the number of shots remaining before his energy pack ran dry, but he knew it wasn't much. In fact, he considered it a miracle the charge hadn't died already though he'd managed to mow down a significant portion of the enemy.

Yet, as the horde advanced down the corridor toward him, the illusion of progress from his initial bursts was erased. The ice-wraiths trampled their fallen brethren without even a glance to be sure their footing was true on the cold dark stone. Those among them who'd taken to scrambling across the walls and ceiling on all fours were nearly upon him, as well, and firing blindly wouldn't do much good against such a heavy press.

No use holding back now, he thought, continuing to fire as he drew the laser-blade with his left hand. *I'll have to cut my way out of here.*

Not if you're smart, Colt told him.

He had no idea what she meant by that and there wasn't time to sift through her riddles. Instead, he hacked the glowing blade through each ice-wraith as they confronted him until the combination of new attackers and fallen corpses was so thick around him that he couldn't be sure whether he was merely attacking the dead. More often than not, the laser made a clean cut and the wraiths fell where he caught them, yet their hardened bones and leathery skin occasionally resisted enough that they didn't drop right away. As a result, those who survived the initial thrust and hack re-emerged from the pileup angrier than before.

You are allowing them to swallow you whole, Colt told him matter-of-factly. She drifted down the corridor beyond the wraiths with her own pale radiance. The sight was somehow more unsettling than the glow of the ice-wraiths' eyes as they descended upon him.

I don't have a choice.

They pressed too heavily for a counter strike. She was right about one thing: their sheer numbers were on the verge of completely swallowing him. Figuratively, at least, even if they had so far been unsuccessful in literally devouring him. They flung themselves at his blade so relentlessly and with such fervor that he could only manage to lock his legs beneath him and occasionally parry their groping claws or snapping teeth.

You have to find a way out.

He glanced over his shoulder in hopes that he'd somehow missed an exit in the darkness, but there was nothing. There would be no miraculous escape, then. No one was coming to help. If he wanted to survive, he'd have to keep dodging, ducking, punching, slicing, and hacking through the hungry horde until he blazed his own way out.

The pile of bodies at his feet spared him any surprise attacks but also prevented him from moving forward. Thankfully, his assailants were only in front of him for the time being. They could only reach him from the waist up, so he didn't need to worry about his flank. It was a small blessing but a blessing, nonetheless. It wouldn't be long before he ran out of room to move his arms, however, and then he wouldn't be able to hack *or* shoot.

Still, the wraiths came, and each new wave learned from the mistakes of its predecessor.

The intelligent ones knew to stay behind, he thought. *They don't have the blind recklessness of the first wave. Those ones almost always die.*

But they also get the most food if they survive, Colt pointed out.

As he ducked beneath the swiping claws of a particularly terrifying ghoul with half its cheek rotted to the gums, Nuri wondered if Colt had a point or if she was merely attempting to break his concentration.

Whether she means to be or not, she's a distraction, he decided, gnashing his teeth. The effort of hacking the blade through an ice-wraith's neck made his shoulder pop out of its socket. An old injury, and one which usually didn't flare up until he'd been engaged with the laser-blade for hours. It shouldn't have been hurting so early in the trials. The weakness was a bad omen. Even if he somehow managed to break through the barrier of ice-wraiths and uncover a path through the tunnels, the mounting injuries would cause him trouble.

"AAAGGHHH!" he screamed as one of the creatures finally wrestled through the tangle of corpses and bit into his thigh. Using force only his mid-battle adrenaline was capable of mustering, he brought the hilt of the blade crashing down on the wraith's head, cracking both its skull and its grip on his flesh with a sickening squelch. Black blood and bluish brain matter splattered his face, but Nuri hardly noticed. Fury had replaced his quiet intensity. He trudged through the pile of bodies with a scream and his blade slicing curtly through the cold air.

Colt's face appeared above the onrushing wraiths with a sour expression.

Hidria do not know rage. They are calculated. Discerning. Lethal. Terrifying in their calm decisiveness. In their detachment.

Nuri thrust the point of the laser-blade through the throat of an ice-wraith and pointedly ignored her despite the implied consequences. She may have been his guide and a part of the trial itself but that didn't mean much to him at the moment, a fact which would surely disappoint whoever judged the worthiness of his performance. Besides, if the Duri Masters' teachings were true, God had already determined whether Nuri would be successful, so there was no point in sweating the details. He was a warrior and there was enemy flesh to hew all around him. *Tainted* flesh. Emissaries of the Evil One. Hidria or no, he was doing God's work.

Use whatever excuses and justifications you need to. Blame it on God.

Colt's ethereal form drifted towards the ceiling. She had her arms folded over her chest and regarded him with a look of cool indifference which contrasted his unbridled emotion, a purely human trait.

Every breath you take pushes you further from the path to enlightenment. You cannot know God until you know yourself, and that means recognizing your limitations.

Still, he continued chopping through the line of ice-wraiths, advancing slowly by climbing the mound of corpses as he struck. His thrusts and hacks had lost some conviction, though, in the wake of Colt's admonishment. Anger gradually drained from him and was absorbed by his adversaries, which *The Unholy Other* also claimed was the feeding method of choice for the Evil One.

But God willed it to be this way, his Duri Master cautioned.

Colt scoffed and drifted down the corridor away from him. Apparently, she'd given up.

You're just like the wretched Duri, she accused. *With free will, God cannot be your conscience. He must be invited. You must build one for yourself.*

Just like who?

For a moment, he ceased fighting altogether, stunned both by her sudden disappearance and the poignancy of her condemnation. Had a servant of God just compared him to the Duri Masters as a sign of ignorance and futility? Had she spoken against the very religious order the Hidria served? It didn't seem possible. He figured he must have misinterpreted her words in some way.

It's a distraction, that is all, he realized. *She's doing this on purpose to test me. To make me doubt myself and thereby learn if I am capable of discerning truth from illusion.*

A sharp pain in his forearm jolted him back to the situation at hand. He kicked away yet another assailant that had wedged between the corpses for a bite.

One of the Duri Masters' mantras occurred to him as he leapt and spun sideways off the wall to his right to avoid a lunging ice-wraith: *Heavy and swift is the hand of God's Judgment.* Their numbers had thinned to a mere handful and he could finally see the doorways ahead of him again. There was no sign of Colt, though. *The righteous hand will not tremble, for such weakness expresses a profound distrust in the Lord's will.*

Utter calm had finally returned. Nuri walked down the corridor, now free of the corpses tangled beneath his feet, and decapitated a wraith just before its jaw clamped down on his throat.

Hidria must never question the will of God. The blood they spill is the blood of redemption, a portion of the debt repaid for the Salvation that the God Man bought for all creatures when the Sinners spilled his blood.

His eyes found a broken door hanging off its hinges a few meters ahead. There was still a faint trace of Colt's luminescence in the frame. With a quick thrust to the abdomen of the second-to-last ice-wraith followed by a slice across the throat of the other in fast succession, he cleared his path and stood before the doorway, panting, trying to make sense of the utter darkness that led to nowhere at all. He knew it *wouldn't* lead anywhere, either, until he passed through to the other side. And who knew what fresh hell awaited him there?

Tscharia waits in every new doorway.

It wasn't a Duri saying. In fact, Nuri wasn't sure where he'd heard that proverb at all. Perhaps it was something he'd picked up as a child before the brainwashing of the Duri had broken him on the distant mountaintop. It didn't matter, though. He recognized the truth of the testament. There was nothing he could do about it, anyway.

Unless he appealed to Colt, the haunting visage of God's chief advocate who had taken the form of a woman. A woman that, perhaps, he knew.

But who was she really?

We are not to question the divine mysteries, his Duri Master told him.

"If I am to know God, I need to *know* Him."

His own words sounded nonsensical off his tongue, but perhaps that was the point. Perhaps he was speaking in his own riddles now because the Duri prayers had filled every part of him. Perhaps that was what it meant to be Hidria.

To be Hidria is to be inhuman, Colt's voice beckoned.

The words gave him some pause. He'd never heard it phrased quite that way before, and he wasn't sure what to make of it.

"It's all meant to confound me," he reminded himself. Somehow, speaking aloud provided the assurance he'd missed internally, perhaps because his thoughts were becoming too crowded. "These are all distractions. Even she."

Thou shalt not suffer a distraction to live.

Yet another proverb that had been obfuscated by time as it passed through new worlds and generations.

Nuri's head swam. He could already feel himself drowning in the swirling doctrines, mysteries, and incantations of the rite. A quest for the nature of God. He couldn't imagine why he'd ever worried over the combat aspect of the trials, although it was possible that the danger would ramp up the further he progressed.

Only one way to find out, and only one place to go to do it.

The path to enlightenment, Colt said. Her voice was close, so close that it made the hairs on his forearms prickle with electricity. *The path to God.*

Gathering his breath, he leaned against the frigid stone wall and watched the tendrils of breath escape his lips. He took one quick glance at the bodies he'd left in his wake—twenty at least, and possibly more—then sheathed his blade and dipped one trembling foot into the darkness on the other side of the doorway.

Grant me complete surrender, he prayed.

And he allowed himself to fall into nothingness.

8

"Sit there and watch until I call you forward," the Duri Master hissed.

A dozen clergymen surrounded a wooden platform in a wide clearing outside the temple. Beyond the twelve men stood two dozen heavily armed Called soldiers in full combat armor. Each warrior's faceplate had been activated to hide their gender and expression, a necessary measure to avoid distraction and favor, which—according to the Duri Masters—were two of the greatest evils to develop in an army. Once a commander favored one soldier over another, the venial sins of that soldier were overlooked, and leniency over discipline was a temptation of the Evil One. Therefore, it followed that camaraderie on the battlefield was an affront to the Divine Infinite, one which was measured in the casualties of His Holy Warriors. Failure on that scale was intolerable.

Nuri sat dutifully on the ground outside the circle and didn't move even when the pine needles dug into his skin. Any sound he made would undoubtedly draw the ire of his Duri Master and lead to additional disciplinary measures, ones even harsher than the penitential floggings he'd already been prescribed for his indiscretion. His presence at the ceremony, in fact, was just as much a punishment as it was a solemn rite to observe the final cleansing of the sinner he'd thrust into the righteous flame.

As with any other unfortunate soul who'd been purified without the decree of a Duri Master, the pig farmer (Nuri still hadn't learned his real name) was about to be memorialized with a funeral pyre. He would not be granted a grave like a pure follower of the faith, but neither would his corpse be left for the mountain scavengers or hung in the village square as a warning to the devout. His was the purgatory of memorials: not quite reverent, but not completely spiteful, either. And because Nuri had taken the man's life without properly consulting his Duri Master, his punishment was inevitable, as well. There were times when the oversight was excused and the warrior was spared (which, in Nuri's mind, only proved the hypocrisy of a religious order which supposedly abhorred favoritism and leniency on the battlefield), but since he was still in training and had yet to be "broken," this was not one of those occasions.

There's no point in my being here, Nuri thought bitterly. *I would do the same thing again if it meant I didn't have to kill the girl.*

He supposed that was his problem. All lay creatures were supposedly equal in the eyes of God so long as they ascribed to the Duri teachings, so in most cases, one murder would have carried just as much weight as any other. However, in this instance, Nuri was still guilty of what his Duri Master referred to as 'the Sin of Preference' and needed the evil predilection beaten out of him before it poisoned his mind completely.

Will I be better off for it? he wondered. *Will it strengthen my faith?*

His Duri Master didn't seem to care much about how it affected his faith, only his discipline.

But it could work the other way, too. It could make me turn against them. Do they not recognize the threat?

The twelve clergymen hummed as the pig farmer's naked corpse was brought forth from the temple. The revered dead were wrapped in hand-stitched tunics of purple and gold before being laid in their graves, but the purged were stripped naked to expose the root of their sins.

Someday, that will be me, he thought.

A servant girl emerged gripping the old man's decapitated head by the hair. The skin had had been cleaned for the ceremony but he somehow looked worse for it. Haunted.

Soulless.

She set the ghastly visage on his belly as soon as his body was laid atop the altar. The hollowed-out eyes stared straight at Nuri, and he couldn't help wondering whether that was by chance or by design. When it came to the punishment of their followers, the Duri allowed few coincidences. They delighted in twisting the knife.

On cue, his Duri Master separated from the circle of esteemed clergymen and approached the corpse. "Vessels of the Divine," he addressed the gathering, "this man was a heretic. A servant to the Evil One. He spoke blasphemy in the presence of a Called Warrior, and though the cleansing of this one was swift and lacked the divine judgment of God spoken through us, His servants, his death was no doubt justified. May his soul forever rot in the nothing space between Omega—the presence of the Divine Infinite—and Tscharia, where the Evil One dwells."

With that, the eleven remaining clergymen advanced in unison, each dumping a modest spray of oil over the pig farmer's body. The Duri Master turned to Nuri and motioned him forward. Seeing no other alternative, he rose obediently and tried to clear his mind with meditative breathing. He hadn't the stomach to guess at what would be required of him. The stone steps were cold on his bare feet, but he pushed the distraction away and took his place at the Duri Master's side.

"You must cast the match that sets him aflame," his scar-faced teacher told him.

Nuri detected more than a little sadism lingering just below the surface of the man's solemn facade. And why not? For the Duri Master, this was a perfect scenario. He was both daring Nuri to openly challenge him and delighting in the prospect of watching the boy sear the pig farmer's flesh. Like all dogmatists, Nuri thought, he was out for blood and argument.

No preferences. No fear. No regret.

His hands shook but he accepted the torch the servant girl offered, anyway, and scrunched his toes together to keep from biting his lip. He couldn't show any sign of weakness in front of the assembled clergymen, least of all his Duri Master. And why should he hesitate to set the purging flame to a man he'd already beheaded? At least he could provide some form of release for the pig farmer's soul, be it to Tscharia, the in-between, or elsewhere in the universe. And Nuri still didn't wholly trust the Duri doctrine that all those deemed unworthy were condemned to one or the other, either. Maybe there was hope for the pig farmer yet.

But not for you if you don't act quickly.

Under the measured watch of the Duri Master, he touched the torch to the oil-drenched flesh of the pig farmer and stepped back as flames consumed his body. His hands continued to shake. Dread frothed in his stomach. It took all his self-control not to vomit when the first whiff of burnt hair and skin reached his nose, but such an indiscretion in the presence of the clergymen would have been just as damning as hesitation before performing the cleansing rite. Perhaps even as damning as admitting that the whole exercise was folly because he shouldn't have killed the pig farmer in the first place. He shouldn't have had to kill anyone at all.

How can it be God's will to destroy His creation?

The question had hung over every combat lesson the Duri Master taught him, yet he dared not ask it for fear of retribution. Even Called soldiers had limits to the level of tolerable heresy the Duri Order endured from them before acting on it. Nuri considered himself to be one of the more audacious recruits among the Called and was more than happy to mutter a barb under his breath here and there, but that didn't exactly mean he had a death wish. He was acutely aware of how easily it could have been *him* spread across the ceremonial altar with his severed head draped across his belly.

And the purging fire erasing all proof of my existence, appendage by appendage.

Once the initial shock subsided and he could watch the devouring flames at work without an overwhelming urge to wretch, he examined the pig farmer's eyes closely to see if they betrayed any semblance of spiritual cognizance. It was a widely held belief among human colonists that a soul bound for purgatory would emit blue smoke during the Duri purging ritual. Nuri saw no such traces of blue, but it was hard to make out anything aside from the bright firelight in the dusk haze. As with all Duri teachings (as well as the contradicting superstitions of the colonists), there was no way to be certain.

Yet, either way, it didn't change his role or the Duri Master's expectations. He had his doubts that the pig farmer was going anywhere save the atmosphere as his ashes scattered in the wind, so why bother worrying? The state of existence between Tscharia and the Holy Realm was a matter of much debate and controversy even among the Duri Masters, but Nuri had trouble imagining the pig farmer's spirit existing in any sort of higher plane: Tscharia, Purgatory, or otherwise.

Maybe you are already in Purgatory, then, the disembodied voice of the girl from the river said. *According to the Duri, there is only one plane of existence between Tscharia and the Divine Infinite.*

"Go," the Duri Master whispered in his direction.

Nuri nodded and bowed his head as he carefully slipped between the shifting line of clergymen, who were now deep in the throes of baritone exaltations and fevered dancing.

They look so strange, he thought. *So childish.*

His Duri Master had never explained why dancing was a part of the ceremony nor what it was supposed to represent, which led Nuri to believe that it had been thrown in solely for the benefit of the outsiders bearing witness to the purge. If nothing else, it added to the order's mystique as well as the notion that Duri Masters were privy to secret knowledge, both of which ultimately kept their followers toeing the line while emboldening the precepts of the Duri Order. So long as the people believed their clergymen were able to tap a conduit to the Holy of Holies, they would fear and obey. Therefore, the existence itself of the ritual didn't surprise Nuri so much as the idea that the Duri Masters hadn't thought to further capitalize on their perceived mysticism by devising another elaborate falsehood surrounding the ritual's origin.

The ritual is already steeped in falsehoods, the river girl persisted. *Perhaps they ran out of energy.*

Nuri carefully avoided the suggestion until he was safely seated at the base of the pine tree again, as though the clergy would somehow read his thoughts and toss him atop the pyre. He didn't want to betray any subtle physiological symptom of unbelief while in their presence.

I shouldn't be questioning the ritual, he scolded. *I'm the reason we are here. Not just for brazenly killing the pig farmer, but because I am guilty of preference. I sinned by allowing favoritism to cloud my judgment.*

To the girl, he directed a cold thought. *You are not welcome here.*

There was a pause as her voice built up from the depths of him, but the three words she directed in response cut right back to his core. They summarized his life on the mountaintop so aptly that all at once he felt dizzy.

Neither are you.

It was the unacknowledged truth underlying both his refusal to kill the girl for his own sin and his rejection of Duri teachings by proxy. He was not welcome among the Duri and never had been. Though neither the clergy nor the Called recruits themselves realized it, Nuri was well aware of his inability to sell out completely for the sake of God's Will—or rather, what the Duri *claimed* to be His will. For instance, he should have felt guiltier for disobeying and misleading his Duri Master than he did, but he'd spent all his guilt on regret over the death of anyone at all by his blade. Coupled with the putrid smoke from the cleansing pyre, it was enough to bring tears to his eyes. Nuri carefully wiped them away and concealed his stare so his Duri Master wouldn't notice the slip.

The weakness, he amended. *Not the 'slip.' Call it as it is.*

One by one, the clergymen completed their ritual aerobics and settled back into assigned positions around the altar. By then, night had covered the mountain and a chilled silence swept over the congregation. Nuri rose and bowed dutifully toward the mountain peak as a show of respect for the departed, then turned from the crowd. The Duri Master hadn't dismissed him directly, but he knew the older man would be waylaid a while by the clergy. If Nuri hurried back to the cottage in the meantime, he might not face as harsh a punishment for his sin simply because the scar-faced monster would be too tired from the hike to bother with him before morning. By then, his anger and bloodlust would both have assuredly abated. Nuri had seen it happen before.

And then what? the girl asked as he quietly slipped through the wilderness, darting between the *suyloc* trees a dozen yards removed from a group of villagers also departing the ceremony. They were oblivious to his presence, otherwise they would have avoided him altogether.

And then nothing, he replied. *I fulfill my purpose by serving God.*

That's a great deal more than nothing, she countered. *Fulfilling what you believe is your purpose and serving God are usually two different things.*

And what would you know about serving God? he demanded.

The girl didn't respond. Before long, he reached the cottage again and collapsed into his bed, expecting it would be a long while before he found sleep. He drifted off as soon as he hit the pillow, however, and slept straight through the night until the Duri Master roused him by searing the flesh above his right wrist with a branding iron.

"Time to cleanse your soul," the old man told him with a scowl that slammed his mouth shut despite the startling pain. "It is God's Will."

9

For a while, he simply floated through space.

He was distantly aware of images passing by, likely devised specifically for subliminal processing but near enough to his consciousness that he was wary of their presence.

Space, he thought. *Nothing, containing everything.*

Colt revealed wonderfully terrible things as he drifted through nebulae, skirted along the event horizon of a black hole that would eventually consume everyone he knew and loved, then passed through and beyond dying stars to witness the birth of new universes, galaxies, planets, and civilizations. It was a supremely humbling experience that he never quite grasped beyond a vague recollection of brilliant, heart-wrenching light and equally poignant darkness. He learned the histories of all alien races and saw every millisecond of time and space from the moment of thundering, explosive creation, but only for an instant. It was a series of great unveilings. Glimpses into the Divine Reality that existed beyond the perception of humanoid creatures and even the most spiritually advanced non-corporeal beings. And it was all punctuated by the realization of a great expansion towards truth, the calling home of his universe to its essence. The outward journey which must eventually end at the source of all things: the Omega Point.

He could not retain the knowledge or the experiences for more than a few seconds otherwise his brain would have simply overloaded, but each separate vision left an imprint on his soul. This, he understood, was the voice of God. This was His face, if He could be said to have a form at all. This was the Beginning and the End.

He didn't need Colt to explain it to him but she was there regardless to ease him back to his reality as the flow of galaxies slowed and he witnessed himself rocketing toward a shimmering planet where city lights gleamed across large bodies of water.

Maberrya, Colt informed him.

He retrieved the planet's history from the fading knowledge imparted to him as he drifted through space: the Divine Body incarnate. And then, the memories abruptly disappeared, yet his brain still felt stretched beyond its limit by the brief perception. He felt the harsh reality of space settle around him again. His breath sucked out from his lungs as the paralyzing cold worked its way into his body.

We won't reach the surface in time, he told Colt without a hint of anxiety.

He knew his body would freeze and his blood boil before they hit the atmosphere even if he didn't suffocate, and then he might burn up before he reached the planet's surface, anyway.

And what a way to die it will be.

Memories blistered through him again. Images from his time on the distant mountaintop with the Duri Master. The countless hours he'd spent studying ancient texts and training for survival in the harshest conceivable conditions to prepare for life among the Hidria.

Trust and surrender, Colt said.

He suddenly remembered slaughtering the men and women of a settlement in the Hiaro System once because they'd worshipped the natural world around them. They had contrived their own deities rather than acknowledge the primacy of the One True God, an action which was unfathomably heretical. Those had been some of his earliest kills, and he still remembered how a young man kneeling before an altar of twigs and carefully arranged grasses had stared at him as he approached. Eyes wide and fearful but not flinching in the face of that fear.

Acceptance.

Surrender.

A just executioner learns much about the nature of God through the salvific conjuring of blood.

It was the first line in the third book of the *Hidria Catechism*, the revelations and doctrine by which all Called were trained whenever they weren't directly reading from the Book. The phrase had stuck with Nuri throughout his time on the mountain, mostly because he thought the phrasing was peculiar. Hidria were not merely executioners. They were God's Right Hand. They were Divine Justice Incarnate. To devalue such a sacred charge to the grotesque misnomer of 'executioner' was jarring, and furthermore belied the import the Duri placed on the role of the mystical Hidria.

Surrender.

Even as he felt the last breath torn away from his lungs and the blue planet rushed up to meet him, Colt's presence reassured him. He refused to believe she would kill him in such a way when there had been so many other opportunities for him to die while he had a measure of control. Here was a problem that he could not solve nor influence in any way. Here was the result of utter surrender, the contradicting imperative of the Duri faith, and he doubted that acknowledging his helplessness in the face of the lethal cosmos would mean that he had failed the trials.

You do have control, though, Colt insisted. Her form appeared before him and matched his speed as he accelerated toward the atmosphere. Her features contorted until she looked more like a serpent than a humanoid creature and she roared an ungodly, soulless howl that made his stomach lurch more than the impossible velocity of his fall. *You are Hidria. You have the power to influence all those around you.*

True surrender is knowing when the All has called you to action, his Duri Master said.

Humans cannot influence the passage of space and time because they do not exist in God, Colt growled in a voice that grew deeper and more intricately layered the nearer they drew to the planet's surface. *You will die before you reach the water if you are human.*

I must not be human, he reminded himself, locking his jaw and bracing against the air that tore through him. *I must be Hidria.*

If you weren't Hidria, you would be dead already, Colt said.

He closed his eyes, trying to decide whether she spoke the truth or was merely attempting to distract him the way she attempted to lead all Called astray during the trials.

Yet before he arrived at a definitive answer, his body smacked against the surface of the ocean and he plunged leagues deep before daring to open his eyes. Even then, darkness enveloped him. He was too far from the surface to see anything beyond a distant glimmer reminiscent of Colt's wavering form. His body ached from head to toe with some regions throbbing with greater poignancy than others, but he knew she had been right.

I am already Hidria or I would be dead.

Except he suspected that wasn't quite true, either. It failed to account for the peculiarly warped reality of the trials. Even Hidria, he presumed, may have burned up in the atmosphere at that or been shattered into a thousand pieces upon impact with the water. The issue of immortality versus invincibility had never been adequately resolved in Duri texts, but his impression was that Hidria could be destroyed under the right—or rather, *wrong*—circumstances. This was something else entirely, then.

Or maybe it's the drugs they used to induce the Hidria Trance.

He suspected that it could have been any number of things. Colt's suggestion, however, seemed the unlikeliest. He did not believe he'd already transformed into Hidria. He didn't feel any different physically than he had on Shehoora. In fact, he still had bite marks in his thigh and forearm from the ice-wraiths to complement the deep gash beneath his ribs from the Jhrupa.

Is it real, then? Is my body truly here or am I lying on the floor of some chamber on the forbidden mountain?

The trials were designed to test the Called's ability to discern between reality and illusion, to draw back the curtain and glimpse the insane, incomprehensible reality that was God's true form.

Then these are all distractions, he warned himself as he kicked his legs toward the distant light and tried to ignore his lungs' cries for breath. *My lungs are an illusion. I do not need air as long as I follow the path laid out for me.*

He ascended from the frigid depths with his eyes locked on the surface, barely noting the mammoth sea monsters passing within a hundred meters of his position. If he was calm and projected an aura of control, he was confident they would leave him in peace despite their well-documented biological imperatives for food and violence. The kraken of Maberrya, he remembered, had awful reputations.

They were made that way, just as you were made to question your path and existence even if the Duri do not wish for you to do so, Colt said.

By the time he reached the surface, he could barely feel his arms and legs, but the towering city of Juriaq was ahead of him with its shining skyscrapers and bright lights, and that raised Nuri's spirit.

He struggled to a wooden ladder, knowing he had to pull himself out of the water before hypothermia took hold. He had no desire to die unspectacularly on a dock in the slums of one of the galaxy's largest cities. Although he'd been protected during his interstellar journey and in the ocean, instinct told him Juriaq would be a different animal altogether. Just like on Shehoora, he would be susceptible to injury once he was back within the trials' sphere of assessment and control. Juriaq would present a different sort of danger, he knew, but it would be no easier to escape with his life than the mountain tunnels on the ice planet. In fact, the location seemed oddly appropriate for religious trials. As far as the Duri Masters were concerned, Juriaq was the most dangerous city in the galaxy as well as the largest. They had long wished to sink the platform-city into the ocean that covered the entirety of Maberrya, but the operation had proved too large and the Called too few to mount a world-spanning strike. Additionally, the melting-pot of galactic species among the populace represented far too many formidable militaries to provoke and have any hope of victory. Still, the tribunal dreamed of a day when the heathens would be brought to their knees and the flag of the cross flew from every skyscraper.

Juriaq is a cesspool of sin, distraction, and vanity, the Duri Master had warned him throughout his training. *No soul visiting that wretched place escapes untarnished. To live in Juriaq is to completely sever your connection with the Divine Omega.*

Nuri felt a superstitious chill as his fingers at last gripped the final rung of the ladder and he pulled himself onto the floating, wooden platform where several fishing boats were tied. Yet lying there on the dock, trying to catch his breath while warming his arms and legs the best he could, the city didn't seem all that terrible. Imposing, surely, with buildings that sprang aggressively toward the heavens in a perpetual, ill-advised challenge of the infinite, but any evil that existed on the floating city lived within its varied inhabitants, not Juriaq itself. He had greater difficulty imagining a modern city as inherently worse than

Shehoora's mountains and temples, which had been built on black magic and wicked intent.

A desire for blind, misguided progress can be as dangerous as any weapon of the Evil One.

He quickly checked to be sure his weapons were still in place and picked himself up from the wood. There wasn't a clear path onward save for the lone dock leading to the city proper, so there was no point lingering to mull over his options. He reminded himself that the longer he was stuck in the trials, the worse the effects would be to his overall psychological health. Now that he'd felt his mind straining to grasp even the minutest aspects of the knowledge shewn to him as he hurtled toward Maberrya, he understood why it had such a lasting effect on Hidrian sanity. Or perhaps the inevitable result of all-encompassing knowledge was a state of being which could only be described in those generalities.

This place is truly a wonder, he thought.

Nuri had never been to Juriaq before, having only visited two-dozen planets in his life. The Duri Masters believed their pupils should live in isolation while they trained and thus were only dispatched from the mountaintop for purging missions to learn how to kill. None among them had ever visited Maberrya to Nuri's knowledge. As much as the Duri Masters would have liked to send an army to the ocean planet and wipe out anything and everything that moved from a comfortable orbit, there were more issues to consider than strictly the death toll. Sometimes, Nuri suspected, politics got in the way of the Duri agenda more than they would have their followers believe. Witnessing the vibrancy of the city and the warmth of the peculiar aliens he encountered as, soaking wet, he limped along the docks, he wondered if that wasn't such a bad thing after all.

Careful, the voice of his Duri Master cautioned. *That's precisely how they lower you to their sinful level. They disarm you with kindness and good humor, yet it's only a mask for the debauchery and Tscharia-worship taking place in their hearts and minds.*

A worker hauling materials from a rusted Laruka Crab ship nodded in his direction, clearly curious how Nuri had survived the ocean and why he'd attempted to swim out there in the first place. Even with the floating city nearby to discourage the largest sea monsters from venturing too close, the water was dangerous, and even the most thick-headed of tourists knew to avoid it without a proper vessel.

Nuri returned the nod before deciding to keep his head down until he exited the docks to avoid engaging any more locals. He didn't feel like explaining his situation if they asked and he wasn't truly certain any of them were real at all.

Then why are you turning away? Colt pressed. *The goal of the trials is to judge whether you can sift through distractions and determine what is real and what is illusion. That is the only way to know the truth of God. You must first know truth in the universe around you.*

The argument sounded like something he might hear from his Duri Master, but it reeked of a trap regardless. To engage the locals would only delay his mission and might lead to further trouble. Yet if the doorway to the next stage of the trials was hidden within the consciousness of one of these creatures, he needed to explore more than just the physical characteristics of the city. The Duri manuals on the trials did not explicitly outline whether one was supposed to interact with the aliens they encountered on each new world beyond engaging them in combat, but Nuri was acutely aware that his trials weren't developing at all the way the others purportedly had.

That's because true Hidria do not reveal the nature of their trials. Their relationships with God are personal and all-

encompassing. If you are to know God, you must forget what the Duri have claimed to know for you.

Nuri frowned and climbed the ladder from the second level of the docks to the lowest level of the city streets, which themselves ascended on platforms into ten interconnected conduits that ran throughout Juriaq.

If I am to know God, he thought towards Colt, who had disappeared from his sight even though he still felt her hovering over his shoulder, *then I will need time to hear Him. You are nothing but a distraction. An illusion.*

He pulled himself onto the street and had his first glimpse of the West Quarter, which comprised the so-called fishing slums of the massive city. He identified the area by its reputation alone in one look though he'd never seen a holographic likeness in his life. Most of Juriaq enjoyed unfathomable wealth, but that meant all the citizens who couldn't afford the cost of living in the three affluent sections of the city were pushed towards the docks, many within reach of the midnight sea monsters. His Duri Master had spoken at length about the misery and corruption ruling the city's lower classes and the West Quarter was at its very heart.

It is a sin to treat them this way, he thought.

Those who do not honor Creator God live in anguish, his Duri Master countered. *They must not be mourned.*

For a few moments, Nuri stood on the wet ground, digesting the view of the imposing skyscrapers. The ubiquitous signs of abandonment and vandalism at the base of each structures were particularly alarming.

This is a godless place, he thought. *His presence has been forced away by the Evil One and these poor souls aren't even aware of it.*

The image of his Duri Master in mid-rhetorical ecstasy suddenly appeared to him. The scars along his cheeks stretched and shimmered in the flickering candlelight as he denounced the sinners of Juriaq and the government that had forced them into the hands of the Evil One, who preyed upon the disheartened and downtrodden.

Am I to save these people then? he wondered.

He couldn't imagine that such a fundamental shift in the culture of Maberrya could occur during the trials. Even assuming it was possible, that sort of large-scale conversion took a lot of time and even more politicking, sometimes even at the end of a laser sword. It also didn't strike him as an occupation that would bring him any closer to Prime no matter how well he convinced his Duri Master they needn't purge the entire planet in the name of God.

A beat-up hover car approached through the street, leaning drunkenly to one side as its undercarriage scraped against the ground. Three blue-skinned aliens sat in the passenger compartment of the self-flying vessel. Each watched him closely.

Fronovs, he thought.

A smooth-talking species by reputation. On Juriaq, the Fronovs in the West Quarter usually ran the local gangs. They capitalized on the lawlessness and desperation of the fishing slums for profit. It was peculiar to see them in such beat-up transportation, but Nuri decided such a vehicle was likely to allay any suspicions of the sparse local law enforcement. Any Fronov seen riding in one of the higher-end models in the West Quarter would likely be pegged as a drug-dealer or arms-supplier right away and be taken in for questioning. Juriaq may have been a corrupt city, but there was only so much the government could overlook in plain sight.

Nuri approached the vehicle slowly as it dragged towards him on its busted lifts.

Your hands must be swift and steady, Colt told him.

He reached instinctively for the holster on his back, then decided a blaster would be far too conspicuous before he had ascertained their intentions. Instead, he gripped the hilt of his laser sword and watched the vehicle gracelessly screech to a halt in front of him.

Distractions, he frowned, glancing toward the docks and noticing that the few workers who'd been hauling crates of fish into loading floaters had made themselves scarce at the sight of the Fronov hovercar. It was a startling indication of just how heavy-handed and audacious the Fronov gangs had grown in the West Quarter. The fishermen themselves were nothing to mess with by the looks of them, yet they had fled before they'd even gotten a look at the passengers.

A moment later, the doors on either side of the cab gasped open and the blue aliens climbed out. Their long, black cloaks skimmed the ground as they approached. The alien at the front—presumably their leader—straightened his black gloves and reached into his shoulder holster for his blaster.

"Stranger," the alien called, letting the blaster swing carelessly in his hand.

He doesn't understand the weapon, Nuri realized. *It is not a part of him.*

He gleaned much about the nature of the Fronov's stature then, and it didn't involve getting his hands dirty. He didn't know how to fire a blaster properly which meant the two others with him were the muscle of his operation. Bodyguards, Nuri wagered, although it was possible the leader was just a low-rung crime-lord. The type who shook the locals for money they didn't have and pushed drugs they couldn't afford.

"Hello," Nuri said as they approached. He focused on the blaster as much as he could while still maintaining eye contact with the Fronov gang leader. His grip tightened on the hilt of his laser-blade with each footstep. "What can I do for you?"

The Fronov flashed a charming, mischievous grin and glanced back at his two bodyguards. Evidently, they found Nuri's lack of fear amusing.

"Well, for starters, we're curious how you managed to survive a fall from the upper atmosphere without a suit."

Both Nuri and the Fronov stopped walking a dozen paces from each other.

"I don't know what you mean," Nuri replied.

"Our scanners detected a meteor strike on the surface of the ocean at over a thousand *kromospheres*. An impact like that would crush anything organic, and yet we watched you climb out of the ocean with hardly a scratch and no armor to speak of." The blue alien leaned closer and eyed him up and down like he was taking inventory of Nuri's injuries, though it was clearly just for show. Gang leaders weren't physicians and anyone scanning him as he climbed onto the docks would have already completed their analysis of his physical condition. "That wasn't *you* that fell, was it?"

Nuri shrugged noncommittally, wanting to avoid a confrontation if possible, though it was clear the Fronov boss would not have drawn his weapon if he expected a friendly exchange. He wouldn't have brought the extra muscle, either.

That won't work, Colt warned. *You need to answer him or things will get ugly in a hurry.*

Nuri was a killing machine with knowledge of all systems in the known galaxy and many cultural complexities archived in his catacombs of memory, but he'd never dealt with a delicate situation like this before. His training only told him to use his weapon before the conversation progressed any further. At the very least, it would buy him some time to find the next doorway and the next stage of the trials.

But what if I'm supposed *to talk to them?* he wondered. *What if learning to negotiate this situation is part of the test of my worthiness to be Hidria?*

It didn't fit exactly with what he knew of the trials and the primary focus of uncovering the true nature of God, but there was enough nagging doubt within him that he decided to wait it out a while longer and explore all possible alternatives before resorting to violence. It would likely come to that eventually—he was almost certain of it—but he might be able to glean some information from the Fronovs in the meantime. They might even provide some profound, hidden message from the Divine that would steer him toward the correct path.

Unlikely, his Duri Master said. *They are nothing but distractions placed in your way by the Evil One to prevent you from reaching Prime and gazing upon the face of God.*

The Fronov grinned and glanced back at his companions again, although neither of the stoic aliens offered any show of emotion or support.

"It would be better for you if you answered me," the Fronov said, raising the blaster. It was a gaudy threat from a man who clearly didn't understand the nature of a weapon or the intimidation of a superior foe, even if he didn't realize Nuri *was* his superior just yet. He would know it soon enough. "Then I won't have to use this." He waved the blaster again.

Nuri released his grip on the laser blade. He wouldn't need it to deal with this one, he wagered, and it didn't seem right to kill the man for being an ignorant fool even if his Duri training told him otherwise.

"I *did* fall into the water," he said, walking toward an abandoned hovercar dealership across the way. He knew the answer wouldn't end the conversation, but he needed to at least *look* like he thought it would while he sought better footing for combat. He didn't want to be backed against the dock despite his confidence that he could handle the three Fronov buffoons, who'd likely never seen battle outside Juriaq gang wars. The two bodyguards, however, quickly moved to intercept him before he reached the open area.

"I didn't say you could leave," the leader said firmly. He didn't move. It was clear he expected Nuri to return to a conversational distance, a subtle and childish power play that likely worked on many of the downtrodden souls he bullied in the West Quarter. Nuri may have been spiritually downtrodden the way that the Duri Masters claimed *all* creatures were spiritually downtrodden so long as they were separated from God's Holy Presence on Prime, but he wasn't susceptible to the intimidation of mere men. The Called were taught to fear two beings and two beings only: God and the Evil One, being one and the same as well as polar opposites. If Nuri had conquered his fear of the Watchmen and their supernatural evils, he wasn't worried about dispatching a few opportunistic thugs.

"Why does it matter?" Nuri asked the Fronov, stepping close enough to make the leader visibly uncomfortable. To his credit, though, he didn't flinch. Someone who hadn't been trained to mark physiological reactions in alien species likely wouldn't have even noticed the twitch beneath the Fronov's taut skin. "My misfortune is no burden to you."

The bodyguards crowded in around him, blocking his exits on either side of the gang leader.

"On the contrary," the Fronov said. "Your presence *is* a burden to us. We don't like surprises dropping out of the sky in our territory, especially ones with a lot of weaponry and very little armor. It makes us wonder if you were sent by the Duchitaw to sabotage our operation." Comfortable in his protection now that the bodyguards were close enough to touch, he leaned forward and grinned in Nuri's face, exposing dazzling white teeth and a blood-red tongue. "We like to take care of problems before they become too big to handle. So what problems have you brought to the West Q? How do you plan to pay for protection if we even decide to tolerate your presence?"

Nuri took a deep breath. The whole introduction by the Fronov was so rehearsed and well-worn that he wondered how many unfortunate travelers had been accosted the same way when they were shipwrecked or wandered into the wrong part of town.

Pitiful creature, the Duri Master's voice growled. *Do not suffer this thing to live. Slit his throat so he may spend eternity in Tscharia with the Clown King.*

Calmly, Nuri reached for the hilt of his laser blade and spat at the ground. In this issue, at least, he agreed with the Duri Master's assessment of the trials and would enjoy carrying out the Divine Sacrifice. The Fronov may only have been one small crime-lord in a practically abandoned section of the West Quarter, but thousands would be spared his tyranny when Nuri ended his insufferable life.

Another will rise in his place, Colt said.

It was true enough, he supposed, but maybe the next one would be better, and maybe he or she would reflect a little more profoundly on the nature of mortality. Maybe Nuri's shadow would live as a constant warning to them. A living nightmare. But only if someone was still around to spread word of his deeds.

For that reason alone, he decided to allow one of the bodyguards to live. While the Fronov droned through the next paragraph of his speech, Nuri glanced back and forth between the aliens, deciding which one seemed a worthier survivor.

"You don't have an answer?" the Fronov continued, daring another step towards Nuri that was clearly for show. His legs were still taut like springs, ready to explode backward at the first sign of movement from Nuri's concealed right fist. "Why don't you come along for a ride, then, and we'll see if you remember once you have a chance to warm up from the ocean? I'll even buy you a drink."

There were probably some hapless wanderers who trusted the Fronov at his word and allowed the bodyguards to lead them into the vehicle, where they were more likely than not driven to a warehouse far removed from life in the West Q and tortured until they revealed whatever insignificant information they had to offer or paid for release. It wouldn't be much if anything at all, Nuri knew, because no formidable crime boss capable of challenging the established gangs of the West Q would be stupid enough to send a lone man into the city section via the ocean. At the very least, he or she would have found their way in through the more affluent quarters of the city. Nuri suspected the Fronov knew as much but enjoyed torturing the innocents anyway, maybe because it made the citizens of the West Quarter more docile but also probably because it made him feel big.

Still, Nuri started walking away, willing to give the trio one final chance to move off on their own.

"That wasn't a request," the Fronov snapped when Nuri tried to push around one of the bodyguards.

"I don't care," he responded truthfully, shrugging out of the nearest alien's grip. The one he'd decided would live. "I don't have any currency and I don't work for anyone you know. I'm not here to cause any trouble unless you make me."

This time, the bodyguards joined their leader in snide laughter.

This won't happen once you wear the armor of the Hidria, the Duri Master told him. *Everyone in the galaxy knows the sigil of the Hidria. They would be pissing their boots right now if they knew who you were.*

He wasn't Hidria yet, though, and he knew even the greatest of the Called were susceptible to underestimating their opponents in battle. Anything could happen once blasters were drawn.

"Hold him," the Fronov said with a scowl.

Deep breaths, Nuri told himself as the burly blue aliens gripped his arms. He didn't resist. His eyes were focused on the glint of the midday sun off the skyscrapers. There was a familiar symbol reflected in the glass across from him, formed by the busted-out windows of a building the Fronov gangs had usurped for their drug trade.

What is that? he wondered, momentarily so distracted by the circular image with markings in its center that he forgot all about the Fronovs. He was jolted back to reality in short order, however, when the leader stabbed him in the stomach with a small device packing a powerful electric charge.

"AAAGGGHHHH!" he screamed as the end of the weapon buried in his gut where his armor had been torn by the Jhrupa.

Bright blue snakes of electricity scorched his veins and rattled his teeth. His stomach started belching blood immediately. Whatever the Fronov had used to break through the tears in his armor, it had broken through his skin just as easily.

Distractions, Colt scolded him.

He couldn't afford to divide his attention in the middle of the battle, even if the sigil of God's Holy Protectorate was evident on the building across from him.

The Fronov laughed. "Does that make you a little more agreeable, friend?"

Nuri stifled a scream as the leader pressed the button on the side of the small, black square and electricity flowed through him again. He forced himself to draw deep breaths, even when he bit down on his tongue hard enough to draw blood and his bones began to ache.

Pain is human pain is human pain is human, he fought the words into his consciousness, using them to ward off the mortal agony of his earthly body. Control returned to him by degrees even as the device continued beating waves of pain through every molecule of his being. Even as his skin began to stink like cooked flesh.

Pain is human.

He opened his eyes and glared at the Fronov. "I am not human," he said.

The alien's expression changed for an instant from triumph to confusion, then morphed into an agonized howl when Nuri kicked him in the chest hard enough to crack his multi-layered ribcage. The device fell to the ground. Nuri swept the leg out from the left bodyguard and rolled in that direction in one smooth motion, hurling the other bodyguard a few meters down the street where he skidded to a halt beside an overturned vending machine which had somehow wandered into traffic.

Before any of the Fronovs could react, Nuri drew his rifle and fired three quick shots into the nearest bodyguard, blasting through the leathery protective armor the alien wore over his chest and burning a hole in his head. The small-minded brute hadn't thought to add any protection there, of course. Muscle rarely cared for brains. It was a swift death and not at all like the damnation he had in mind for the Fronov leader, who not only lacked morality as a creature purporting to safeguard his community from outside threats but who also lacked skill and honor as a warrior. As far as the Duri (and therefore, the Hidria) were concerned, those were two unforgivable sins.

Calmly, Nuri rose and stepped toward the Fronov leader, who was gasping for breath and writhing in pain on the littered street. "You are a sinner," he said, shifting the rifle so that the gang leader was reminded of its presence. "It is the will of God that we must not suffer a sinner to live so long as his actions conflict with the best interests of those around him and prevent any man or woman from reaching the Divine Truth." As he spoke, Nuri felt the world flexing. The symbol of God Infinite on the first and last planet glowed white-yellow within the building across the way. Beckoning him.

The sight was invigorating. It sharpened his focus and strengthened his resolve.

"It is the will of God that I kill you now as a symbol of His first sacrifice that saved all mankind from Tscharia."

These were the ritual utterances each Called recited prior to taking a life and offering it to the All God, but Nuri knew he wouldn't need to remember them much longer. Those who failed the trials were not bound to such pompous recitation, and the Hidria did not speak at all. Not with their lips. They were silent killers and purveyors of justice, for theirs was the voice of God.

"Stop," the Fronov wheezed. He crawled away from the docks, possibly trying to make it back to the hover car before Nuri made good on his threat and ended the despicable creature's life. But Nuri was patient. He knew that he had time before the crime boss reached the door, and he didn't intend on letting the machine run ever again. He would cut it to pieces with the laser blade himself rather than see it used by the lone survivor of the Fronov trio, who was currently unconscious and crumpled against the wandering vending machine.

"It's too late. I'm running out of time," Nuri told the alien with genuine sadness. His eyes wandered up to the lightshow through the broken windows of the building across the way, knowing his path to Prime and the true nature of God led him through those haunted hallways and the stores of drugs the West Q gangs stocked up for sea transport throughout the other sections of Juriaq.

"I can pay you," the Fronov persisted. He'd finally managed to get enough breath to level his voice, but the desperation was still evident as he backpedaled toward the beat-up hover car. His eyes never left Nuri, but Nuri's focus had been drawn elsewhere. First to the God symbol, then further down the street towards the city's center, where the more affluent neighborhoods (everywhere but the West Quarter) were no doubt bustling with midday activity as the system's center of commerce and entertainment welcomed new promises and opportunities brought in by the afternoon crowds.

Godlessness, the Duri Master seethed while the neon lights caught Nuri's attention and drew him toward the heart of the city. *Sinners.*

Seeing that Nuri was otherwise occupied, the Fronov eased his way onto one leg and began to shuffle away as quietly as he could manage with his ribcage cracked and his insides bleeding.

"Not yet," Nuri said. He fired one shot into the Fronov's side without taking his eyes from the gleaming city and stepped over the alien as he cried out in agony.

This is the perfect opportunity to prove yourself, his Duri Master insisted. *You can wipe out this whole godless city. It is clearly an outpost of the Evil One where corruption and debauchery reign.*

Moaning softly, the Fronov collapsed face-first onto the street. Defeated.

Kill them all. That is the way of the Hidria.

He could picture himself doing it. One billion souls were a lot to sacrifice, but in the grand scheme of things, they were nothing. His training had prepared him to deal with large cities on a solo mission, since Hidria always operated individually to prevent a tainted collective perception. It was even said that, sometimes, one Hidria was even tasked with assassinating another Hidria if he or she fell too far beyond the veil of reality and could no longer distinguish truth from illusion.

You know what to do. Work your way down into the giant repulsorlifts that keep the city afloat. Blow them to pieces and all of Juriaq will be swallowed in the redemptive waters like Atlantis of old.

It was simple when he really got down to it. If he devoted himself, he could accomplish the task in a matter of weeks, and yet no Called or Hidria before him had done so.

Why?

Distractions, Colt warned. *You're straying from the path. You know where to go from here. Do not confuse the voice of men for the voice of God.*

Nuri froze and shook his head. *She's right,* he thought. But why would the Duri Master be the one to distract him from killing the despicable crime lord groveling at his feet?

Because he doesn't just want to see one or two sinners in Juriaq die. He wants all of Maberrya to burn.

He stared at the building again. The God symbol had disappeared, leaving only empty windows and a faint crunching sound that whistled out through the open doors. He'd never felt so utterly alone in his life, and it was a peculiar feeling considering that he was surrounded by the most heavily populated city in the known galaxy.

"He's left me," he whispered in horror, as he stared at the building. "I'm all alone."

"Please," the Fronov begged, reaching out in supplication.

Nuri didn't even look when he pulled the trigger, but he felt the splatter from the alien's exploding head against his skin.

There is no greater lie than Death, Colt whispered in his ear.

Her mist-like form swirled around him. He closed his eyes, holstered his rifle, and followed her toward the building, forgetting all about the unconscious survivor he'd left by the vending machine.

You need to learn how to avoid distraction, she told him as he walked unsteadily toward the open doors of the massive, abandoned building. *These are all illusions.*

The idea made his eyes widen, but surely there couldn't be *pain* in his shoulder and legs then, could there? If none of it was real?

You are not really here.

But it couldn't *all* be illusion. Some of it was true or there would be no way for him to discern reality from the obfuscation of the veil.

"Prime," he muttered as he reached the sidewalk. A swirl of wind carried colorful debris past him.

It should have occurred to him earlier, he supposed, but now he believed the trials could only have one endpoint, and it was also the beginning. He had to reach Prime, the last planet, and ascend the Holy Mountain to reach the Divine Infinite. It was the only way he would know God, to gaze upon Him on His throne and allow reality to envelop him.

"Prime," he said resolutely.

He took one last look at the defiled streets of Juriaq, feeling a pang of sadness that he hadn't gotten the chance to see the true majesty of the famous city during his time in the West Quarter, then stepped through the open doors of the abandoned building to surrender himself once again.

10

This is not how Time has remembered it, but this is how it was.

The howling of the jackals kept Nuri awake well into the witching hour. He heard his Duri Master through cracks in the wall of his bedchamber, mumbling passages from *The Divine Incendiary*. The text was a forbidden follow-up to the written word of God and was purported to contain Divine revelations from beyond the Milky Way galaxy.

The words inexplicably disturbed Nuri. Everything about *The Divine Incendiary* disturbed him, in fact, though he couldn't quite explain how even to himself. He supposed some of his apprehension owed to the temperament of his Duri Master when he read the book, which usually coincided with his secret alcoholism and a general rage at the state of the despicable creatures of the galaxy. It almost always ended with his Duri Master sobbing off into another corner of the hut, cursing God and his own sinful ways where he assumed Nuri couldn't hear him. Afterward, he would mutilate himself as punishment. It happened often, and each scar on the Duri Master's face was uglier than the last.

Tonight, he obsessed over a particularly controversial book in the middle section of *The Divine Incendiary*, one that detailed the nature of the physical God in the physical universe, and how He might be reached through the means of an exploratory spacecraft.

"And Man will set foot on that Holy Mount, and he will see that God has, indeed, created all things from the beginning of Time. And by reaching the Omega, he shall be saved."

Chapter seventeen, verses nineteen and twenty, Nuri thought. He was forbidden from reading the book as well, of course, but his curiosity had gotten the better of him and eventually he had committed most of the passages to memory. They disturbed him but they were *delightfully* disturbing, much the same way the Divine Book *Revelations* sent shudders through him and awakened a unique brand of cosmic paranoia and insanity which delighted the intellectual buried beneath his Duri training.

There was a crash from the other room as the Duri Master pounded his fist on the wooden table and hurled something into the fireplace. The jackals continued to howl up and down the mountain.

Nuri squeezed his eyes shut, knowing he was expected to wake at the first sign of dawn to complete his chores and meditation before he departed to participate in the sacred purging of a moon colony that worshipped an alien deity instead of God. It was no use trying to fall asleep, though. As long as his Duri Master was in the next room, sweating out a private catastrophe of faith at the bottom of a flask through the words of a forbidden book, Nuri couldn't drop beyond consciousness even with the aid of his strongest meditation techniques. Resigned, he opened his eyes and looked out the window at the towering yellow moon illuminating the valley.

The village was quiet. The murder of the old man had been all but forgotten now that Nuri's exile and humiliation had ended. No one spoke about the incident openly anymore, which was little help to Nuri's search for answers to his endlessly multiplying questions. He still could not grasp the distinction between killing the old man and killing entire colonies of innocent settlers for their beliefs. Colonists who likely had never been exposed to the Divine Word in the first place.

It's all fake, that's why, he thought bitterly. *Dissent is forbidden so no one acknowledges the glaring inconsistencies in Duri dogma. The village has been bought and paid for. The citizens are mindless followers who take everything at its surface value, which may be the greatest sin of a follower.*

He rolled away from the window, struggling to quiet his discontent. For years, he'd had no choice but to indulge the falsehoods of the Duri religion, and slowly his mind had begun to dull from the injustice of it all. He was terrified that eventually his own complacency would win out and he would transform into a soulless creature like the masses asleep in the valley below him.

It is all illusion. None of this is real.

As he stared at the sagging wooden beams over his head, pale smoke began to swirl through the cracks and took shape before his eyes. A creature, or maybe a spirit.

Chapter thirteen, verse nine: The fog of Illusion is the nature of Evil.

A face formed and hovered over him, staring raptly at his unflinching expression. When he reflected on the apparition the next morning while boarding a Duri Fighter bound for slaughter, he was stunned by his own lack of terror. In the moment, however, he wasn't the least bit surprised to see the face of the girl by the river—the one whom he'd refused to kill—emerge from the tangled mist.

"You're alive," she whispered to him.

It wasn't until years later that he wondered whether it was a question or a statement, and what the implications might have been for either meaning depending on how he interpreted her visitation. At the time, he simply nodded. "You are, too," he whispered. "Did you make it to the forbidden mountain?"

Her form swirled again and she drifted to the floor, where she solidified in the girl's physical form. "Yes," she said, "and no."

He sat up, carefully avoiding the telltale creaks of his wooden bedframe so the Duri Master wouldn't hear him while in the throes of desperate fury toward his own lacking faith. "What do you mean? Did they kill you?"

The girl sat down on his bed, heedless of the loud crackling of the floorboards beneath her, and shrugged. "No one ever truly dies. Our bodies merely transfigure into the perfect form of energy that encompasses the universe."

Nuri shuddered and moved his legs away from her. "That's heresy. They'll crucify you for speaking it and leave your body for the *shuloc* Crows. You'll be an example to the rest of the villagers."

"I am not a villager," she said.

He fell quiet, trying to guess her true nature and intentions while they held stares.

"We were born to suffer," Nuri said finally, once the gleam of her human eyes bore too deeply into his soul for comfort. "We cannot reach Prime without suffering. Our own misery purifies us, and that of the ones we offer up to God to honor his blood sacrifice."

She took his hand. He was shocked by the frigidity of her grip. "Where is Prime?" she asked.

He scoffed, trying to mask his confusion over their physical proximity. "No one knows where Prime is. If we knew, we would be there already and there would be no more suffering for any of us."

"You sound like you're quoting *The Divine Incendiary*. You could get into a lot of trouble for that."

His expression soured at once and he withdrew his hand from hers. "Why are you here?" he demanded. "What *are* you?"

She continued staring at him for a moment, then slowly rose from the bed and crossed to the other side of the room. She looked out the window through the heavy, purple leaves of a *loolom* tree that obscured the view of the ancient ruins, where it was said that God's angels had crashed millennia ago on their way to a human colony. The girl turned her back on him and gestured through the window-frame.

"There are ghosts here," she said. "Victims."

Swallowing hard, Nuri rose and tossed aside the bedclothes. The floor was warm against his feet. Warmer than it should have been on a mountain night, even in the summer. Nevertheless, he shuddered when he put his weight on the wood and stepped carefully to the girl's side.

"Are *you* a ghost?" he asked.

She turned with her eyes glowing and her hair waving in the breeze through the open window. The cries of the jackals had risen in pitch and volume. They seemed closer to the cottage on the mountain than Nuri ever remembered them.

"What do *you* think I am?" she asked.

Her brow furrowed, as though she truly relied on his judgment to grasp her identity rather than merely playing at mysticism.

Nuri carefully considered her visage, ignoring his human preferences in favor of his Higher Judgment as one of the Called. Once he'd worked out the spiritual arithmetic, he frowned and turned toward the window. "You are a distraction, whatever your nature may be, and therefore you are a sin."

"How do you define a distraction?" she asked, turning his shoulders with her frigid touch so that they faced each other again. Inches away from touching lips, he realized. More intimate than Nuri had ever been with a girl.

A *woman*, he amended.

"Is the classification of 'distraction' subject to the weaknesses of the beholder?"

His eyes widened. All breath had sucked out from his lungs, though he wasn't sure if it was the girl's presence alone or the shock of her cold touch. "I don't know," he said truthfully, despite his Duri training and despite knowing better. "I suppose so."

"Would I be considered a distraction to one who did not find me appealing in a physical and intellectual capacity?"

Nuri shrugged out of her grip and turned away, hanging his head in shame. "No," he said. "You would not."

"Do you believe me inherently evil? Do you think I am an emissary of Tscharia because you prefer me over the other villagers? Over an old pig farmer?"

His stomach lurched at the mention of the old man he'd killed to spare her life. He clenched his fists at his sides and dropped to his knees, stifling the guilt and embarrassment that had draped over his shoulders like a cloak of misery since he'd taken the farmer's life in front of the villagers. "No," he confessed through pursed lips. "I am weak."

The girl knelt before him, brushing hair from his forehead. "Do you care for me?"

The jackals howled beneath his window. Outside his bedroom door, the Duri Master cursed and sloshed a wine bottle as he frantically expelled the uncertainty that had usurped his heart like a cancer through *The Divine Incendiary*.

We all have secrets, he thought. *Secret hearts and secret sins. There is only one who sees through them.*

"Do you?" she persisted.

He nodded, averting his eyes. Not daring to say the words aloud lest the fury of God and his Duri Masters condemn him.

Unshaken, she nodded back and rose abruptly to her feet. "Then I will go now to the forbidden mountain. Not because I am a distraction to you but because you care." Her physical form began to waver and then pull apart, reassembling in the pale smoke that hovered over his bed.

"You will see me again," she whispered, then ascended through the cottage roof toward the heavens.

Nuri did not bother watching after her. He merely remained kneeling on the warm wooden floor, listening to the cries of the jackals and the feverish recitation of verses from *The Divine Incendiary* drifting through the cracks in his bedroom walls.

In the morning, he rode the Duri ship to a moon colony and slaughtered its inhabitants in the name of God.

11

This was entirely different.

Nuri had stepped through the open door of a building in the West Quarter of Juriaq, but he wasn't on Maberrya anymore. He wasn't on Prime, either. He was back in the stone hallways where the trials began, back where he'd encountered the Watchman. It was a different section of the temple and Colt was nowhere to be found, but the corridors were otherwise identical to the ones he'd previously explored. They extended in both directions with wooden doors on either side of the hallway and no indication of which he was to open next.

Humans are always seeking overt signs of where they must go to fulfill their destinies. You must not be human.

He drew his laser blade and ignited the beam to get a better look at the faintly glowing walls. There were no roadmaps to guide him this time. Not even grooves from countless millennia of Hidria exploration into each portal. Just uniform blocks of stone seamlessly mortared one after another against each other.

A man who does not know the correct path to follow has lost sight of the God King. He is in danger of wandering into the perils of Tscharia.

Nuri brushed the wet hair from his forehead and started down the hall, ignoring the frantic voice of his Duri Master spouting passages from *The Divine Incendiary*. It didn't seem to matter much *where* he went since there was no indication of a pre-ordained path and Colt was gone, but as he walked, he wondered yet again whether that meant he'd already failed the trials. Maybe this was his slow preamble to waking life, a settling designed to ease him back to consciousness rather than cause irreparable brain damage during the journey back through the veil. At least this particular brand of failure was preferable to being killed by Colt during the trials. At least he would have his life.

Why would you want to go on living if you fail the trials? Wouldn't you prefer that your consciousness reaches Prime as soon as possible?

It was the great dilemma of a devout life to have such a deep need for communion with the Divine Infinite and yet delay the transfiguration as long as possible. The Duri Masters refuted the so-called paradox exposed by those outside the Duri faith by claiming that one could only achieve transfiguration and communion with the Divine Infinite through a lifetime of service to God's Holy Agenda. Nuri believed that wholeheartedly, yet even he acknowledged that some of his belief was tainted by the very human fear of death and the unknown.

Hidria know no fear. Hidria are fear and death.

You are still human.

His muscles tensed. His pace quickened without thought. It was devastating to have endured so much misery in the years since arriving on the mountain to begin his Duri studies only to be reminded that he had not yet transformed because of selfish *human* preoccupations. He was shaken, but he couldn't show it. He couldn't allow himself to feel the devastation because that very awareness of his human fears and insecurities was what held him back in the first place, anchoring him to a universe that could not possibly be the ultimate achievement of Creator God.

There is something more, he reminded himself firmly. *There is a greater truth.*

Colt's face at last appeared before him. *Yes, and it's right here for you to see*, she told him. *All you must do is look. Follow your path and know where you are going.*

102

He opened his mouth to reply but the apparition faded into the stone before he'd devised an adequate retort or settled on one of a dozen pressing questions. It didn't matter, he decided. She wouldn't have provided a definitive answer, anyway.

That's not why she's here, he thought. *She's here to make me question, not to make me see.*

He buried himself in that harsh truth for a time, troubled by the apparent goodwill of the trickster being which had been painted so unflatteringly in his studies of the Called trials. In person, she seemed anything but evil. Maddeningly vague, perhaps, and eerie in her ubiquity, but otherwise helpful. More advocate than adversary.

Was it possible that the Duri Masters had radically misinterpreted her nature when they assembled their teachings on the trials?

Perhaps, but the Hidria *would have known. Maybe she appears differently for each of the Called.*

He'd never met a Hidria, of course, and therefore couldn't say for certain one way or the other. If he'd met a Hidria, he would have been dead already.

The great paradox...

But if they'd killed him, he also would have found Prime, assuming those killed by Hidria wound up on Prime rather than Tscharia. And who knew if souls survived the Hidria cleansing at all?

Before he could ponder the issue any further, a shadow passed through the corridor ahead of him. The quiet presence reminded him of the ice-wraiths on Shehoora and sent a shudder down his spine. He stopped abruptly and extinguished his blade, more out of reflex than a belief that he could possibly avoid detection in the ancient structure, where no living souls had ever passed except during the trials. The hair on his arms stood on end. He felt electricity in the air, although he guessed he could have been feeling leftover jolts from the Fronov's weapon on Maberrya. The wound had been cauterized by the device, but it still stung. His skin felt too tight over his bones.

This was a different sensation, though. Familiar, but different.

The Evil One, he decided, scowling. *Watchmen.*

Careful not to draw any more attention than he already had, he crept slowly down the hall toward the shadow. He felt at least one additional presence stalking him nearby, and with each step, he grew more convinced there was another Watchman in the corridor and possibly a few of them. His instincts warned that the masked devils had laid a trap in the darkness to finish him off before he managed a retreat.

Footsteps shuffled loudly toward him. Evidently, they no longer cared to conceal their presence, which was especially troubling given how discreetly the Watchmen typically hunted. It meant that they knew he couldn't escape and didn't care whether he was aware of it. They likely preferred he was, in fact, since agents of Tscharia sustained themselves on fear and suffering.

He had to act fast.

On impulse, he felt along the wall to his right until his hand found a doorknob. He didn't bother puzzling over whether it would bring him any closer to Prime. He only knew that he needed to escape the corridor quickly no matter what awaited him. In the weakened state brought on by his marathon swim on Maberrya and subsequent confrontation with Fronov gangsters, he didn't think he could overwhelm two Watchmen at once—let alone three or more—so his only hope lay through the doorway.

Put your trust in the Architect of All Things, his Duri Master told him. *He will guide you true.*

The footsteps closed in on both sides, but he didn't dare ignite his laser blade to get a fix on their exact positions. It was too late to matter, anyway, and he couldn't spare the time it took to draw the weapon and point it toward the Watchmen.

His hand found the knob just as a warm, dead grip settled on his wrist.

Surrender, Colt said.

He slammed his shoulder into the door and fell into darkness, dragging the Watchman with him through the portal.

Too late, he thought as he fell. *My mind is too muddled by doubt. My own consciousness is a distraction. I am my own adversary.*

Unseen, the Watchman growled and thrashed above him as they hurtled through nothing-space.

Space, he thought. *Nothing, containing everything.*

Nuri kicked at the air rushing past them, trying to separate himself from the foul creature. He didn't make much progress, though. The fall seemed to have no end.

What if it doesn't? he wondered. *What if I've opened a door into an unpopulated universe? What if I've opened the door to Tscharia?*

Tscharia is its own universe, his Duri Master recited. *Tscharia is complete separation from God, a universe the Divine Infinite created to fall beyond his sight. There is only one planet in that miserable infinity, and that planet is Tscharia.*

Nuri stifled a scream as the Watchman's grip seized on his ankle, burning through the protection of his layered armor. He forced himself to stop squirming long enough to descend into a meditation exercise.

If this fall is indeed forever, he reasoned, *I can at least rid myself of fear. If no impact comes, what is there to fear?*

Colt's voice suddenly shot through his brain with such intensity that his mind was thrown back into chaos.

The greatest fear of all, she warned. Her voice was loud, frantic, and soulless in the never-ending abyss. *The absence of God.*

The Watchman pulled itself up by Nuri's leg. He could hear the creature wheezing with fury, desperate to reach his neck and choke the life out of him.

Distractions, Nuri told himself. *Agents of the Evil One.*

These are reality, not distractions, Colt said.

It only made the situation more confusing.

Surrender surrender surrender surrender.

The Divine Imperative. Surrender to the will of the Divine Infinite but enact His will no matter the cost.

"It doesn't make any sense!" Nuri shouted.

The Watchman's grip released and the darkness was instantly replaced by a glowing rectangle of light ahead of him.

A new doorway, he thought.

He didn't feel the Watchman's presence anymore. Or Colt's, for that matter. He wondered if his confusion had ended the trials prematurely, since confusion of any sort betrayed a dour lack of faith in the teachings of the Duri Masters. God was clarity. Incomprehension came from the Evil One.

You've been abandoned in this godless universe because you failed to fully surrender yourself to your lack of understanding, his Duri Master told him sadly.

He stood where he had fallen until he realized that he wasn't *standing* at all but lying flat on his back, and that the object in front of him wasn't a doorway but a rounded rectangular object blocking a bright light from above.

He shifted and tried to identify the cold material at his back. It was soft and smooth. Clearly some type of cloth, though he couldn't see it in the darkness aside from a purplish hue revealed by the faint traces of rectangular light.

Where am I? he wondered.

The more important question, he thought, was where had the Watchman gone? He couldn't see the creature nearby, nor could he smell its foul stench or hear its rasping breath.

What are you waiting for? Colt asked. *You're wasting time and every second lessens your chances of finding Prime.*

Nuri tried to lift himself from the soft surface but found he only had about six inches of room above his head to work with. Worse, the object he'd initially mistaken for a door was too heavy for him to casually toss aside.

Push.

Grunting, he shifted his weight again and pressed his feet against the flat object above him.

Push.

He did, and managed to lift the stone slab a few inches from its resting place, revealing a dull green haze overhead and a buzz of wildlife before it settled back down. He wiped sweat from his brow, panting, and stretched out his legs for another attempt to break free.

Where am I? he wondered again. Now that he thought it through, it seemed impossible to be facing *up* after falling for so long, but the dull green haze he'd glimpsed while the stone slab was in the air was more disconcerting than the displaced gravity. Wherever he was and whatever planet he was on, it appeared to have a toxic atmosphere and his damaged suit didn't have a sealed helmet to compensate for the environment. The moment the slab fell away, he would be breathing unfiltered toxins, assuming he'd be able to move it any further than he already had. Even from that brief exposure, the tight air around him seemed tainted by the fog on the other side of the stone.

You won't be killed by such trivialities during the trials, his Duri Master reasoned. *The trials are designed to discern your holiness as well as your worthiness to gaze upon the Divine Infinite, not to test the endurance of your human lungs.*

But it could be a test of your true nature, Colt countered. *If your human lungs require oxygen, you will die the moment the headstone of your crypt falls away. You, therefore, cannot be human if you wish to survive. You must be Hidria.*

"Distractions," Nuri growled, positioning his arms and legs for another push. "You're all distractions."

With a shout, he threw all his weight upward and to the right, driving the stone slab as far up and over as he could to keep it from dropping back down on him. It fell with a tremendous crash over the side of the rectangular box, though not as violently as he had expected.

Gripping the sides of the rectangle, Nuri pulled himself into the green haze and took a deep breath to test the atmosphere. After a few seconds of deep inhalation without any ill effects, his muscles relaxed and he quickly scanned the area.

"This figures," he muttered with a deep frown, seeing the rows upon rows of monoliths in each direction.

There were graves everywhere he turned. All shapes, sizes, and colors of tombstones dotting the damp, moss-covered earth. Hills stretched off in the distance to his right and even *they* appeared to be covered in the mess of wood and stone comprising the graves of three-dozen alien cultures. He caught movement in his periphery every so often as he scanned his surroundings, but it was always either too far off to get a lock on or deliberately evaded close inspection.

Who are they? Nuri wondered. *What planet is this?*

You won't catch them standing still or suddenly discover what planet you're on simply because you will it, Colt told him. *You could be on Prime right now, for all you know.*

Grimacing, he pulled himself out from the crypt and dropped onto the soil, instinctively taking cover behind the stone rectangle in case the Watchman (and whoever was wandering the graveyard) searched for him. Not that he'd been particularly tactful in his arrival, of course. He was beginning to sense a pattern to the trials in at least one aspect: no matter where he went, he was exposed and almost always at a severe tactical disadvantage.

That's the whole point though, he reminded himself. *If it weren't difficult, then none of the Called would fail. Everyone in the universe would be transformed into Hidria.*

Though the notion should have been reassuring, it vexed him instead. None of the challenges had been particularly difficult, or rather, more difficult than he would expect from normal combat. Taxing to a certain extent, especially the initial fight with the Watchman and the attack of the ice-wraiths on Shehoora, but nothing that rivaled the intensive training he'd completed in hostile environments while preparing for the trials. So far, he considered the challenge somewhat of a breeze.

Only if you consider it solely a test of strength rather than spiritual fortitude, Colt said. *But that is not the purpose of the trials, and you should not be overly confident in the ease of the journey. There are evils you've never dreamed of waiting behind the ancient doors. You never know what card you will draw next.*

He drew his rifle anyway, amazed that the magnetic lock had kept it strapped in its holster during both the drop into Maberrya's ocean and the long descent from the stone corridors of the ancient structure to the crypt. Scanning his immediate vicinity again, he rose and crossed the aisle to the next grouping of tombstones. He had to keep a close eye on the passing rows to spot additional hostiles, but his attention was mostly drawn to the sheer number of graves surrounding him. Any one of them could be the doorway to the next phase of the trials, and he couldn't devise a manner of checking each one without activating the sensor equipment built into his battle armor. The Called were strictly forbidden from using technology beyond their two pieces of weaponry during the trials, just as it was forbidden to desecrate the grave sites of any creatures on a Rest Planet, as the dwarf-planet cemeteries like this one were called.

I could be anywhere in the galaxy right now, he thought.

At least with Shehoora and Maberrya, distant though they were, he'd been able to identify them quickly and orient to his relative placement in the universe. There were hundreds of moons and dwarf planets designated solely to apolitically honor the dead of dozens of alien species, however, perhaps extending even beyond Nuri's quadrant of the galaxy. For all he knew, he could be in Andromeda.

Why does it matter? Colt prodded.

Nuri examined one of the gravestones, frowning, unable to decipher the alien script glowing across its surface. *It matters because I need to reach Prime and I need a ship to get there.*

Why do you think you need a ship? You don't even know where to go.

He sighed and shook his head, turning back toward the distant hilltop to see if there was any sign of a relay station or hangar. He couldn't be too far off from some type of landing field considering the cemetery's custodial crew needed an efficient method for transporting alien bodies across the terrain. Whoever the caretaker was, he or she likely had some sort of landspeeder or hovercar, but Nuri still didn't think the outposts would be too far from the actual burial sites. Otherwise, it would be nearly impossible for visitors to pay respects to their loved ones. No space-faring ships larger than three meters in width could land between tombstones, and vessels of that ilk were extremely few and far between given that they were typically short-range shuttles.

I'll just have to walk until I find a landing pad or outpost, Nuri decided, poking his head out from cover to examine the nearest aisle once again. He couldn't shake the feeling that someone was watching him, and though it didn't necessarily feel as ominous a presence as the Watchmen or their dark lord, it was disconcerting, nonetheless. *Let's hope nothing hunts me down in the meantime.*

It wasn't like him to avoid combat. Hiding simply wasn't the way of the Called, who'd been trained to believe that anyone willing to raise a weapon against them was undoubtedly a steward of the Evil One and therefore demanded an agonizing death. But he recognized the importance of haste in his predicament. Already, he felt his mind tearing away at itself, desperately fighting to keep up with the constantly shifting realities and illusions projecting before him.

Be strong, he told himself as he angled toward the hilltop. He kept his rifle at the ready in case a welcoming party for the eerie dwarf planet jumped out from behind a tombstone. The green-yellow haze enveloping the rows tasted bitter and burned the back of his throat, but that was to be expected. The atmosphere drew from tens of thousands of decomposing bodies and the myriad preservation chemicals used by diverse alien cultures as a tribute to their honored dead.

Nuri's feet felt heavier than usual in the increased gravity. The ground was so soft beneath him that he sank each time he brought his heel down. In addition to his degrading mental state and the overwhelming (though barely acknowledged) dread that came with being surrounded by generations of the dead, the constant shifting of his weight like he was ankle deep in an ocean was enough to convince him he was hallucinating the whole ordeal. The experience had a similar feel to his tour of the cosmos before he'd dropped on Maberrya, and though the implications of a cemetery planet weren't quite as incomprehensible and foundation-altering as momentarily grasping the nature of all universes, he felt the same disorientation. The same flexing of his brain beyond the limits of his mortal self.

"What *is* this place?" he asked aloud, wondering how his voice could be so hoarse and phlegm-blocked if he was truly on a spiritual plane outside his physical body.

Some things are better left unknown, his Duri Master told him.

"Another falsehood," Nuri countered. His legs began to wobble beneath him, and his steps wandered first to the right, then drunkenly over-corrected to the left. "To know the nature of God is to know all, therefore Hidria know everything. Every truth of the universe. If I'm not supposed to find God and look upon His face to know the prevailing Cosmic Truth, then what is the purpose of the trials? How do the Hidria know that their judgments of life and death and morality are just?"

You're getting weaker, Colt stated.

She seemed detached from the philosophical argument between Nuri and the Duri Master. He couldn't tell whether she was referring to his waning faith in the Duri teachings as he sank deeper and deeper into the trials, or the way the atmosphere of the cemetery planet seemed to suck the life from every part of him.

"I am Hidria," Nuri responded, exhausting every ounce of mental energy at his disposal to keep his hands from trembling over the trigger of his assault rifle. "I have no weakness. I am fear and death."

He wanted to believe the words.

The planet, he thought. *It's poisoning me.*

He didn't think he'd be able to reach the nearest hill, let alone the land beyond it, but he kept walking anyway. He didn't have a choice. Even if he wasn't in the middle of the trials, staying in place meant certain death. Eventually, assuming the chemicals in the atmosphere didn't kill him first, he would need food and water.

It's a trap, he thought.

No, Colt persisted. *You don't need to breathe. You are not human.*

Nuri scoffed weakly and kept his eyes locked on the hilltop. He sensed a great deal of movement around him now that he was visibly faltering, but he tried to ignore its presence. He didn't sense that his visitors were Watchmen, and any other threat could be handled by his rifle if they came too close. More than likely, they were curious custodians or families visiting the graves of their loved ones. It was rare that a cemetery planet was completely devoid of visitors, although Nuri was not so naïve as to believe the volume of traffic around him was typical for a toxic dusk like that one. Cemetery planets, by rule, were off-limits for three months out of each solar year (aside from new burials) to allow the custodians to complete renovations and general maintenance. The schedules varied widely so Nuri couldn't be sure whether his impromptu visit to the dwarf planet fell within that window, but his gut told him that it had.

They don't want you here, Colt said.

"I don't want to *be* here," he muttered.

You must control your body. You must know *that you are Hidria, then you won't need to breathe. The atmosphere won't affect you at all.*

The idea sounded great, but Nuri wasn't sure how to accomplish it, especially since his body very clearly *was* affected by the atmosphere. It seemed impossible to simply *will* himself not to feel the toxins in his body, although he was fairly certain he'd managed it at least twice during the trials so far.

Both of those instances could have been illusions, though. This could be the real *thing. I could be dying right now.*

You are Hidria. There is no such thing as death.

At last, the burn in his veins was so severe and disorienting that he had to stop walking or he would have fallen over and likely smashed his skull on a gravestone in the process. He felt the soft earth beneath him yielding, eager to swallow his body and add him to the graves sprawled across the planet's surface. More troubling were the sounds of a dozen unknown creatures pressing in around him, seeing that he was too weak to resist their advances. He didn't dare guess their intentions, but he had his rifle and laser blade to sort it out when the time came.

You must get off this planet, the Duri Master said. *Find a ship and get to Prime. That is the only way you can see the face of God.*

"Fight it," he growled, summoning all the strength left in his body to rise to his feet and survey his enemies.

Indistinct, expressionless alien faces regarded him beneath silver atmosphere masks. Each of them carried a heavy-looking blaster rifle and wore dull gray suits with black armor covering their chests, arms, and abdomens. Their legs were protected by heavy-looking boots that stretched all the way to their hips where they intersected with chest plating. There were at least twenty of them in all and more emerged from behind the gravestones with each passing moment. When they saw Nuri marking their approach, they froze in unison and regarded him suspiciously.

"*Chizuuma shul,*" one of them declared, raising a fist in the air in the universal sign to 'hold.' Evidently, it was the leader of the group, for they all fell back into defensive positions upon his command, seeking any available shelter while keeping their blaster rifles locked on Nuri in case he had any designs on a pre-emptive strike.

"You're not supposed to be here," Nuri said, addressing the alien who'd given the 'hold' order.

"Neither are you," the creature responded with a heavy, guttural accent.

Nuri tried to suppress a cough but gave up when the burn in the back of his throat threatened to make him vomit instead.

"Why did you come here?" the alien asked, lowering his blaster rifle. Clearly, he was confident Nuri posed no immediate threat to him or any of the other masked soldiers, and Nuri didn't blame him. He didn't look like much just then and they outnumbered him at least fifty to one when all was said and done.

Once Nuri had his breath under control again, he steadied his legs and looked the leader in the eye. "I didn't *mean* to come here," he said. "I was brought here."

Reflexively, a half-dozen of the soldiers glanced over their shoulders, in the opposite direction that Nuri had been traveling.

The landing pad, he thought, stifling a grin. Naturally, a few of the troops had gotten spooked at the idea that another ship was in the area and wanted to make sure they hadn't missed anything on their sensor sweeps. In doing so, they had unwittingly provided Nuri with directions to the nearest ships, and that positive return outweighed any struggles he could possibly have with the small army surrounding him. A chance to get off the planet quickly was priceless no matter how many bodies he left in his wake.

Any man who raises his fist against the Hidria is a servant of the Evil One and should be killed without question or court judgment. One who would impede the will of the Divine Infinite cannot exist within its framework. He must be removed to Tscharia, the decaying planet in the universe of darkness.

He couldn't remember which sacred text the passage was from, but it certainly wasn't *The Divine Incendiary*.

"What do you mean? Who brought you here?" the leader demanded, raising the blaster rifle again and sidestepping in Nuri's direction.

Slowly, his battle instincts began to take over. Without thought, he'd assessed the layout of the graves surrounding him as well as the nearest soldiers. The toxins from the atmosphere had begun to filter out of his bloodstream as his

Hidria form emerged from hibernation into a rage and surety of purpose.

"God brought me here," he said.

Several soldiers scoffed and turned to each other to share mocking glances even though their expressions were concealed. The leader of the group, however, didn't flinch.

"Why did God bring you here?"

"Why are all of *you* here?" Nuri countered. "And why are you armed?" Then, realizing that the chemicals in the atmosphere were part of the cemetery planet's clean-up, he took another step closer to the commander. "No one's supposed to be here when the planet's shut down. Are you grave robbers?"

The commander matched his steps. Soon, they stood toe-to-toe, though Nuri was slightly taller than the alien and wound up looking down on him. The other soldiers moved in closer as they sensed the tension. Those among them who had allowed their weapons to relax during the banter now assumed offensive positions with their blasters aimed at Nuri's chest.

You are Hidria, Colt reminded him when the first wave of fear began to manifest in the pit of his stomach. He didn't need her reassurance now that he'd willfully filtered the toxins from his bloodstream. Hidria didn't need to be afraid of a small squad of alien soldiers, only large armies built by the Evil One. If it came down to it—and Nuri guessed that it would—he could dispatch the aliens easily enough.

"How are you able to breathe?" the commander asked, ignoring Nuri's question.

Now that he was glaring down at the alien soldier (who was clearly made of sterner stuff than the rest of his crew), Nuri sensed the fear pervading the creature, and that meant the rest of his men were even worse off by comparison. If he could play on those fears, he might not even need to kill them all. Maybe making a few examples would suffice.

As long as they're willing to give me their ship, he thought. No matter how intimidating his combat prowess would be to them, he couldn't imagine they would willingly concede their vessel without one hell of a fight. Cemetery planets were barren during the off months, and even if the life-support systems in their suits could hold out until the end of the toxic wave that purged the atmosphere, they would run out of food on the surface long before then.

"You'd better answer quickly, human, or I might lose my patience," the commander growled, pressing the end of his blaster into Nuri's chest.

"I am Hidria," Nuri answered. "I don't need to breathe."

"Hidria?" the commander spat, taking a startled step back.

The rest of his soldiers immediately retreated to cover behind gravestones once again.

"Hidria."

Almost immediately, the blaster bolts began to fly, creating spectacular swirls of color as they crackled through the toxic atmosphere. If the shots hadn't been aimed at Nuri, he might have even admitted that they were beautiful.

Aesthetics, his Duri Master sternly cautioned. *Distractions.*

As he rolled away from the first wave of blaster bolts, seeing everything around him with senses beyond his normal human perception and reacting faster than the soldiers could compensate for his movements, he realized that the Duri Master was right.

And yet he was still alive.

12

"**Use only your blasters** on the surface. You've not been trained well enough to use your blades. Blades require proximity to your target, and face to face, your margin for error is miniscule. Always remember that the deaths must be impersonal, otherwise they will not be viewed as objective judgment. If the public thinks a subjective vendetta is involved in this cleansing, or that you are godless savages unable to fulfill your charge with due solemnity, there will be backlash, and *you* will be the ones who pay for it."

Nuri nodded to the commander of the Called recruits, one who still wore scars across his neck and forehead from his unsuccessful journey into the ethereal realm.

"All right," the commander continued, flipping the switch on his spacesuit to lock his helmet in place and obscure his features beneath the purple mask. "Make sure your blasters are charged and hit the gates as one unit. Kill everyone, but don't rush. Remember, the root of our power and mystique is our reputation as cold, remorseless death-dealers sent by God Himself. If you rush or if you hesitate, we lose our veil of lethal indifference."

Nuri stole a quick glance at the other Called recruits who'd been assigned to the mission, trying to decide if any among them were as apprehensive as he, but they had all been well trained. Their expressions betrayed nothing but calm detachment.

"You'll have three hours to finish the job and then a ship will touch down outside the colony for extraction."

"Yes, sir," the Called answered in unison.

The commander nodded and moved to the front of the ship to provide instructions for the pilot on where to skim the surface to best avoid detection. He had to be certain that a ship was never seen transporting the Called to a colony cleansing. Since Dublokee, the Duri Masters had invested a great deal of their tax collections and plunder on stealth technology so that the Called could arrive unannounced in their featureless masks, as though they'd been transported from Prime itself to drown the heresy of the colonists. For, as much as the Duri insisted they didn't need theatrics to prove they'd been sent by God to rid the galaxy of sinners and all affronts to His Holy Name, Nuri had marked the extreme, brutal measures they employed to remind the heathens of their supernatural endowments.

No measures more extreme than this, he thought, gripping his blaster and willing away the butterflies in his stomach. He'd run kill missions before, but he couldn't imagine ever getting comfortable with them, especially when the Duri Masters themselves admitted that only a few colonists out of the hundreds on the moon were guilty of heresy. On top of that, Nuri was still reeling from his encounter with the girl from the river the night before, or perhaps her ghost. He still couldn't decide what exactly he'd seen or whether he'd dreamed up the whole interaction, but the state of his Duri Master in the morning assured him that at least *his* drinking and cursing about *The Divine Incendiary* had truly happened.

"Beginning approach," the pilot reported.

Nuri flipped the switch on his helmet and the painted visor snapped shut over his face. The readings that projected across the interior of his visor were disorienting at first, if only for the dizzying swirl of unrelated information, but he adjusted quickly enough. He had to. He would rely solely on the readings from his suit's sensors to track down and eliminate any colonists who tried to hide or break for the mountains on the heretic moon.

The other Called soldiers—utterly faceless now with the purple visors filling their helmet shells—began to adjust their suits for the dive from the shuttle, checking to be sure that their internal life-support systems were functioning properly and that their phase shields were set to the correct frequency. The colonists would have primitive, predictable weapons that emitted uniform pulse blasts or bullets, however, so there was no need. The research teams employed by the Duri Masters (they avoided the term 'scientists' at all costs) had devised adaptable shield modulation for their troopers to minimize the damage of each impact to negligible amounts.

"Two minutes to drop point."

Checking to be sure his comm link had been turned off for the time being, Nuri sighed and finished calibrating the pressure equalizers on his suit. His Duri Master had warned him that if he programmed them incorrectly, his suit was likely to explode before he reached the moon's surface. Yet he was still distracted by anxious rumination as he performed the checks, not the least of which involved the substantial mental preparation necessary to slaughter men, women, and children as they begged for their lives.

I wonder what she *would say about this,* he thought, remembering the not-so-subtle condemnations from the girl's apparition.

He looked at the young woman beside him, who could just as easily have swapped places with another Called soldier while he was immersed in his own ponderings and he never would have known the difference. The suits were designed to mirror the act of the cleansing: uniform and impersonal. It was disappointing. He'd caught the girl's glance a couple of times when they'd first boarded and thought she might have been feeling the same doubts that he was, but she'd quickly adopted the numb, expressionless demeanor of a devoted Called soldier. Now that they were in the thick of things, he didn't dare engage her on a personal level.

Still, he couldn't help wondering about her background, specifically what circumstances had brought her to the shuttle bench beside him preparing to launch an attack on unsuspecting colonists. These days, his own past was hazy any time he attempted to reach beyond his arrival on the mountaintop for training. The others on the shuttle had surely come from other planets and other mountain villages, but their training regimen would have been similar. The Duri always chose mountains for training because they felt it was an appropriate homage to the Divine Infinite, who Himself was said to reside on the first mountain of the planet Prime. It was also a reminder that the heavens were attainable, since the night skies from the mountaintop overflowed with stars that seemed close enough to touch.

And yet you are told to keep your eyes to the ground.

"One minute to drop point."

Two-dozen Called soldiers rose dutifully from the benches, Nuri last of all. They drew their blasters and checked to be sure the safeties were off and the charges full. They carried laser blades for show, but as the commander had instructed, they were only to use the blasters once they reached the surface, and none of them wanted to be caught without a weapon. That would jeopardize their carefully formulated image, and other colonies might get ideas about resistance once footage of the cleansing was leaked throughout the galaxy. Any Called soldier would rather take his own life than allow that to happen.

Any Called soldier, that is, except Nuri. He wasn't yet willing to lay down his life for the cause, although he considered it a failing of his own rather than his Duri Master's teaching. As for the others, the Called were not permitted to communicate with each other outside of missions, so he might never know if any of them had doubts about their commitment to the Holy cause.

"Thirty seconds."

The commander joined them again in the rear cabin to oversee the drop. There were no windows on the shuttle, but Nuri could tell they were near the surface both by the turbulence and the patter of rain over the outer hull.

"Fifteen seconds," the commander told them, punching a button to retract the side door. The moon's surface streamed by too quickly to catch any meaningful glimpses. It was night and they appeared to be skimming just above a jungle, although Nuri arrived at that supposition mostly by the intel provided in his mission briefing.

"Begin drop," the pilot called back.

The commander nodded to the first soldier in line and the faceless Called began to drop from the shuttle, one by one, with Nuri anxiously awaiting his turn at the back of the line.

You must separate from the act, he told himself, trying to assuage the doubts that rose nearer and nearer his tongue as an outright refusal to go through with the mission. *You are doing God's work. Surrender to His will and let His judgment be your strength.*

Soldier after soldier disappeared into the nighttime storm over the jungle until finally it was Nuri's turn. He nodded once at the commander and then stepped out into the whistling, concussive wind.

The impact with the rushing air was more severe than he'd expected. He was knocked nearly unconscious against the side of his helmet even with the equalizers in his suit at maximum. He spun completely out of control for a moment with the rain pinging violently off his armor, catching a glimpse of the commander dropping a quarter mile ahead of him down the shuttle's trajectory, and then the vessel vanished while Nuri calmed himself enough to punch the adjustment pulses on his suit to right himself.

Even once he faced the right direction, the jungle rushed up to meet him at an alarming rate. A *lethal* rate. He didn't think he could trigger his parachute in time. The jungle canopy was about to tear him to pieces.

Breathe. Breathe and pray.

Panic threatened to paralyze him. He tried to think of a Duri prayer for strength during combat, but in the heat of the moment, he couldn't remember a single one. All he could do was frantically slap the release button for the parachute in a final desperate attempt at salvation, and then he was yanked backward so abruptly that his neck would have snapped if not for the carefully calibrated equalizers in his suit. Even so, he suspected he'd feel the jolt deep in his shoulders for weeks.

But at least he was alive, he reminded himself, and his descent was steadily slowing, the jungle floor seeming less an inevitable grave and more like the rendezvous point it was supposed to be.

The rendezvous point, he thought. His stomach dropped at the thought. He'd forgotten to reactivate his comm link after shutting it off on the shuttle. He might have missed critical information during his radio silence, or worse yet, been directly contacted by the commander. If that was the case, he would face severe punishment from his Duri Master once the commander filed a detailed report of his field performance.

"...miles from rendezvous point. Should arrive within fifteen minutes, sir."

"Understood," the commander responded, then fell silent as he neared the jungle canopy.

"Ten seconds to impact," the AI voice in Nuri's suit informed him. He didn't need the reminder since he could almost reach out and touch the tops of the trees with his toes at that point, but it still made the crash through the canopy less jarring somehow.

He braced his body the way he'd been trained to do. He pulled his legs close to his chest for the initial impact, then triggered the release to hit the ground running before his chute tangled in the trees. Despite the rain, which made him slip twice as he landed, everything went according to plan. Better, in fact, than any drop he'd completed during training. He released the chute before it could jolt him back again, then retrieved it to erase evidence of his entry if any curious parties visited the colony's remnants to investigate the cleansing.

Once he'd broken down the chute and was safely out of sight from any passing aircraft, he initiated the self-destruct mechanism on the pack and it burst into a brief, brilliant ball of flame.

He'd ignored most of the chatter over the comm link while he'd taken care of the chute, but now he cranked up the volume again to report that he'd successfully dropped and would proceed to the rendezvous point as scheduled.

"This is Twelve," he said. "Chute has been destroyed. Proceeding to the RP from a quarter mile out. Will arrive in five minutes."

"Understood, Twelve," the commander's voice crackled back over the comm line.

Five minutes was an irrelevant estimation, seeing as he was the closest of the twelve Called soldiers to the commander's position. Those coordinates were the de facto rendezvous point since they neared the mission's destination of any drop. Even if he took his time, he would arrive at the commander's holding location at least a few minutes before the others.

That allowed ample opportunity for self-doubt to consume him in the meantime, and for him to consider defecting before he was forced to senselessly take another life.

I would die in the process, he reasoned. *I wouldn't be able to take all twelve of them, even with the help of the colonists. They're all just as skilled as I am, and the commander has me beat in experience if nothing else.*

Yet he wondered if it was worth it, nonetheless. At least if he stood up to the massacre, he would die knowing he'd done the right thing by fighting for the innocent.

And then I'd be condemned to eternity in Tscharia for forsaking the Will of God.

He frowned, but he recognized the futility of his internal debate. His allegiance had been bought and paid for, and despite his reservations, the idea of eternal torment finally sold him on proceeding with the mission. The Duri had bred a formidable fear in his soul for the righteous wrath of God and the grotesque pleasures of the Evil One. Dying at the hands of the Called soldiers through swift justice was one thing. Suffering for the cosmic eternity while enduring unimaginable torture and utter separation from God was another monster altogether.

His heart and mind fell somber as he trudged through the thick jungle, barely noticing the branches and plants he picked through on his way to the commander.

Why don't they just send the Hidria for missions like these? he wondered for perhaps the thousandth time since he'd begun his Duri training.

He knew the answer, of course. Or, at least, the answer the Duri Masters were comfortable providing to inquiring young recruits who didn't know any better. The Hidria only concerned themselves with heresies of the highest order. Insufferable Heresies, as they were termed. The Duri Masters did not command them any more than they commanded God, though their interests were so intermingled that they were often viewed as one and the same. That was the official word, anyway.

Aside from that, though, Nuri suspected a more logical explanation was simply that the Duri Masters wanted the Called to perform the smaller missions for the sake of their training. Perhaps, even, to test their resolve, as Nuri's resolve was being tested on his journey to rendezvous with the commander.

Better get it together soon, he told himself. *They'll see right through me like this, and I know exactly what they'll do if they find out I'm having doubts.*

For Nuri, it was well-worn territory. First, they'd beat and practically starve him for weeks or perhaps months. Much longer than he'd been punished for killing the old man in place of the river girl, in any case. In that time, he would be brainwashed through several invasive psychological procedures and branded over and over with the mark of the Divine Infinite. If it were then decided that he still didn't have faith in the Duri teachings, he would be publicly executed as a message to all other Duri followers.

Public execution.

The thought made him shiver. He'd seen enough of the hangings, crucifixions, and decapitations to know just how disgraced the victims were. Unlike the cleansing of heretic planets and colonies which were cold and impersonal by design, the punishment for the Called who sinned against the Duri faith was to discourage rebellion against God and the Duri and therefore necessitated the ultimate act of desecration.

Focus, Nuri thought. *Don't work yourself up or the mission will fail.*

He glanced behind him as he walked, trying to decide if other Called soldiers were close enough to see him with his guard down and his rifle hanging limply at his side. Such an egregious breach of protocol in the middle of an actual mission would have been reported immediately. He would have been hunted through the jungle well before the strike team worried about the colonists. Eradicating defective Called always took precedent over the Holy missions. The Duri didn't want any sign of weakness or dissension among the ranks of their killing machines to leak, otherwise they were liable to have an anti-Duri revolution on their hands. The tribunal was perpetually terrified by the prospect of media outlets uncovering the truth of a failed cleansing and then spreading the information throughout human systems. Over the years, they had skated dangerously close to that reality as it was, even without the benefit of indisputable holo-vid evidence.

"Checking in," the first Called soldier reported over the comm link. "One point five miles out. Should arrive in ten minutes."

"Understood," the commander said. The flood of reports was about to begin in earnest, and that meant Nuri had to be close to the commander's position since he'd been the closest Called soldier to begin with.

"Checking in," the second soldier panted. "One mile out. Should arrive in seven minutes."

"Understood."

Just as the third soldier called in her report, Nuri spotted the commander with his back against a giant tree. Red, banana-shaped fruit hung over his helmet.

He flipped his comm link to mute and approached the commander with flawless combat protocol. "Twelve reporting, sir," he said. His voice barely broke through the heavy rain beating against the jungle leaves and the whistling wind that snaked between branches, but the commander had already spotted him and likely identified his designation from his sensor readings.

"Fall in, Twelve," the commander said.

Nuri did as he was told and took point for the designated approach vector. He could see the dim glow of the colony a mile off through heavy jungle. His heart leapt in his throat with dread and a peculiar excitement he didn't dare acknowledge.

For the most part, the commander ignored him. The Called were not encouraged to adopt discernible personalities, particularly on missions, and they did not engage in small talk. The silence led Nuri's mind to wander, though, which wasn't a good thing considering all the questions and doubts nagging at him. Briefly, he considered turning his blaster on the commander right then and there, wondering how the mission would proceed without its leader and with little evidence to prove Nuri had been the culprit. Perhaps the rest of the Called soldiers would decide that completing the mission would be too risky if the colonists were aware of their arrival and had used guerrilla tactics to kill the commander before they could assemble and march on the colony.

I'd be the de facto commander, then, he realized. *Protocol dictates that the lead takes command if anything happens to the CO in the middle of a strike.*

Nuri shuddered. He didn't like the idea of being at the helm of the kill force. It was strange how committing the same number of murders in the colony seemed so much different when he was the one leading the Called to the slaughter. It made him feel more culpable for the deaths than simply being a mindless blaster rifle aimed where the Duri Masters had pointed him.

Unless I purposely command the Called to fan out and isolate themselves, making them easier for the colonists to deal with.

The prospect had its own allure, mostly because so many unknowns existed in that proposed future once his ties with the Duri Masters had been severed. By then, however, the opportunity for action had passed. The next

Called soldier—designation Eleven—appeared a dozen yards ahead of them and clicked off her comm link. "Eleven reporting, sir," she said.

"Fall in, Eleven," the commander said.

Nuri grimaced beneath the shelter of his featureless faceplate and shifted so that Eleven could tuck in beside him.

For a moment, he thought that she was staring at him, waiting for a response or some conspiratorial gesture. It was the girl who had sat beside him on the shuttle, after all. The one he'd originally thought looked just as troubled as he felt when they boarded the vessel. It was impossible to tell where her gaze was fixed under the expressionless armor though, so he kept his mouth shut and waited for the others to arrive.

As the minutes passed, the commander became visibly impatient for the stragglers. He broke combat protocol and began to pace back and forth around the clearing, tapping his blaster rifle against his leg armor anxiously.

"Ten, report," he said into the comm link.

"Ten reporting, sir," the Called soldier replied. He didn't need his comm link because he was standing in front of the commander, followed closely by Nine. "Sorry, sir. My chute got tangled in the trees. I had to manually cut and fold to get rid of it without starting a fire."

The commander stared him down for a moment, then seemed to relax as Eight came into view. "Should have called it in," he said coldly, then turned back to the assembled Called.

Nine and Ten fell in without comment. Eight lingered for a moment, watching for Seven in the brush behind him, then the two Called dropped into line together.

"As soon as Six arrives," the commander told Nuri, "move out."

"Understood," he responded, biting back a protest. It didn't seem like sound strategy to split the group in two as long as they were entering the colony through the same gate, especially with the commander falling in the rear group rather than taking point, but it wouldn't do any good for Nuri to argue. At least, not now that there were so many witnesses who could report back to the Duri Masters on his insubordination during a critical juncture in the cleansing.

A moment later, Six checked in and Nuri nodded to Eleven. "Let's move out," he said.

The five other Called soldiers comprising his half of the dozen followed obediently.

The journey through the last stretch of the jungle before the flatlands passed too quickly for Nuri's liking. He was still struggling with the notion of participating in the slaughter at all, let alone being the first through the gate with the first kill. He'd never asked for that sort of responsibility, and truly, he didn't think the commander should have put him in that position in the first place.

Unless this is a test. Maybe he sensed my wavering convictions and is forcing me to command the others to prove my loyalty.

Beneath his faceplate, Nuri clenched his jaw and inhaled deeply. It seemed like a reasonable assumption. The Duri constantly employed mind games to root out the weak for public execution, and it would be just like them to use command of a questionable cleansing operation to test Nuri's resolve.

They also could be testing to see whether I'm ready for the Hidria trials, he thought, then quickly brushed the notion aside as utterly ludicrous. He was too young to be taken in by the Hidria, even if he somehow managed to pass the trials.

"Twelve reporting, sir," he said into the comm link once they were within two hundred yards of the colony. When they reached one hundred-fifty, they'd be detected by the proximity scanners, and then their cover would be blown. Not quickly enough for the colonists to realize what was happening, but enough to sound an alarm somewhere, and that would undoubtedly make Nuri's job more difficult. By rule, it was the first soldier who assumed the greatest risk in a frontal assault, even with the element of surprise on his or her side. "We'll reach the detection point in twenty seconds."

"Understood, Twelve," the commander responded. "We're just leaving the RP now. We'll double-time and fall in right behind you. Feel free to easy pace the next fifty."

"Yes, sir," Nuri said. Then, switching his comm link to Called designations Seven through Eleven, he turned and held up his left hand for a stop. "You heard him. Stall for time, but don't do anything to attract attention."

All five of the soldiers nodded back to him, not questioning his command role in the least even though at least one of them must have sensed his preoccupations leading up to the drop.

That's just paranoia, he assured himself, kneeling in the moon mud and trying to ignore the assault of raindrops rattling his armor. The other Called soldiers followed suit, waiting out the storm in silence until they saw the first reflection of their comrades closing on their position.

"All right," Nuri said, taking a deep breath with the comm link on mute to prepare himself. He switched the channel back on. "Weapons at the ready, shield modulators checked, let's go."

He stood and motioned for them to follow, gazing up at the high walls of the open-domed colony buildings, which used rain as its primary energy source. The curved, stone structures were especially imposing with the view of the moon's orange gas giant looming large and menacing overhead. Lights glowed from observation windows dotting the side of the colony walls, but the stealth armor and approach of Nuri's soundless boots were too advanced for the primitive colonial scanning systems. They wouldn't be able to track heat signatures until the soldiers were close enough to sprint through and disable the gate, and they had fallen into formation to camouflage their movements as indigenous predators.

This is it, he thought as they passed the one hundred fifty-yard proximity mark. He winced, staring at the readings projected inside his faceplate to see if any alarms rang inside or if any colonists approached through the gate. *What if they shut the gate before we reach them?* he wondered as they skulked closer to the settlement. *What if this is a trap?*

His blood ran cold at the notion, and even when he rationalized away his prevailing paranoia, the chill remained. A false mission of that magnitude seemed a large expenditure on the Duri's part simply to get their Called soldiers killed outside the public eye, but the Duri often operated unpredictably. For all that Nuri knew, the Duri could have orchestrated an ambush on the Called so word of their sacrifice would reach the press and politicians and justify a *jihad* against all pagan or atheist human colonies throughout the galaxy. At least that would explain why the commander had fallen in with the rear group rather than running point for the assault.

"One hundred yards," Nuri reported over the comm link.

He paused, waiting for the commander's response, but none came.

Hmmm...

"Twelve reporting, sir," he said over the comm again, thinking maybe he'd forgotten to switch back to the correct frequency to raise the whole group. "We're one hundred yards out and closing. Should we proceed?"

Again, there was no answer.

Nuri continued advancing slowly, risking a quick glance over his shoulder to get a read on the second group while keeping as much of his attention as possible on the gate.

Eleven had stopped behind him, staring back toward the other half of their unit. "What's happening?" she asked.

Nuri finally stopped as well and went to one knee in the mud with his blaster resting on his thigh. He swallowed nervously, sure that the colonists would stream through the gate with pistols and pulse rifles any moment for a pre-emptive strike. "I don't know," he said weakly.

Only one soldier approached them through the glow of the gas giant, and the raindrops illuminated his faceplate poignantly enough to draw attention from even the most dimwitted guards along the colony gate.

"Who is that?" Eight asked.

All six of them were kneeling in a staggered line and their attention was focused on the Called soldier with his weapon smoking from blaster charges, oblivious to the searchlights that suddenly fell on his position and the shrill alarms blaring throughout the colony.

"Twelve reporting, commander. Can you confirm your status?" Nuri said into the comm through a thick knot of dread that had formed in his throat.

Whoever it is must have killed the commander already, he thought when he didn't hear a response. *This is not going to end well.*

Shadows appeared in the gateway to the colony. They were out of time.

"Everyone, retreat!" Nuri shouted to the other soldiers. "Don't let them see us!"

The imperative to keep the Duri name separate from a failed mission had been drilled into his head for years, and it was his primary, reflexive concern when he saw colonists filing through the opening. Now that they had been given enough warning to gather weapons and block the gate, it would be foolish to proceed. Even if the cleansing were successful, the risk that one or more colonists managed to flee before they rounded them up was too great, and if the galaxy heard about the Called making a mistake during the cleansing, it would call their spiritual and tactical authority into question.

Yet the other five Called soldiers in his group were frozen, clearly confused by the lone figure with the smoking blaster approaching them from the rear. They didn't want to run blindly into the hot point of the weapon, even with the colonists closing in the other direction. It was combat instinct. Facing a civilian with a pitchfork was a hell of a lot easier than a trained killer with a weapon he wasn't afraid to put to good use.

"Fall back!" Nuri shouted again, trying to rouse them—and himself—from a stupor.

By the time he got his legs moving and started sprinting toward the jungle, the unknown Called soldier had taken aim at Seven without breaking stride.

"What's he doing?" Nine shouted.

The soldier pulled the trigger and blew a hole in Seven's helmet. Her body jerked backwards and she dropped unceremoniously in the mud with smoke billowing from her suit.

"Go!" Nuri screamed. He started running then, firing a few wild shots in the direction of the renegade Called soldier—who was running toward the colony with equal determination—that failed to cause any damage.

The four remaining soldiers in Nuri's group finally took his lead and began running toward the jungle, giving the renegade a wide berth in their confusion and desperation to leave the colony without evidence of their presence. Yet that was a moot point, Nuri realized, since they had left Seven's corpse in their wake.

"Damn it," he growled.

He glanced back and saw that the colonists were in pursuit. It wouldn't take them long to find Seven's body, and that meant they would realize that the Called could be killed. Worse yet, they'd realize that the Called weren't supernatural beings at all, merely flesh and blood humans that could be defeated with the right kind of weaponry.

"AAAAGGGHHHH!"

He turned just in time to see Eight shot down by the renegade, who was also in pursuit of the remaining Called soldiers and ignored the colonists completely.

Nuri returned fire, this time getting closer to the mark but still flying wide with the renegade anticipating his shots.

"We have to go back!" Eleven shouted to him over the repetitive click of the machine guns chasing them from the edge of the colony.

"We can't," Nuri told her, still running. "We'll all die."

"We won't," Eleven said firmly. "And that's not what matters."

Nuri rolled away from the renegade's aim, digesting Eleven's words.

What does she mean by that? he wondered.

"We can't go back," Ten told them. He'd just about reached the jungle and was trailing fire behind him to ward off the colonists. "We're done now, either way. We've got to call in an air strike to salvage the mission."

The renegade soldier shot Nine in the back of the leg, then quickly put three blaster pulses through his helmet from such close range that brain and glass sprang into the air and reached Nuri's suit from two-dozen yards away. The renegade turned to him and they locked stares through featureless faceplates for a moment, then the rattle of gunfire from the colonists became too deafeningly close to ignore any longer.

"*Fury*, this is the strike team!" Nuri shouted into his comm link once he'd connected to the ship's frequency. An IED skimmed off the mud towards him. He dove and rolled as far from the object as he could manage, narrowly avoiding the impact. "The mission has been compromised," he managed to communicate between gasps. "We need an immediate air strike on the settlement. Someone's gone rogue. They know we're here. We've already lost most of the squad."

"Understood, ground team. Proceed to the extraction point and the shuttle will assess whether it's safe to get you out of there."

Assess who among us is the renegade you mean, he thought, *or whether we deserve saving after what happened down here. Maybe they'll blow us to bits with the rest of them.*

Nuri staggered to his feet as bullets tore past, spraying the mud around him in geysers. Sooner or later, even untrained colonists would manage to hit the mark by pure luck. He didn't intend on sticking around to find out how many shots they wasted before finding a target.

"Hurry!" Ten shouted, issuing covering fire for Nuri and Eleven from the shelter of the jungle. "They're gaining on you!"

Nuri crouched and forced himself to run harder even though his legs felt like they would snap off with another step. Two bullets pinged off the armor plating over his midsection and the impact jolted him sideways, nearly sending him face-first into the mud. Somehow, he held his footing and the suit held together. It was designed to take much heavier firepower than the archaic machine gun bullets the colonists carried, which had somehow survived generations of moon-hopping by colonial vagabonds.

They're easier to stop than blaster bolts at least, he thought.

When he reached the jungle border, he dove into the brush, swiveling as he landed to return fire for Eleven's sake. She'd started lagging behind, and that was hardly a surprise. She'd taken more bullets than he had—the holo-display on his faceplate told him so—and it slowed her down considerably. Enough that the renegade was within a dozen feet of her now with his blaster aimed for the kill shot.

"Down!" Nuri shouted into his comm link.

Eleven obeyed without hesitation and the bolt sailed over her head, igniting the mud at Nuri's feet. Ten turned his attention back to the renegade and began to fire, but once Nuri took his eyes away from the action for a split-second to mark the colonists' progress, he could no longer tell the two soldiers apart. He didn't know what to shoot. Instead, he started gunning down the front line of colonists at a feverish pace.

The battle-calm took over. It steadied his hands and focused his shots, so he was constantly moving to the next target before the last had hit the ground. He was startled by his own accuracy and precision in the field after training for so long. Exhilarated, even, though he denied it once he returned to his studies on the distant mountaintop and reflected upon the cleansing gone awry.

"*Fury*, where's that air strike?" Ten shouted into the comm link. He repeatedly checked the ammunition display on his blaster. His charge had to be running low from laying down such persistent covering fire.

"Everyone fall back *now!*" Nuri shouted.

He'd oriented enough to the battlefield to distinguish Eleven from the renegade again (at least, he was fairly certain of it), but they were too close together to risk blaster fire. The last thing he wanted to do was drop the wrong target and leave himself at a disadvantage while he sorted it out.

What does it matter? his Duri Master's voice demanded. *Better to kill both and ensure the heretic dies than risk bringing his poison back to the lifeblood of our faith.*

Nuri caught the renegade's helmet in his crosshairs briefly and his finger squeezed on the trigger, then Eleven's head popped right into his line of fire and he hesitated.

"Damn..." he muttered.

Luckily, the renegade had his hands full for the time being. The colonists nipped at his heels, unaware that he was the very reason they'd survived so far or that he likely shared their views on God and eternity (which were still a little hazy to Nuri). It was clear that the defector wanted to engage Eleven, but for the moment, he was too busy covering his own flank to line up a shot. That left him exposed to his former squad mates.

"Down!" Nuri yelled again. He recognized the futility of calling out over a comm frequency that the renegade soldier was also accessing, but he couldn't see any other options in the moment. As soon as Eleven dropped, he squeezed the trigger again, this time all the way down. The renegade's shoulder and left arm blew off in a white flash, smacking the stomach of a charging colonist five yards away.

"Got him!" Nuri exclaimed, feeling a mixture of relief and sadness as reality sank in. Under other circumstances, he might have joined the renegade's cause, but the attack had caught him so off guard that he had no other choice.

The renegade staggered drunkenly but kept running, and Ten's fire into the onrushing wave of colonists inadvertently cleared his flank of any hostiles that might have overrun him.

"Firing now," the tactical officer of the *Fury* announced just as Eleven reached the jungle border.

A blinding, white-yellow beam of energy thundered down and struck the heart of the colony. The walls exploded outward, sending a shockwave that catapulted Nuri, Ten, Eleven, the renegade, and a half-dozen angry colonists deep into the jungle. The rest were killed instantly.

When Nuri landed in a bed of giant, pink-petaled flowers, he scrambled to his feet and dropped the remaining colonists that pinged a pulse on his sensors. Like most Called missions, the work was so easy that he felt guilty doing it.

It's better than dying.

His suit had taken the brunt of the shockwave in addition to dimming the visuals, but the colonists would have been as good as dead from the radiation, anyway. He'd just spared them a negligible amount of additional suffering.

He checked his sensors again to be sure no other colonists had survived in his immediate proximity, then cautiously approached the remaining life-sign readings for his squad. There were three others, meaning the renegade was still alive even with his left arm gone.

"Ground team, any survivors should proceed to the extraction point immediately. We're leaving the system in ten minutes with or without you."

"Understood," Nuri replied, eyeing the dazed Called soldier before him in the thick jungle with suspicion until he realized she still had both arms.

The soldier noticed him appraising her and nodded slowly, rubbing at her lower back even though there was no way she could reach the source of her pain through the suit. "Eleven reporting, sir," she said weakly.

"Get up, Eleven. We've got five minutes to make the extraction point or they're leaving us."

"Yes, sir." She started running without him, glancing back once at the settling cloud of mud and debris that had splattered their approach vector and covered the corpses.

Suddenly, a clamor rose from the bushes directly behind Nuri and she froze in place.

"Behind you, sir," she said calmly.

Nuri turned and watched the renegade soldier stagger toward him, right hand pressed against the hole where his left arm had been moments earlier.

"Twelve," he wheezed.

Nuri scowled and raised his blaster.

The renegade fell to his knees in the mud and hung his head. "I thought you would join," he gasped. "I thought you would listen."

Aware of Eleven watching him and Ten somewhere nearby, Nuri ignored the comment and advanced on the unarmed, injured traitor. Once he was within reach of the dying soldier, he knelt beside him and replaced his blaster in the holster on his back.

"Why did you do it?" he whispered.

Ten stumbled into view opposite Eleven and froze, watching the two soldiers kneeling in the mud.

"I thought you would help," the renegade mumbled, his head lolling from one side to the other. "I didn't save them."

"Why did you *want* to save them?"

The renegade paused, slipped lower in the mud. He was clearly losing consciousness, but Nuri needed answers before that happened.

"Why did you want to save them?" he repeated.

Slowly, the soldier removed his trembling hand from the cauterized skin at his left shoulder and pressed the release button on his faceplate.

Nuri winced. Eleven gasped. Ten cursed.

"Commander?"

The commander grinned wide, looking every bit the Devil that the Duri painted him to be in the aftermath of the disaster with fire from the air-strike glowing beneath a gas giant on a jungle night. "You don't know what you'll see. At least I listened," he said.

Then, in one motion, he pulled the blaster from Nuri's holster and blew his own head off, leaving nothing of his face for the Duri Masters to identify to ensure his memory was sufficiently desecrated. As long as no one was able to pinpoint *who* had committed the treason, the commander was just another unfortunate battlefield casualty who'd died in honorable service to the Divine Infinite. A fate to which all Called soldiers aspired, even those who'd failed the trials.

The three remaining soldiers stood in silence for a moment, staring at the smoking hole where the commander's face had been while trying to digest the impossibility that he'd willingly turned against the Duri and his Called brothers and sisters.

"We're going to miss extraction," Ten piped in after several seconds had passed.

Nuri nodded, retrieved his rifle, and led the other two soldiers to the extraction point. Later, he learned why the commander had turned. Aside from the hysteria brought on by his failure during the trials, he'd also lived among that group of colonists before being abducted as a teenager.

At least he'd died with his family.

13

Before the first volley of blaster bolts whizzed past his head and scorched the tombstone behind him, Nuri drew his rifle and took shelter behind an imposing crypt with alien script chiseled across its walls.

This is a waste of time, Colt told him. *You're taking lives for the sake of taking lives.*

They're the ones shooting at me, he protested, creeping his blaster rifle around the edge of the structure and dropping two alien soldiers in fast succession. *I don't have a choice. If I don't kill them, I won't make it out of here alive.*

You are Hidria. What is death to Hidria?

He grimaced as a blaster bolt glanced off his forearm plating and made his bones ache. *A useful occupation.*

The alien commander shouted in a coarse tongue and the remaining soldiers fanned out to flank him, advancing in turns while others covered their movement. Nuri emerged from the crypt to return fire, but the barrage was too heavy for him to get a look at how far the aliens had advanced, let alone fire an accurate shot.

What now? he wondered.

He may not have gotten a precise read on the soldiers' positions, but they hadn't been far off when the shooting started, so even though he'd cleared enough of a path to buy himself some time, he knew they were close. In fact, when he held his breath, he could hear their movements in the squelching soil. He could feel the Hidria form leaving him, making him susceptible to the weapons fire of the remaining soldiers. In a matter of moments, he'd be surrounded and they would either kill him or take him captive. He couldn't spare the time for either fate. Even if he made it out of the trials alive, at this point, he'd likely be insane by the time he reached Prime and beheld the face of God.

And then what?

All at once, the blaster bolts ceased, followed by several seconds of silence. Nuri's pulse pounded in his throat.

Now! his Duri Master said. *Attack now! Kill these heathens!*

But Nuri knew the element of surprise would only last a split-second if it emerged at all, considering the soldiers expected a counterattack.

They're probably baiting me out, anyway, he worried.

Yet it didn't seem likely considering how easily they could have surrounded him. Perhaps there was some sort of barrier preventing them from doing so, but he sincerely doubted that was the case, either.

"Lay down your weapon and come out," the commander said.

It's a trap. If I go out there, they'll shoot me on sight.

"You will not be harmed if you come quietly."

Nuri stood from his crouch, frowning, and holstered the rifle. The crypt still shielded him from enemy fire, so he had a moment to collect his thoughts. He hadn't completely made up his mind whether he would oblige the alien officer, but the break in active shooting at least gave his legs some respite from crouching against the stone.

The aliens whispered to each other in unsettling hisses. He didn't understand their language, but occasionally he caught the word *Hidria* falling from their lips and knew they were either mocking him or expressing disbelief that he truly was a member of the fabled, indestructible fighting machines. For that, he didn't blame them. He'd declared himself Hidria and then promptly backed himself into a corner, only managing to drop a half-dozen alien soldiers in the process.

I still thinned their numbers though, he thought, reminding himself that they wouldn't take the losses kindly. Come to think of it, the invitation felt less and less like a true call to parley with each passing second.

What choice do you have? Colt asked. *If you will not attack and you can't find another way to move on, then you must play their game. They won't just leave without dealing with you properly. No warrior is stupid enough to expose his back to a threat.*

Nuri knew she was right, but he still hesitated before finally emerging from the crypt's shelter with his hands in front of his chest to show he was unarmed. He was also testing whether the movement drew any fire. It didn't, and that made him feel slightly encouraged about trusting the alien commander's word. It appeared he *would* allow Nuri to speak with them again without immediate retribution, after all.

"I'm coming out." He edged into the open aisle, bracing himself for another attack. He was confident that he could retreat behind the crypt again before sustaining too much damage as long as they didn't manage a headshot. But considering how many soldiers had blasters pointed at him, he thought the chance of at least one blowing a hole through his temple was too high.

Yet not a single soldier fired, and Nuri ventured another two steps toward the commander without incident. They might have allowed him to creep even closer if he'd kept going, but he didn't dare abandon his lone prospect of reliable cover just yet.

"You're not Hidria," the commander said, eyeing him up and down.

Nuri said nothing. He didn't feel up to formulating an agreeable explanation of the trials or the transformative nature of knowing God. It wouldn't do him any good in the short term, and in the long term, it would actively degrade his mind with the seconds and breaths he wasted on heathen, alien ears.

Recognizing that Nuri had no taste for argument, the commander handed his weapon to a nearby soldier and paced thoughtfully around him. "What brings you here?" he asked.

"God," Nuri answered.

The alien scoffed but, likewise, didn't argue.

"We haven't detected any other ships since we landed. *How* did you get here?"

Nuri turned to stare into his mask. "God brought me here," he said firmly. "Through Colt."

"What's Colt?"

He shook his head. "Not what. *Who*."

The alien commander gaped at him with arms folded over his chest. After a few moments, he started pacing again. This time, however, he wasn't looking at Nuri at all. He was scanning the rows of grave-markers for some clue only he would recognize. "Are you here for her?"

"For Colt?"

"Is that what you call her?"

Nuri frowned. "I don't understand."

"The Corpse Queen."

He stared at the alien blankly. "I don't know who you're talking about."

The commander stopped and turned back to regard him. "Are you here for the Corpse Queen?"

Nuri shook his head. "No. I've never heard of the Corpse Queen. I'm here for God." He took a moment to assess the soldiers' reactions, many of whom had lowered their weapons with this new development. "I don't even know what planet I'm on."

"Operandom," the commander told him. "It's the Dikoval word for *ending place*."

"I've never heard of it."

A murmur rose from the soldiers, but the commander continued unperturbed. "There aren't many visitors to Operandom, especially ones who don't know where they are or how they arrived. Did your ship crash?"

Nuri shook his head. "I told you. I came here for God, through God."

The alien stepped up so his face was within an inch of touching the Called armor plating, although Nuri still had to look down on the shorter creature. "What business does God have on Operandom?"

Nuri shrugged. "None, as far as I can tell. Or plenty, depending on your faith in *The Divine Incendiary*. The Duri Masters still argue over the Divine's obligation to the bodies of His departed souls."

"Duri?" the alien groaned. "Murderous imbeciles. So, you *do* serve the Duri, then, even though you aren't Hidria?"

Once again, Nuri said nothing. He sensed that telling the truth would mean more trouble and lying would be an affront to God, particularly during His holy trials. He didn't even bother correcting the heresy that the Hidria served the Duri. The Hidria served only God.

"The Duri represent everything that's wrong with this galaxy," the alien declared. He raised his voice to a theatrical shout, although Nuri didn't think he'd done so purposely. Many heathens were similarly riled up by the mention of Duri teachings, since the Called were a constant threat to their planets and customs. It had been a slow expansion by the Duri Masters, but with the support of human colonies throughout the galaxy, they had quickly gained strength in key trade worlds as well as footholds in strategic communication relays. Enough to make examples of several smaller planets and civilizations with a few carefully orchestrated attacks.

"Terrorists," the alien continued. "Spewing fear and hate-speak to every world and killing any weak settlement that opposes them." He turned back to Nuri, and though his face was covered by the atmosphere helmet, the creature's derision was palpable. Nuri could *feel* his scowl through the darkened faceplate. "If you serve the Duri, it wasn't any god that brought you here. It was slavery to a belief in supernatural drivel." He stepped back to Nuri's side and wrapped an arm over his shoulder. "You're one of the Called then, aren't you?"

Nuri didn't respond, but that was all the answer the alien needed.

"How old were you when you were taken?" he asked quietly. The malice had abruptly vanished from his tone, replaced by sincere pity. The implication that Nuri had been trained against his will appeared to resonate with the commander.

"Young," Nuri answered stiffly. He didn't like the alien's arm over his shoulder, nor the condescending attitude which implied he was somehow a pitiful creature because the Duri chose him to carry out the will of the Divine Infinite.

"They've brainwashed you," the alien said, shaking his head slowly. "You've been misguided."

"I've chosen to follow the will of God. That doesn't make me misguided."

"God doesn't exist," the alien countered, but softly enough that it was clear he hadn't meant the assertion to spark further argument. Still, fury rose in Nuri's chest unbidden. He fought back the urge to snap the alien's neck through the suit and take his chances with the rest of the godless heathens on the cemetery planet. He'd dropped more enemies with heavier weaponry on his own before and could do it again, especially with the considerable rage he felt hearing the alien mock both God *and* the Duri faith.

"Why are *you* here, then?" he asked sharply instead. "Why are you looking for a Corpse Queen?"

Removing his hand from Nuri's shoulder, the alien beckoned the subordinate holding his blaster. The weapon was promptly presented to him. "My people are at war," he said. "We're losing. Badly." A few soldiers flinched at the frank assessment of their dire situation. The movement was subtle, yet still telling to Nuri's trained eye. They were desperate. The cemetery planet must have represented one final opportunity to alter their fates before they were enslaved or exterminated by their enemies.

They're all going to die, Nuri thought. *Otherwise, a man who condemns God as superstition wouldn't be walking among the dead searching for a Corpse Queen to change his fortune.*

His expression softened. The annihilation of a species was always troubling. The alien commander may have considered him a pitiful creature for growing up in a forced faith, but Nuri found *his* situation much more pitiful. Seeking knowledge of God was a nobler pursuit than seeking out the dark magic of a dead witch. Just by searching for her presence and meddling with evil forces, the entire squad had assured themselves swift passage to Tscharia once they were reduced to dust by their enemies.

"If we find the Corpse Queen and raise her from the grave, she will serve us in the war. No mere army can stand against her."

"An army of God can stand against anything," Nuri countered. "You should repent your sinful ways and pray for salvation from the Divine Infinite instead. If you seek help from your witch, she will fail. You will all burn in Tscharia."

The soldiers laughed cruelly (a little *too* quickly and cruelly by Nuri's reckoning), but he sensed unease among them. Mistrust, even, as though some of the soldiers weren't as devoted to the cause or convinced of the mission's merit as the commander believed.

Maybe the commander himself has his doubts.

The alien watched him closely as the laughter died down among the others. He was trying to decide whether he should take the suggestion seriously or if Nuri was merely mocking him under the guise of naivety. "God doesn't exist," the alien reiterated flatly. "Tscharia doesn't exist. You've been brainwashed and I don't have time to make you see the light."

"Nor do I."

The alien nodded. "Then at least we agree that we don't have time to be enemies, although I could have had my warriors kill you by now. I'd rather let you live so you can learn your way out of your foolish beliefs on your own."

"I appreciate the gesture," Nuri said, though he felt anything but appreciative for the mockery of his beliefs.

"However, I can't let you off on your own," the alien continued. "I'm not foolish enough to take that risk. If you want to live, you'll have to come with us. Once we find the Corpse Queen, you can go back to wandering this horrid place as it pleases you."

Nuri scowled. "I won't take part in searching out agents of the Evil One unless the aim is to kill them."

"She's already dead," the alien pointed out. "And besides, you don't have any choice. The alternative is we open fire on you here and now. And I doubt even a Called soldier could escape three dozen blaster bolts aimed at his head fast enough to stay alive."

Nuri raised an eyebrow defiantly and held the alien's stare. "You might be surprised."

The tension held for a moment, then the alien stepped back and clapped his hands together. "You're strong," he said. "The Duri train their murderers well. I'll grant them that. But we both know that you're coming with us. You can be a conscientious objector if you would like. If it makes you feel better, you can tell yourself that you're being forced, and you'll be correct."

Heathens! his Duri Master said. *You cannot search for this dead harlot with them! You have been called to a higher purpose!*

Nuri said nothing. Two alien soldiers bound his wrists and confiscated his weapons. His jaw clenched as they carelessly tossed his deactivated laser blade into a hovering crate of supplies they had concealed behind a tombstone, but at least none of the creatures had defiled the holy weapon with their curious, heathen hands.

You're allowing yourself to be distracted, Colt said. The sound of her voice inside his head was startling after so much vocalized conversation with the alien. The Duri Master had spoken up since then, but the strength of that voice was fading the further Nuri was removed from the onset of the trials. He wasn't sure if that meant he was falling further and further from God or further and further from reality, although he acknowledged the two possibilities were not mutually exclusive. *You've lost sight of the true path of God. You've lost His voice and His teachings.*

You said it yourself, he countered. *I don't have a choice.*

Colt's voice fell silent again, although this time he suspected it was because she'd left him to ponder her admonishment and meditate on the true purpose of the trials. His outlook and the trials themselves had certainly ventured down a different road than he'd expected when he'd eagerly dove into the ancient structure, the place where he'd symbolically offered the severed head of the Evil One to the Watchman as both an insult and a threat.

I was quoting scripture then, Nuri recalled as the soldiers led him roughly down the aisle to an unknown gravesite. *Scriptures and Duri dogma. I've been too preoccupied with myself and the perceived dangers of the illusory world around me to remember why I'm here.*

You say you're here for God, the Duri Master agreed, *and yet you have forgotten your purpose. These are nothing but hollow words for you now.*

He swallowed and closed his eyes, surrendering to the direction of the alien warriors to meditate on his selfish fall from his Duri Master's teachings. There was a rebellious voice buried deep within him that protested that *all* Duri words were just that: hollow, pointless, self-glorifying words, and he was an imbecile to follow them.

A younger, foolish self, he thought, suppressing the rebel who'd considered betraying the Duri Masters on countless missions while he was an adolescent. *Through trust in God, I have seen the light of faith. I will never stray again.*

His foot knocked the edge of a tombstone and he was yanked roughly back to the center of the aisle.

"Watch yourself," his alien guide snapped.

He offered no apology.

Those of faith will be delivered from the hands of the Wicked, and the Wicked shall see the awful glory of God through His swift retribution. Do not trouble over the hour of your death, for the Lord will not permit the unholy to take the life of one of His precious emissaries.

It was a common Duri prayer that was to be spoken in times of capture and despair. The words normally stirred Nuri to the verge of tears, but on Operandom, he'd forced his body to become inhuman. There were no tears or breath for him to waste on pointless sentimentality.

"Do you have any idea where you're going?" he called to the alien commander.

"The way will reveal itself," he responded without turning from the holographic map he studied as he walked.

"That seems a lot of faith in the supernatural for someone who claims God and Tscharia do not exist."

Something caught the commander's attention before he could respond. The bait Nuri had lain was left untouched.

Distraction yet again, Colt scolded him. *A religious or philosophical debate at this point would only delay you.*

Ironic, he countered, *considering you, yourself, are a distraction designed to cloud my thoughts from the Divine Infinite.*

If that is how you understand my purpose, then you are a hopeless case. You will never be Hidria.

You claim that I already am.

"Spread out in groups of four," the commander shouted to his troops. "We're running out of time."

The soldiers began to separate wordlessly as the commander cursed and slammed his fist on the door to a large mausoleum, splintering the Khduovian wood. Along with splinters of bark, Nuri noticed bits of blue light piercing the toxic atmosphere from beyond the door. Immediately, he knew that Colt was inside.

"I know where you can find your Corpse Queen," he shouted to the commander as two more alien guards pulled him down another row of headstones.

Lying is an affront to God, the Duri Master told him.

Is it still an affront to God if I lie to perform His will?

He knew that if he could infiltrate the mausoleum and find the portal Colt concealed within, he could leave the planet entirely and be transported to yet another reality. Even if it didn't bring him any closer to finding God on Prime, he wouldn't needlessly waste any more time with the doomed aliens or their sacrilegious quest. If lying was the only way he could resume his mission for the good of his soul—and, potentially, the good of the galaxy so long as he passed the trials—then it would have to be a lesser sin.

We are all sinners, Colt reminded him.

The commander turned and approached him slowly, clearly erring on the side of caution while he worked out whether he believed Nuri or if the human was merely distracting them out of spite. "I thought you said you'd never heard of her."

"I haven't, but I can see that she's in this mausoleum," he told the alien, nodding towards the splintered door.

The commander glanced back where Nuri was pointing and shook his head. "You're lying."

"I see blue smoke curling out from the doorway," he said quietly. "She's in there."

Without turning, the alien motioned for two of his soldiers and pointed them toward the mausoleum. "Check it," he told them.

What if they search it first and can't find her? Then the lie will be for nothing.

"I can check it for you," Nuri said. "If you can't see the smoke in front of that door, then I doubt you'll see the signs of her inside, either."

The alien nodded as though he'd had the same thought and had merely waited for Nuri to suggest it on his own, then pointed to the splintered door and pushed the small of his back. "It doesn't hurt to look," he explained, more for the benefit of the murmuring soldiers, Nuri suspected, than himself.

The soldiers made way for Nuri as he trudged ahead of them through the toxic atmosphere and descended three steps to the mausoleum's entrance.

"Go with him," the commander directed two aliens standing near the doorway. "Keep your blasters on him."

Nuri glared at the alien commander, yet he didn't blame him for taking precautions against deceit, especially considering deceit was exactly what he planned once he stepped through the doorway.

Too risky to move right away, he thought. *They'll be expecting it. Better to wait until their guard is down, then take these two out and bar the door.*

He stepped through the narrow doorway (clearly built for a taller, thinner species than either one currently inhabiting the planet) and tried to clear his head while his eyes adjusted to the darkness. Colt had been through the mausoleum—he could feel it—but her trail had gone cold. He supposed she'd purposely diminished to get him to cooperate with the aliens though he did not understand why. Still, he held out hope that he'd find another doorway into the ancient, labyrinthine temple so he could continue his path toward Prime and God.

You don't even know where you're going, Colt mocked.

He ignored her voice and tried to focus on her presence.

"She's not down here," one of the soldiers reported back to the commander.

"Hold on," Nuri told him.

He opened his eyes. He could barely make out a thin trace of billowing, blue smoke from the back of the building, but it was there. The sight of her essence made his muscles clench. "There," he said, pointing toward the smoke. "Do you see it?"

The soldiers moved forward with blasters drawn, examining the air in the mausoleum in all directions so closely that Nuri could tell they couldn't perceive it. "There's nothing," the first one said. "He's lying."

The commander appeared in the doorway and looked in at them, shining a light from a spherical object that had materialized on the right forearm of his suit.

"I'm not lying," Nuri told him, holding his hands up to show he wasn't attempting a quick play for freedom.

At least, not in the way he thinks.

"Show me what you see," the alien responded.

He didn't seem as skeptical as the other soldiers, Nuri noticed, and that would at least buy him enough time to figure out what Colt wanted him to see in the mausoleum if he couldn't find a doorway back to the ancient temple.

"There," he told the commander, gesturing toward the area where the blue smoke snaked toward the high ceiling. "Do you see it?"

The alien stared intently at the air before them. Unlike the other two soldiers, however, his gaze was fixed in one spot, and as far as Nuri could tell, he was in the right vicinity.

Does he really see her? Nuri wondered.

For a moment, he forgot all about searching for Colt's hidden symbols in the mausoleum. He was more intrigued by the idea that this hostile, heathen alien could pick up on signs which only one of God's Called soldiers should see. The very notion went against everything the Duri had taught him since he'd been brought to the distant mountaintop. The Duri insisted that only God's chosen ones could see His presence, and that included the ethereal vessels, like Colt, that He used to facilitate the trials.

He can't, Nuri reasoned. *It would undermine all Duri teachings and, therefore, the trials themselves would be a farce, which cannot possibly be true.*

The alien commander breathed heavily and made a noise Nuri didn't recognize. "Is it blue?" he asked.

Nuri's heart leapt into his throat. He took a few steps forward without realizing his legs were moving at all. "You can see it." He meant for it to sound like a question, but his voice came out flat.

"It's just smoke."

"It's *not* just smoke," Nuri protested. His legs shook. He could feel the toxins from the atmosphere seeping back into his lungs, burning his esophagus on the way down. "It's *her.*"

The commander eyed him carefully for a moment, then looked back at Colt's remnants at the far end of the mausoleum. "That's not the Corpse Queen," he said. "It's something else."

"It's her," Nuri said weakly. He felt like sitting down. Or falling over.

But everything I've seen in the trials is real, he reasoned, *which means the Duri faith is real. How could we see Colt otherwise?*

The alien commander walked to the far end of the mausoleum and traced the blue smoke with his fingers.

He sees it.

The soldiers who had accompanied Nuri into the building stared at their leader with heads tilted inquisitively. Evidently, they thought that he was crazy, or perhaps just putting them on. They made no attempts to spot the anomaly for themselves, even with the aid of their suits' sensors.

They only trust their eyes, Colt said. *They don't understand there are senses that can detect realities beyond their own.*

Nuri crossed the room to the alien commander on unsteady legs, trying his best to recall his meditation techniques as he fought back the toxins worming into his blood.

This isn't real, he thought. *This can't be real.*

The reason you are here is to see if you can distinguish illusion from reality. Can you be sure of anything during the trials, then? Can you be sure of anything back in your flawed reality? How will you know where God is present and where it is the Evil One in disguise?

"What is it?" the alien asked again uncertainly.

"I told you. It's *her*. Colt."

The commander stepped back and watched the blue smoke swirl through the stuffy air, then turned to his soldiers. "Bring the offering."

They hesitated, glancing at each other to see whether either was willing to voice a protest, then quickly exited the mausoleum and shouted to the other soldiers.

"You're sure that this is the place?" the commander asked.

"See for yourself," Nuri replied curtly.

You don't have much time, his Duri Master cautioned. *Kill these heathens and find your way off this wretched planet! You have God's work to do, and it begins with cleansing these creatures of their iniquities.*

Nuri scanned the room for exits or any other symbols Colt had left behind for him, feeling a little more clear-headed each moment as he got his breathing under control and the toxins began to slowly suction out from his bloodstream. Before he could focus enough to detect additional clues, however, the alien commander gripped his shoulder and exclaimed in his native tongue.

"Something's happening."

Nuri turned back to the electric blue air. He was right. The smoke wasn't swirling with the aimless nonchalance he'd previously observed. It began to rapidly spurt out from nothing into a shape that solidified as the smoke increased.

"She's here," Nuri whispered, his heart pounding heavily in his chest. He felt an other-worldly presence manifesting around them. The sensation was as exhilarating as it was alarming.

It's not you, he said to Colt.

A shudder rocked his body as he watched the figure take form.

"Hurry!" the commander yelled in the direction of his soldiers. "She's already here!"

A moment later, a half-dozen aliens burst into the mausoleum carrying a purple-haired primate that struggled against their hold.

"Lay it in front of her!" the commander demanded.

The soldiers stopped running and stared at him, obviously confused. "Where?" one of them asked.

"What are you talking about? Right there!" he pointed toward the woman-figure's face. She had nearly assumed full physical form.

Still clueless, the aliens advanced toward the general area where the commander had pointed and dropped the struggling primate to the floor.

The glowing, blue smoke that was now a woman looked down at the beast and hissed.

"The book!" the commander shouted.

Another soldier burst through the doorway with a large, weathered text clasped against his chest and handed it over as reverently as he could manage at the end of a sprint.

The smoke-woman had at last become a full being, with glowing, pupil-less eyes, rotted hair, and a loose robe to cover her flaking, gray skin.

"*Iesu halla gokan*," the commander read from the text while the soldiers glanced back and forth between him and the seemingly empty air. "*Ack alahoo depon.*"

The Corpse Queen scowled at the alien, curling back her pale, blue lips to expose a worm-like tongue and cracked, yellow incisors.

Nuri's body was frozen in place. He wasn't sure whether to engage the hateful apparition whose very breath was sin and abomination, free the innocent primate who'd been brought as a blood sacrifice to the witch, or use the distraction to attempt an escape so he could find his way off the planet.

"*Iesu domi muham, Iesu domi iham. Bukara*," the commander continued unabated, even when the Corpse Queen moved toward him with a dragging limp and Kileran flies circling her rancid breath.

"Sir?" one of the alien soldiers whispered.

"Do you see her?" Nuri asked.

Again, the soldiers glanced back and forth, perplexed.

At least only one among them is privy to other realities.

Nuri nodded. "Then you should all leave now. Your commander can handle the rest. You won't be any good to him if you can't see your enemy."

The alien stopped reading abruptly and snapped his head toward Nuri. "She's not our enemy," he growled, venom dripping from his voice.

"She's a courtesan of the Evil One," Nuri argued. "She's enemy to all living things. Her presence here is an affront to God and all creation. We have to destroy her now before she becomes too powerful to contain."

The witch turned her soulless eyes to Nuri and growled a deep, phlegm-thick challenge.

"Then *you* can be her sacrifice," the commander told him. He resumed reading defiantly. "*Iesu domi Tscharia, kinoman lisan.*"

Heathen! his Duri Master shouted. *Kill them both* now!

Waves of heat rolled off the Corpse Queen, driving Nuri back toward the entrance. They didn't seem to have any effect on the alien commander.

I don't have my weapons, Nuri protested, edging sideways. He wasn't about to give up on finding a portal back to the ancient temple, even if it meant suffering the witch's presence even longer. It may not have been Colt's signs that had led him to the Corpse Queen's chamber, but he wasn't ready to dismiss the notion entirely considering he'd been too distracted to seek out alternative exits.

"*Ipatsu meno kolahando, kokkola opearandi hermanisk,*" the commander finished, dropping the text carelessly to the floor the moment that the last word left his lips—or whatever his species used for verbalization. For all Nuri knew, the sounds could have been manufactured completely by telekinesis. He'd seen such adaptations in other heathen species during his missions throughout the galaxy as a Called soldier while cleansing heretics of their sins and delivering them to God.

"My queen," the commander declared, falling prostrate before her.

"I am Death," the Corpse Queen hissed. "I will cover your universe in darkness."

Pride dwells in the tongue of the dead man, Nuri thought, remembering the seemingly nonsensical passage from his Duri teachings. But he couldn't stop the life from draining out of him when the wretched creature turned her glowing eyes to him again and roared with such terrible strength that he shrank back furtively. He could feel her thick saliva burn holes in his suit.

"You," the witch growled. "You stink of the Omega worshippers. I feel their poison in you."

"Poison?" he gasped. "It's *your* presence that poisons me."

"I've brought you back from the land of the dead to help my people," the commander persisted, ignoring the exchange between Nuri and the Corpse Queen entirely. "You're the only one who can save us from destruction."

The witch, likewise, ignored the alien, crossing the mausoleum to Nuri and sending rivulets of cracks like infected veins through the ground as she approached. "You wish to be Hidria," she said mockingly. "Hidria are not what you think they are."

Nuri attempted to backpedal but found that his limbs were paralyzed by malfunctions in his suit. The creature's poison was causing widespread system failures. "Hidria are servants of God. They protect all realities from your dark reign."

"It is not *my* reign, Omega fool."

"No, it is the Clown King's. You are nothing more than his consort. A harlot corpse. An abomination."

The Corpse Queen laughed, shaking the walls of the building so violently that even the alien commander fell to one knee and shielded his head in case the roof collapsed.

"Do you believe that God exists?" she asked.

Nuri gaped at her incredulously, forgetting her terrible power for a moment at the shock of having his faith questioned so openly without any prefatory argument. "I don't just *believe*," he said. "I *know*."

"Then that is your ultimate flaw," the Corpse Queen responded. "Your faith cannot be tested because faith requires an unknown. You *know* that God exists, therefore you don't have faith in Him."

Nuri scoffed, but the notion rattled him.

Could she be telling the truth? he wondered. *Is it even possible for me to be Hidria, then?*

Of course, his Duri Master argued. *The Hidria know that God exists more than any other living creatures because they* know *Him. If you become Hidria, it is impossible for you not to know that God exists.*

Nuri frowned, barely noticing the witch as she limped closer to him. *Then it's also impossible to say that Hidria have faith or are faithful. Is it possible for them to serve an ideal when it is no longer an ideal but a fact?*

"Please," the commander begged, crawling across the floor to her feet, yet not daring to stand in her presence without permission. "My people will die if you don't help us. You *must*! We brought you back to life solely to vanquish our foes. Please! Save our people."

The Corpse Queen stopped limping abruptly and scowled at the alien. "You raise a *corpse* queen and appeal to her to spare the living?" She laughed and theatrically changed direction to limp back to the commander. "What do you think a *corpse* queen is, fool? Did it ever occur to you that I *need* more souls from your dead to grow in power?"

Slowly, the alien pushed his way backward, erasing her progress with each shuffle of his hands and feet. But there was a wall not far behind him. It wouldn't be long before a confrontation was necessary one way or the other.

He's done this to himself, Nuri thought, once again using the opportunity to scan the mausoleum in case he'd missed an obvious exit or Colt's sigil while he'd been distracted by the Corpse Queen. He knew that he wouldn't be able to leave the mausoleum through the doorway they'd entered so long as the soldiers lingered, and the Corpse Queen's attention was angled in that general direction. Even if he managed to evade the soldiers, he wouldn't get far. As it was said, the dead traveled fast.

They both deserve to die.

The witch's head snapped back to him as soon as the thought echoed in his consciousness. "Are you one to pass judgment on who lives or dies?" she mocked. "How can you kill a Corpse Queen? I own death. I *am* death."

Rising, Nuri shook his head slowly. "*I* am Death," he said resolutely. "Hidria are Life and Death, and I am Hidria."

"You have to save my people!" the commander shouted. "Forget him! I'm the one who brought you here!"

"No, you're not!" the witch roared, forcing the alien to cower against the wall. "*He* brought me here, whether he knows it or not."

The alien turned to Nuri. "You?"

"She's lying," he said. "I know nothing about her."

"I do not lie."

"You are a queen of lies," Nuri retorted. "Death is the greatest lie, so a corpse queen is the greatest liar of all."

The witch snarled, then turned back to the commander. "I cannot save your people. Your planet is doomed no matter what you do. Not because of me but because of the maniac plans of *his* god." She stabbed a crooked, rotting finger in Nuri's direction, then curled her upper lip over her teeth again and brushed at the air in front of her face. "The stench of that foul creature is all over him. He's *drenched* in it. It's offensive."

"I'll kill him for you," the commander pleaded. "He can be your sacrifice. The sacrifice that you deserve."

The witch made a crude honking sound and spat black acid at the floor. "I deserve more than one of Omega's disciples. You insult me with the offer."

The alien stood and held out his hands imploringly. "I meant no offense, my queen."

"Stop groveling!" she shouted. "Offer *yourself* as a sacrifice. Then I'll know you truly value the fate of your people and not just yourself."

He fell quiet, considering. The Corpse Queen turned back to Nuri.

"You," she said. "You should offer yourself as a sacrifice for *his* people. Isn't that what your Savior God Omega would do?"

"They are not my people," Nuri responded.

"If the Duri truly lived the lifestyle they preach, they would be offering themselves as sacrifices for *all* people, regardless of their constitution, rather than eradicating anyone and everyone who challenges their beliefs. They are like children who cannot bear the thought that there are people in the galaxy who are better off than they are, and their jealousy drives them to kill indiscriminately." She waited a moment to see if Nuri would argue the point, then laughed when she realized he was speechless. "You must agree, then. In your head if not your heart. But the heart cannot be trusted with matters of faith and common sense. You shouldn't worry, though. The Duri do a great service to the Evil One by merely existing. Every day, they drive more souls into the corpse fields of Tscharia. They do his work more readily than even his self-proclaimed disciples."

She's lying! his Duri Master's voice shouted in his head. *She's trying to trick you! She wants you to forsake your holy calling!*

Silence hung heavily in the air. Nuri stared into the ground while the witch watched him. The alien commander held his breath with poorly suppressed despair.

"Please," the commander eventually muttered again. "You have to save my people. I'll do anything."

"Will you let me crucify you upside down and keep you alive in that state for one-hundred years while your people prosper?"

Again, the commander fell silent, glancing at the other soldiers in the mausoleum who could only hear the words spoken by their leader and Nuri. Even with a helmet to hide his expressions, Nuri sensed the guilt radiating from him. He was likely wondering if the soldiers could hear the witch's words or if their ocular perception of the apparition was the only sense affected.

"You are a weak, pathetic thing," the witch continued disgustedly. "What do you expect I can do for you? Why did you come here? I cannot raise armies of the undead in this reality. I do not have ships or weapons to offer you. If you wish to use the soul-summoning magic of the Evil One, then seek his Watchmen and find his unholy relics. You're more offensive than the Omega fool. At least he understands his doubts and deficiencies. At least he is willing to die for the will of God, even if he does not understand what that entails."

"Death is a lie," Nuri said defiantly before the alien commander could protest.

The witch moved back toward him. Her limp had diminished somewhat since she'd appeared, and that troubled Nuri. It made him wonder if she was gaining more and more strength the longer she was outside the realm of the dead. "Death is *not* a lie. It is a lack of comprehension for your finite minds."

As she moved, her shape began to lose constitution. Her rotting skin pulled off her body and swirled into tendrils of smoke that reached out to Nuri like tentacles. They beckoned him toward her, and the sensation was unsettling.

"You are on a quest to know the nature of God, or so you claim," the Corpse Queen continued. Her voice had changed as well, Nuri noticed. He couldn't even be sure that she *was* the Corpse Queen anymore. "But a human being cannot know the Divine Infinite. A human being cannot understand His nature because your minds aren't built for it. You can only comprehend things in terms of a beginning and end point. An Alpha and Omega, but never one and the same even when you picture them as a circular line encompassing everything."

Her flesh continued to rot away into smoke, and that smoke turned the metallic blue Nuri had grown accustomed to seeing in the trials.

She is returning, he realized. *This was never the Corpse Queen. This is Colt Incarnate.*

She knelt in front of him but her legs were swept away before they grazed the ground. She gently cradled his chin and drew him closer to her glowing eyes. Despite his training and his knowledge that the hideous face before him was nothing more than an illusion designed to distract him from the trials and teach him a lesson, Nuri shuddered and shrank from her touch.

Colt continued unabated. "No matter how hard you pray or train or wish, you will never be able to understand the true nature of God." She paused as her fingers melted from his beard then swept back into her hair and turned to a brilliant, alluring white. "Not as a human."

"Who is this?" the alien commander demanded. He turned to his soldiers. "This is not the Corpse Queen. Shoot her!"

The soldiers only stared. They couldn't see this emanation of Colt any more than they'd been able to perceive her guise as the Corpse Queen. It wouldn't have done them any good to see her, anyway. Blaster rifles wouldn't harm Colt, nor any entity from the other realities.

Nuri stood and stepped away from her. "I will not be human, then," he said. "I will be Hidria."

Colt had reverted completely to her smoke form. She shook her head sadly at him, stirring the air with half-realized light. "You say you know God exists, but that is not enough. You do not understand how closely knowledge opposes belief. You see them as two separate ends, meaning that knowledge and faith are mutually exclusive, but they are not. Only Hidria truly understand the paradox of faith versus knowledge in this reality, and that is only because they have access to other planes of Truth."

Nuri shook his head in frustration. "You were sent here to confuse me. It is your sole purpose in this reality. You are here to obfuscate the truth and make me question myself and my faith."

"That's how *you* understand my role because that's the way that the Duri Masters have described it to you. Just remember that I cannot muddle unshakeable knowledge or faith. My purpose is to pose these questions to you to judge whether your faith is a true extension of self or merely the result of Duri indoctrination."

"The Duri are dogs," the alien spat, fuming. "You will all burn with your bloodshed and false mysticism!" He turned to his soldiers and gestured toward the door. "This dog has led us astray. This is not the Corpse Queen, and he is not Hidria. We need to leave this filthy place and find the true Queen before it's too late."

"What about the stranger?" a soldier asked.

The commander turned back and regarded Nuri and Colt for a moment. "Leave him be. He won't give us any trouble."

With that, he left the mausoleum and never looked back. His soldiers lingered a moment longer, watching Nuri and debating if they should follow their commander's orders after hearing him interact with a being they could not see.

That's the trouble with faith, Nuri decided. *That's why he could see her and the others could not. They lacked both knowledge and faith.*

Finally, the soldiers followed their leader into the aisles of tombs, although one of them promptly returned and dropped Nuri's laser blade and blaster roughly on the ground beside the confused primate sacrifice, who apparently was free to go, as well.

"Thank you," Nuri said. He felt much more himself now that he was in the familiar presence of Colt's ethereal form. The panic and doubt that had risen in his chest had receded. He was comforted by the idea that he'd caught up with the right path to God's infinite divinity somewhere on the cemetery planet.

Colt began to drift toward the lone tomb at the far end of the mausoleum and Nuri retrieved his weapons so he could follow her.

"Do you understand why you were brought here?" Colt asked.

Nuri nodded. "To show me that I cannot meet God as I am because His nature is beyond human perception." He nodded back toward the entrance as he followed. "The soldiers couldn't see you because they lacked both faith and knowledge. The commander only had faith without knowledge, but that was enough for him to see you. If my faith is truly unshakeable, I will be able to recognize the Divine Infinite and know His ubiquity, even if I do not know His existence."

"You claim that you already *do* have knowledge of God."

He inhaled deeply. "Misguided arrogance," he admitted. "Pride dwells in the tongue of the dead man. I thought that I truly understood, but I did not. I am still human."

Colt drifted into the closed tomb. The top slab melted away to reveal a black hole beneath it that stretched beyond his vision. "You cannot know God as a human," her voice echoed up to him. "To survive the trials, you must be more than human."

Hidria, Nuri thought grimly.

He closed his eyes and fell into the emptiness of the tomb in her wake, surrendering to the fall even as he realized that he felt much further from his destination than when he'd started the trials with the severed head of the Evil One in his curled, hungry fist.

Prime. I need to figure out how to reach Prime.

But was Prime *truly* his destination, he wondered? What if Prime itself was an illusion? What if the true reason Colt had brought him to Operandom was because she *was* a queen of lies and had devised an ingenious, tautological argument with no answer to distract him from his calling?

That is why you must have faith, Colt's voice flashed into his head. *Whether your faith is in me or your own instincts, you must follow that faith to its logical conclusion. You can have doubts and still be strong in faith, but you cannot be weak in faith and juggle your doubts without crumbling beneath the weight.*

"Nonsense," Nuri groaned in the blackness. "Drivel."

He supposed she was right.

The darkness swallowed him whole.

14

It was morning. The entire village had assembled in the temple for the Duri Master's sermon. As his pupil, Nuri was required to assist with the rituals preceding the service and then dismiss the congregation once their minds had been freshly saturated with what he liked to call *scarecrow wisdom*, or thoughts that appeared full-bodied but were nothing more than broad generalizations of relatable struggles.

Ghosts of the pulpit, he thought as he straightened his garments and prepared for the service. *The spiritual equivalent of hot air.*

Granted, Nuri had only been released from disciplinary cleansing the prior morning. He was still bitter and the wounds were fresh on his emaciated body. Therefore, every aspect of the Duri Order was subject to reflexive cynicism, and even with the threat of torture and starvation looming just as large as his scars and bruises, he found it difficult to keep those opinions to himself. In fact, the fatalistic urge to detail aloud the contradictions in Duri doctrine had nearly overwhelmed his survival instincts more than once that morning.

Maybe I'll call it out during the service for all villagers to hear.

He imagined the fleeting seconds of bewilderment among his superiors, and for a moment, the fantasy seemed worth the shameful public execution that would inevitably follow. At least if he died, he wouldn't be forced to make the choice that kept him tossing and turning each night.

It is not a difficult choice, the river girl assured him.

His gut told him she was right. Yet even on the heels of the order's brutal punishment, his soul was torn between its purported destiny as a Called warrior and the identity he'd left beside his parents' unmarked graves on Dublokee. At times, he thought he must escape his de facto imprisonment even if he failed in the attempt, but then he would wonder if God were merely testing his faith through misery. There was joy and godliness in suffering, the Duri said, and so by torturing Nuri both physically and spiritually, perhaps Omega was merely purifying him with greater intensity than his superiors.

At times, the idea of a special, targeted suffering gave him pause. Enough, at least, that he dared not venture too far along the path of doubt for fear of retribution. He may not have always believed in the Duri, but he believed wholeheartedly in the Divine Infinite and had no desire to incite His righteous wrath, especially through willful negligence of a sacred duty.

The trouble was, unlike many among the Called, Nuri didn't know what sort of path Omega had laid for him beyond the Calling, and if he dwelled on it long enough, he was prone to interpret any pull one way or the other as the Evil One's deceit and thereby debate himself into apathy. Since the first seeds of doubt had arrived, he'd convinced himself any decision in which a choice appealed to him was a trap set by the Watchmen, and so even acts of charity made him suspicious of his own motives. There was simply no way to win. If, for instance, he helped an old woman in the market struggling to carry her food, he wondered whether it was truly out of the goodness of his heart or because he wanted to be perceived as the type of person who helped the needy? Was it for the purification of the universe or to stockpile his own credit in the Great Unending? In other words, were his 'good' actions driven by ego or selflessness? Were humans capable of complete selflessness in any action at all?

Whichever the case, he always managed to convince himself he was in the wrong regardless because there was no good in him and the realization was terrifying. He felt similarly reading the Old Book with the context of the New Book. Depending on the chapter and verse, he could make an argument that God was either inherently evil or inherently good depending on the reader's predilections, and so in his weaker moments, he wondered if there was ever any difference at all or if it was merely a matter of semantics.

Heresy, he thought. Yet so long as he was tied to the Duri, there was no way for him to be certain it was not the truth. He could only answer the questions in his soul beyond the influence of the Duri faith.

So leave, the river girl suggested.

It isn't that simple.

He knew freedom from the order could only be achieved through unprovoked bloodshed, which was evil by nature. Yet acquiescence to their decrees meant even *more* bloodshed and becoming lifelong accomplice to religious genocide of the New Manifest Destiny. He saw no benefit in choosing one side or the other so long as he still had his doubts. As with the cleansing missions, he thought it was always best to play it safe. To keep his options open.

Not now, he reproached himself. Distraction was getting the better of him again. He turned his attention back to the gathering crowd inside the temple.

There weren't enough seats to accommodate the full population of the village, so Nuri had been charged with overseeing the requisition of chairs from the village proper. Although the lack of seating had been an issue for as long as Nuri could remember, the Duri Masters had never made an effort to remedy the situation and he suspected they never would. Doing so would have run counter to their theology, largely owing to the idea that servants of the Divine Infinite were purged through the solemn act of suffering to hear His Holy Word, and therefore, anyone who did not arrive on time to honor God deserved to atone for their sins by standing through the duration of the service. It was a noble fantasy, perhaps, but Nuri figured the order had ulterior motives which superseded the notion of self-sacrifice.

Typically, the order wouldn't have tolerated such an oversight when it came to a sacred ritual, but the ultimate effect of crowding villagers into the temple three times each lunar cycle with hardly any room to breathe was that the sermons were perceived as nurturing an insatiable community hunger. Undoubtedly, it was the Duris' aim to quietly strengthen the perception of space within the temple as a valuable commodity, which endowed the faith itself a political economy that further strengthened their grip on the locals. And with each favor gained by a smile or nod or any other display of the preference for which Nuri himself had been flogged and branded, the people were driven further to extort those affirmations. In this case, the Duri Order looked the other way at the sin of preference, for this was how the clergy emptied the coffers of their zealous, confounded followers. As with any religion tainted by man, Nuri supposed, all behavior was permissible as long as you were the one doing it.

Due to the perpetual shortage, therefore, villagers arrived early to secure proper seats. It was a fascinating social experiment. Those in closest proximity to the altar were inevitably allotted premier social status and assigned to the highest echelons of holiness in the eyes of their brethren. Just as inevitably, those who prided themselves on this manufactured yet proportionally irrelevant relationship with the Divine through pew numbers then condescended upon the others, and those in the rear of the church or those who cared little for the social perception of their reverence for the Duri Masters had no choice but to accept this condescension from their betters. After all, they reasoned, these people sat closer to the altar, so they had a better understanding of God than anyone else. In this way, perception of holiness became reality within the hive mind. The men and women in the front pews became the elders, the heresy watchdogs who served the Duri under the guise of serving the community and serving God.

Standing at the rear of the church, therefore, was as far removed from the Duri Master—and God, by proxy—as a humble villager could get, and the Duri Masters were all too eager to encourage that unspoken belief. It followed logically that the lack of proper seating was an issue of supply and demand for the order, one which only thickened their veil of power and mystique. Had there been enough pews to accommodate the entire village populace, any empty seat would have been glaring. Even if the idea never materialized to the villagers on a conscious level, they would wonder whether someone knew better than they did about the rituals and if maybe they were fools for buying in to the Duri theology merely for the sake of a modest life protected by the Called soldiers.

Therein dwelled the problem, of course. Much like the rest of the human colonists who'd succumbed to Duri theology since its emergence during the New Manifest Destiny, the villagers hardly catalogued or questioned the motives of the Duri Masters once they passed a decree, especially with the Pontificates of the Front Pews shaming them into submission. Through great pain and years of ineptitude, humanity had once adopted a reflexive skepticism to anything and everything related to the Crown government and its Royal Space Armada, yet they forgot those hard-won lessons the moment that they were abandoned on the Galactic Frontier. Now, they simply accepted whatever the Duri Masters claimed the Divine

Infinite had told them, no matter how seemingly trivial the shewing happened to be.

Yet how could Nuri blame them? What was wrong with desiring safety or a connection to God? Why would the villagers feel a need to question the lack of proper seating at the temple beyond quiet rumblings whenever they were the ones left standing against the cold stone walls or ruining their backs in the uncomfortable chairs Nuri fetched from the village proper? At face value, they would not have seen a great conspiracy hidden within the mundane discomfort, nor in the assignment of social standing based on proximity to the altar during the tri-lunar sermon. Yet to Nuri, it was another example of the way the Duri Masters controlled the populace in every subtle aspect of life until they were utterly broken. Until they lapped up anything and everything the order threw their way. Until they were too dependent on the order to speak against it.

The trouble for Nuri, however, was that, although he never would have admitted it aloud, he took an absurd level of pride and satisfaction in being included in the rituals. He cherished being front and center in his assigned role for all the villagers to see and know his importance. Put simply, he was proud of his assumed proximity to God through service to the Duri Masters, as much as he protested his belief in the Duri Order's methods (if not their theology).

In more enlightened moments, he recognized how his Duri Master was carefully winning him over with each menial task he assigned to oversee the successful performance of the Duri rituals. Participation was agreement. Despite the decree that praising and reflecting upon the Divine Infinite should not be done for personal gain, he couldn't help but enjoy an elevated feeling of self-importance when he made decisions or assisted the Duri Master in public, no matter how trivial the endeavor truly was. In that sense, he understood the Pontificates of the

Front Pews. Respect and awe were addictive and immersing himself in each for long enough got him to believe the external perception of his status was reality. He was Holy. He was God's Chosen. He was Better.

The Duri Masters enjoy the same selfish longing, he often thought. *I haven't met one among them who joined the order out of a fervent desire to serve God's interests. Those who did would long since have been silenced by the purging blaster bolts and laser swords of the Called.*

Still, was that alone reason to entirely dismiss the basic tenets of the faith? The Duri did a lot of good in worlds who obeyed them, after all, and it was an inevitable truth of any religious institution that it was subject to the corruption of man. In fact, in Nuri's eyes, a pure faith was utterly impossible. Yet so long as he stood on the winning side of the ideological war in the colonies, he was loath to speak such heresy openly.

"Brothers and sisters," his Duri Master began.

The murmur of the overflowing crowd died down until the stone temple was silent aside from the steady rush of the river current just beyond the pulpit. Nuri took his assigned post to the right of the altar facing the congregation and bowed his head with his hands clasped behind his back. A light rain had begun to fall over the mountain range, tapping a rhythm off the forest canopy and the rushing river. Faced with such atmospheric profundity, he felt a chill build from the base of his spine to the hackles of his neck: the surest sign of God's presence he could fathom since it only emerged when he contemplated eternity. Circumstantial evidence or not, it certainly did little to diminish his fear of angering the Duri Masters. If there was even a chance that they had the Divine Infinite on their side, who was he to question the veracity of their doctrine?

"Today is a difficult day," the Duri Master continued. "A tumultuous day."

The congregation collectively leaned forward. With eight words, he had won their complete attention. Most men and women were afraid even to breathe, and children were afraid to make any sound that might draw the wrath of their parents. Noises in the quiet moments of the service were viewed as shameful, just as failure to sing during the ceremonial utterances was a sin. Entire families would be relegated to the Back Pews in the favor of God at the slightest misstep.

"Today, we acknowledge that we have failed the Divine Infinite." He cleared his throat and adjusted the hulking red and white robe so his hands were free to point out the failures of individual believers. "You are all sinners. We are all sinners. We have failed, and we must be purged of our iniquities."

A nervous exhale swept through the congregation. They were always stunned by the direct, though vague, accusations from the pulpit, having only the thrice monthly exposure to it. Nuri was immune to the sting, however. He endured similar condemnations on an hourly basis as the Duri Master attempted to strengthen his faith and resolve.

"How must we be purged?"

His scarred, angular face peered over the edge of the raised platform and he scowled. The tension rose in the room until Nuri was certain someone would let out a nervous cough or a swallow that would necessitate the reassignment of pews, but no one did. Instead, the Duri Master leaned so far over the stone railing that Nuri marveled at his balance, then stabbed a long, bony finger at the huddled masses. "You must purify yourselves through agony to atone for the agony you have inflicted upon the Maker by your disobedience. By your self-servitude. We were not put here to endlessly chase personal pleasure. We were brought into this universe to purify it for the next iteration of the Divine Incarnate."

Nuri scanned the faces of the Front Pew Pontificates. Most of them hung on every word of the sermon to the point that he considered their attentiveness suspect. There was a difference between listening and straining to assume the expression associated with deep concentration, which appeared closer to the look Nuri adopted while agonizing through a bout of serious intestinal distress than the one he wore while saying his evening prayers in the privacy of his cot. The ones who seemed most engaged often wore blank expressions, he thought, since their minds were filled to the brim with the reality of God's Eternal Presence. This was not a universal truth, of course, nor was the idea that those closest to the altar were merely looking for the clergy's approval or a higher social standing.

Still, despite the favors doled out by the Duri Masters themselves, Nuri had his own ideas about who truly absorbed and applied the manufactured message of the sermon to their daily lives and who was merely in it for the status points. And since he heard the Duri Master's rehearsals of the sermon each night leading up to the ceremony in the cottage they shared, he used the opportunity to inventory the congregation itself, if for no other reason than to prepare himself for the day when he would need to separate truth from distraction in the trials.

The Duri Master had once asked him to report back on what he noticed about the men, women, and children who imbibed his self-congratulatory calls for self-flagellation to offer suffering to God. To be just like him, in other words, and thereby legitimize the radical stupidity of injuring oneself because the Loving Creator of the Universe desired it.

Nuri never felt comfortable relaying such arbitrary judgments based on posture and eye contact, though, so he rarely reported his findings. He never saw how slumped shoulders correlated to a relationship with or belief in the

Divine Mystery, the Beginning and End. Besides, the temple worshippers he considered the most suspect and least Godlike were the ones whom the Duri Master chastised him for fingering, and he'd never felt comfortable at all rendering judgment on others while his own faith was in such perpetual turmoil. Casting judgment seemed like a particularly self-indulgent practice. Excusing those in the Back Pews simply because they didn't exhibit the desire for perceived holiness that those in the Front Pews displayed was dangerously close to the same trap as judging them the other way around. It was a convoluted mess, one for which he saw no reasonable solution, and it only added to the stratification of the people.

But he supposed that was the whole point of these ceremonial gatherings. Not to offer conciliatory wisdom to the downtrodden or to reinvigorate the villagers' faith, but to remind them of the purging flame while simultaneously marking those whom the order deemed potential heretics and establishing an unspoken social hierarchy in the mountain community. It was less a ceremony and more an inventory. A test. A culling.

A cleansing.

Nuri felt the shudder at the base of his spine again and suppressed the urge to convulse. He wasn't sure if he could trust the impulse anymore. Surely, God couldn't be present in such a convoluted mess of political and self-serving aspirations. Surely, the minstrels were not solely performing to glorify God but to glorify themselves, shaming others into action by telling them that you didn't *truly* love God unless you accompanied them in song. Surely, God would be more likely to condemn those who mocked true faith by shaping it to suit their individual agendas than those who crouched in shame in the back pews or against the cold, stone walls.

Wouldn't He?

Nuri still wasn't sure, and so he remained silent.

Men are the folly of religion, he thought.

It might have been a phrase from *The Divine Incendiary* or maybe just an idle pseudo-intellectual musing. That was the trouble of being drowned in philosophy and theology every day while considering the effect of each mundane task he performed on his soul. He sacrificed the grace of the moment for the unwavering long view. By eliminating distraction and preference, he could no longer identify the notions that came to him based on experience and a true understanding of his place in the universe versus those he'd merely read in one religious text or another. The metamorphosis of perception had nearly blinded him, to the point that he now wondered if some distraction from the mysteries of the universe, or at least appreciation of them in their physical form, was actually a *good* thing. If, then, appreciating beauty in his mountain surroundings and in his distant love for his murdered family was itself glorifying the Divine Infinite since He created all things.

Shouldn't distraction be considered a blessing from God—a grace—rather than a willful corruption from the Evil One?

No, he quickly responded. *Distraction glorifies self, not the Divine.*

Another phrase from another book. Another layer added to the ever-thickening veil between the Living All and theology. Where did the thread between the two begin and end?

In God, the river girl's voice assured him.

He frowned and shifted against the wall, too frightened by his own blasphemous, circular thoughts to scan the temple. He might lock eyes with someone in the congregation if he did that, and then they would know that he wasn't hanging on every word of the sermon. He was a fake. His relationship with God was nothing more than illusion.

So, like the Front Pew Pontificates, he turned his gaze back to the Duri Master and squinted his eyes in a show of fervent concentration.

You are a fool, the river girl admonished him. *You grow further from the truth each day. This isn't God. This is politics.*

He clenched his teeth and forced her from his thoughts.

Years passed before he felt the chill at the base of his spine again. He never noticed the difference.

15

Nuri awoke face-down in an alley between two tall buildings.

Juriaq again? he wondered. The air was heavier than before and lacked the ubiquitous sea-salt smell for which the floating city was famous, but the skyscrapers alone were enough to give him pause. After gathering his bearings and closely inspecting the architecture, however, he determined that despite the similarities, it wasn't Juriaq after all. In fact, he had no idea *where* he was.

His legs were unsteady from the fall and he felt more than a little disoriented by the constantly shifting worlds beneath his feet, but he managed to stagger out of the alley onto a wide avenue. A wave of smoke immediately enveloped him. He coughed until his eyes watered and stomach ached.

If you had truly learned surrender, you wouldn't need to suffer this transformation on each new world, Colt admonished.

He squeezed his eyes shut and clenched his jaw in fervent concentration, willing the smoke from his lungs along with the biological imperative for pure oxygen. Now that he was familiar with the process, it was only a matter of moments before he could breathe again (or at least ignore his lack of breath), and then the root of his cough switched from smoke inhalation to the grating exhalations of his damaged throat.

I am Hidria, he told himself.

Even in his head, he uttered the words with a newfound reverence. The simple declaration had become a prayer, an acknowledgment of the truth of God in the universe and his power to overcome the distractions of the Evil One.

I am Hidria.

Once the final wave of coughs sputtered out and his vision settled, he turned his attention back to the street.

Almighty God, he thought as he surveyed the area. *What happened to this place?*

The city block was pure carnage. The sidewalk platforms were filled with overturned vehicles. Debris from the scorched buildings and corpses from two alien races were sprawled over top of them. Now that his transition fugue had lifted, Nuri recognized the sound of blaster fire in the distance along with the heavier pound of artillery tearing chunks from the skyscrapers. High powered ordnance, too, by the sound of it.

Where am I? he asked Colt and his Duri Master.

He didn't recognize either alien species, and his suit was too battered to research its database even if the action had been permitted in the trials.

I'm not here to satisfy your curiosities, Colt replied coldly. *I'm here to make you question your faith until you either arrive at an answer or you don't.*

Does it matter *what creatures these are or what planet this is?* his Duri Master said. *Your only objective is to reach Prime and learn the nature of the Divine Infinite. Investigating planet names and alien species are trivial distractions. They have nothing to do with the fundamental truths of Creator God. Leave this place as quickly as you can and trouble no more over such insignificant details.*

Nuri stared at the bodies uncertainly. A sickness welled in the pit of his stomach at the sight of so much death and destruction. Unlike the cleansings, this operation lacked precision and cleanliness. Alien blood and guts were splattered everywhere. The dark clouds overhead and the smoke rising from the scorched streets only added to the macabre scene.

Is this Tscharia? he wondered.

The dead and mutilated corpses made it seem possible, yet he couldn't imagine being transported to the isolated universe of Tscharia without feeling the fracture in his mind. Tscharia, after all, was said to afflict each of its miserable inhabitants with insanity by the complete removal of all realities containing God before the bodily torture even began. It was difficult to say with any certainty, but he didn't believe he'd fallen quite that far.

Yet.

It seemed strange that both ends of the spectrum—Hidria and Watchmen—involved a descent into lunacy, but it also made a poetic sense. The weight of reality was simply too much to bear.

Distraction.

He stepped carefully between the bodies and attempted to make sense of the peculiar native technology. The buildings were connected by retractable walkways with glowing green lights and blue surfaces. He spotted figures moving along them high above and an occasional blaster bolt illuminated the darkening sky, but they were both too far off for him to properly assess. Curious, he stooped and examined the uniforms of two warriors who had died with blasters pointed at each other's throats.

Must have fired at the same time, he thought.

The nearest alien was an arachnid of some sort with a long, curved snout, a massive mouth, and tiny eyes buried behind cheekbones as sturdy as any combat armor. Its exoskeleton was slimy and red, its actual armor an odd mixture of webbing and the bones of fallen enemies.

Judging by the tread-wear on the second alien's combat boots and the heavy pack it carried, Nuri figured it was part of an invasion force. Its gray-brown tentacles hung beneath a wide nose and bald head, but unlike the arachnid creature, it had humanoid arms and legs. Its armor looked like it had been forged from Durakian steel, though it hadn't done much to stop a giant shard of glass from piercing the invader's chest. Judging by the breather attached to its nose, its body wasn't accustomed to the atmosphere, either.

I wonder why they're killing each other, he thought.

Each would probably say it's for a god or a communal ideal, Colt said.

He found the suggestion unlikely given that most arachnid species that humanity had encountered beyond Earth's solar system so far were atheists, ascribing only to the worship of their Queen Mother or an elected official within their planet's political hierarchy.

Perhaps atheism is what caused this, then. Perhaps it is considered an insult to the god of the invading species, or an edict from their spiritual leaders spurred these creatures to conquer as many planets as possible and forcefully convert the inhabitants to their faith.

Nuri was familiar with the idea of forced conversion, having participated in dozens of cleansings himself. In fact, it was difficult to consider any other possibility when it was all he knew of political and faith-based conquest.

How can you suggest that Omega is behind such senseless violence and destruction?

Not Omega. The men who pretend to know His mind.

Nuri was about to argue the point when a blaster bolt caught him in the back and flung him into a heap of alien corpses. Another flurry of energy blasts erupted a moment later from the opposite direction, followed by fearsome shouts in two distinct languages.

It looks like the battle has come to me, he thought, casting aside his human revulsion to delve deeper into the pile of bodies for cover. His armor had blunted the severity of the blaster bolt to nothing more than a painful bruise, but his head was wholly unprotected. He knew the battered plating on his torso couldn't sustain much more abuse.

What now?

The shooting around him quickly intensified. The ground shook as both armies charged toward each other in a heavy cloud of blaster fire. The stench of charred corpses and alien guts became sickening. Nuri had to meditate yet again just to avoid vomiting, and the melted-conduit smell of the overheating blasters did little to blunt the urge's potency.

Wheels groaned as heavy tanks crushed bodies on their way to the enemy line. A steady din of battle cries resounded between the two armies, all unintelligible to Nuri.

This world isn't a part of my galaxy, he realized. *I'm a long, long way from the ancient temple.*

Only in terms of the physical dimension, Colt said.

Nuri groaned and began to dig his way out from the bodies, realizing stealth wouldn't do him much good if he was trampled before either army had a chance to shoot him. His only hope was to take refuge in a building where he could collect his thoughts and plot his next course of action, assuming he survived long enough to reach one.

As soon as his head was exposed to the smoky air, however, the front lines of both armies slowed as did the volleys of blaster bolts. They didn't die off altogether—they never quite did—but enough soldiers were confused by the appearance of the small, ugly alien emerging from the pile of corpses and rubble that their attention was momentarily drawn from the task at hand.

Kill these horrible creatures! his Duri Master shouted. *They will destroy you if you don't! They do not know God!*

Desperate for cover, Nuri scrambled overtop an abandoned vehicle that resembled a military-grade hoverspeeder. When he turned his attention from one army to the other, he noticed a few soldiers on each side had already trained their blasters on him and were hurling taunts in their native tongues.

Trapped, he thought.

On a whim, he leapt through the roof of the speeder and dropped into the control seat. Blaster bolts pinged off the armor covering the controls as soon as he hit the leathery pilot's chair. He didn't waste time searching for operating instructions. Instead, he punched the speeder's control panel as hard as he could, then clicked and flipped every button and switch he could find until the engine whined to life with a nasally drone.

On instinct alone, he managed to kick the throttle and send the vehicle hurtling at breakneck speed for a full three seconds before he crashed through the side of a building and was violently catapulted against a rubbery wall, which flexed to catch him and then lowered his body to the floor. He didn't witness the deployment of its technology, though, and wasn't aware of the crash's immediate aftermath until he rolled to a stop on the cold ground. He tasted blood and singed hair from his beard, but most of the pain pulsed along the back of his head and into his neck.

Whiplash.

Considering the velocity of his impact with the building, it was a miracle that his injuries seemed relatively minor, yet that was a small consolation as he struggled to one knee and felt the ensuing waves of pain envelop his body.

"AAAAGGGHHH!" he shouted.

The furious thunder of war machines raged outside the broken windows, but it was the booted footsteps approaching over the blaster bolts and the heavy, repeating artillery rounds that concerned him.

They were coming for him.

Who? he wondered.

He raised his neck to peer out, gasping in pain with each hard-won centimeter of movement. A dozen tentacle-faced soldiers from the invading army began to storm through the hole he'd opened in the building's exterior.

This will not end well, he realized.

At least they were content with capturing him for the time being, he thought, rather than shooting him on sight the way he suspected the locals might if they caught him in the alleyways. The defending army would inevitably suspect he was an enemy spy since he was fairly certain a human fell well outside the scope of known species in this particular galaxy, wherever it happened to be.

I'll have to fight, he thought. *Even if they don't kill me right away, they will eventually if they can't glean any useful information from me regarding their enemy.*

On top of that, he knew he didn't have nearly enough time to learn the language and propose a diplomatic solution to work himself off world. Bloodshed seemed inevitable.

He scowled at the onrushing troops and activated his laser blade.

"I am Hidria," he growled. "I am fear."

The confused aliens sought cover as soon as the weapon ignited, unsure what to make of the energy beam, but they quickly regathered their nerve and started firing. Nuri rolled behind the speeder and waited until an explosion outside the building distracted the aliens, then leapt out from behind the vehicle. "I am Death!" he screamed. Ignoring the pain alighting up and down his body, he launched into the nearest alien and sliced clean through its neck, quickly turning the body to absorb blaster fire from the others.

"I am Hidria!" he shouted.

This time, unbridled rage filled him rather than the battle calm. He roared and tossed his first kill at three alien soldiers clumped together behind a large piece of debris either from Nuri's crash or one of the explosions on the street. The impact stalled their blaster-fire just long enough for him to pounce on the trio. He stabbed the point of his blade through the throat of the first, spun around to separate the second at the waist, then sliced open the last from gullet to groin in the span of a few heartbeats.

Senseless and savage, his Duri Master snapped. *There is no grace in a violent kill.*

Just as Nuri turned to confront the rest of the attackers, though, a blaster bolt caught him in the shoulder and sent him sprawling over a mound of debris.

Death, he thought. It was the only word he could manage in his state of shock. White-hot pain seared the left side of his body where the pulse blast had found purchase between tears in his suit. He pawed gingerly at the cauterized wound and hissed beneath the sound of persistent blaster volleys. He didn't realize that the wound had likely saved his life until he scrambled completely behind cover as a whole battalion of locals suddenly stormed through the opposite side of the building and besieged the invaders with giant, cylindrical cannons.

That doesn't mean it gets any better for me, he thought grimly. *It only ever gets worse.*

The wound had sapped most of his combat rage to the point that he felt absurd for his useless bravado, but the fire slowly began to reassert itself as he watched the invaders realize they were flanked, as well.

God, be my strength, he prayed. *Be my blade and my resolve.*

In the best-case scenario, he was about to be caught in a deadly crossfire between the two armies. Even if he procured a hasty alliance with one side or the other amid the battle, which was itself a practical impossibility given the language barrier, there was still no conceivable way he'd escape the warzone with his life.

If you were truly Hidria, you would manage to escape. You could oppose entire armies on your own.

Nuri shrank deeper into cover as the invaders turned their attention to the battalion at their flank with the aid of flame cannons and blaster turrets mounted on the shoulders of cyborg aliens.

If you cower away from what you know you must do, then you are not worthy to be called Hidria. Hidria place all trust in God and are righteous in their surrender.

A fresh volley of blaster bolts skimmed past Nuri's head and suddenly the rage was on him again.

"I am Hidria!" he shouted. None of the creatures heard him over the drowning din of battle, but they certainly noticed when he leapt into the middle of the fray with a blaster in one hand and a laser blade in the other.

You are insane, his Duri Master chastised him in palpable disbelief. *Your mental degradation is complete.*

He started firing before his feet hit the ground, alternating between the invading army and the locals without any clue which direction was ideal for escape. All he knew was a panic unlike anything he'd ever experienced had swept over him. The calm demeanor that he normally possessed in spades during the heat of battle was nowhere to be found.

Foolish. Proud. Insane.

It wasn't long before he faced more than just the risk of inadvertent crossfire from diving out into the mayhem. Soldiers from both armies quickly aimed their weapons at him and started firing, trying to mitigate the damage he inflicted on both parties. Each was certain he'd allied with the other.

He hit the ground hard and felt his shoulder pop out of socket beneath his armor, but a fresh surge of adrenaline was enough to keep him moving. He let his momentum carry him into a roll with his finger pressed down on the trigger the whole time, landing more shots than he missed due to the tight grouping of enemy forces in the cramped building.

You're wounded, Colt said matter-of-factly.

Nuri tried to ignore her, but it was difficult when he felt the impact of blaster bolts beating into him. He knew he was in trouble. He managed to cover himself just enough to avoid any headshots, but it seemed a futile exercise in the end. He was getting hit over and over and his armor wasn't doing much to dull the impacts. It was only a matter of time before it gave out completely.

I'm going to die, he thought, continuing to fire at both armies out of helpless anger and spite.

Hidria cannot die.

Colt's suddenly booming voice stunned him enough that his grip on the trigger momentarily relaxed, mercifully drawing the shots away from him. The aliens must have thought he was already dead and didn't want to waste ammunition hammering his corpse. He still wasn't completely out of the woods (although he supposed he could play possum long enough to find a window for escape), but it gave the pain of a dozen blaster wounds ample opportunity to fully set in.

Except, it didn't. When he concentrated on the nerves in his body, he realized that he didn't feel pain at all anymore. Not even in his shoulder, which he knew without a doubt he'd separated when he hit the floor.

What's happening? he wondered. *Am I paralyzed?*

He scrambled to tear free of the armor plating to see if there were any burns from the blaster bolts.

There were, and plenty of them. In fact, his skin was still sizzling where there was enough of it left to sizzle. Most of the wounds had burned all the way to the taut strings of his muscle. By all rights, he should have been dead.

And yet, he felt nothing.

Am I in shock?

Another flurry of blaster bolts caught him, this time in the back of his head and the side of his face. His neck snapped sideways when they hit. He smelled scorched skin and melting brain matter, but otherwise, he was no worse for wear.

He stared up at the peculiarly warped ceiling in disbelief, trying to come to terms with his new invincibility, working out whether it was his entire physical form or solely the nerve receptors in his body.

I may still be dying and just unable to feel the pain.

It seemed farfetched, yet not nearly as farfetched as being shot more than a dozen times from ten yards away and still breathing.

You aren't dying, Colt told him as he lay there, startled by his own breath and thoughts. *You cannot die. You are Hidria now.*

He swallowed hard and was awed by the sensation of his tongue sliding against the roof of his mouth. If he couldn't feel the blaster burns, he thought, how could he possibly feel a sensation as subtle as swallowing?

I am Death, he told himself. *I cannot be killed.*

It didn't explain the contrast between his lack of pain and everything else he still felt other than the notion that Hidria could *control* what they did and didn't feel, but it was enough to get him moving again with renewed resolve.

I have to leave this place, he thought, rising to one knee and ignoring the blaster bolts flying around him. *I have to get to Prime.*

His internal clock had begun to tick loudly. He understood he was running out of time to reach the Divine Infinite on the first planet, yet the surreality of feeling the impacts from blaster bolts without ensuing agony had pushed him over the edge of sanity. And once he dipped his toe into those deep and poisonous waters, he knew that there was no hope to re-emerge from the trials unscathed.

That time has already passed, Colt told him. *You have already been marked. There is no going back from Hidria. You have already been transformed.*

Nuri stood to his full height, allowing the blaster bolts to smack into him while he steadied his legs against their impact. It was a cathartic sensation, feeling his body shift and juke with each shot, yet still keeping his feet.

Then I have to get to Prime as soon as possible to learn why I have been deemed worthy, he decided.

He inhaled deeply, then holstered his blaster and swung his laser blade in a wide arc.

More energy blasts turned in his direction. The aliens' palpable fear mounted in the face of a seemingly indestructible being.

"Hidria!" Nuri shouted. He turned toward the invaders and launched into the front of their line with his blade a swinging blur in front of him.

The soldiers responded with battle cries of their own and concentrated fire in his direction, but they scrambled away when he landed atop two tentacled faces and drove his blade downward through the head of another.

Immediately, the locals saw their opportunity to make a press and triggered the flamethrowers for a full five seconds before stopping to allow the infantry to press forward and assist Nuri. By the time they reached the invaders' line, Nuri had cut his way through a dozen of the alien soldiers, not even bothering to twist and turn to avoid the shots as they came at him. He just absorbed each impact, dug in with his boots, and fought his way forward with slices, stabs, and hacks. A few soldiers stopped firing altogether when he got close enough to finish them off. They simply stared with crumpled expressions which he assumed were awe or disbelief, and that made killing them a little bit more difficult because it humanized them.

But only a little.

He'd killed more than his share of unarmed civilians with the Called and they'd each borne similar expressions when they met their end. He'd learned over the years to detach himself from the horror of it all, but somehow the sight of these alien creatures stirred enough of an emotional response that he regretted every life he'd taken all at once.

What have I done? he thought, lowering his weapon in despair.

Now is not the time for regrets, Colt reminded him.

He knew it was true and was himself surprised that emotion should hit him while he was still a primary target. Perhaps it was the sight of the aliens' collective realization that they were powerless to stop the beast among them. Their weapons were useless. Resistance of any kind was hopeless. Even the colonists he'd killed over the years had an idea of what was coming and must have taken comfort knowing their killer would get his just due eventually because he was *mortal.* The look in the eyes of these alien invaders was different, he realized, because they faced something utterly beyond their comprehension. It seemed an unforgivable sin to kill a creature with no hope of defending itself.

It never bothered you while you were cleansing planets, Colt said. *You killed thousands of innocent women and children. Perhaps tens of thousands.*

That was in the name of God, he protested. But in his heart, he realized it was an insufficient justification, and not a true justification at all. He hadn't killed all the heretics and sinners because God had told him to do it. He hadn't received a divine revelation detailing how those specific individuals were an affront to God and His Holy Name. Each mission had been mandated by the Duri Order, who claimed to speak for God but who also had not heard from Him directly since the scriptures were written millennia ago.

Why? he wondered, deactivating his laser blade as the battle raged around him. *Why am I only realizing this now?*

Colt's form suddenly appeared among the invaders, glowing with such vibrancy that he could see her clearly through the tangle of bodies.

You see now because you are no longer human. You are Hidria. The Duri no longer have a hold on your mind.

The invaders began retreating into the street. The locals advanced jubilantly in turn, giving Nuri a wide berth. It was clear by the way they regarded him as they passed that they would have liked to capture and study him had it not been the middle of a battle, but he met their gazes without fear and they moved on in hopes of trapping the invaders between their two ground forces.

Find a ship, Colt told him, taking his hand and pointing out the window. *There is a hangar down the street where you can have your pick of fighters. Don't take anything too big or you will need a full crew to operate it.*

Nuri nodded and stepped through the hole in the side of the building where he'd crashed the alien speeder and inadvertently triggered the skirmish inside. Colt released his hand and sucked backward into the smoke with her glowing eyes still locked on him.

The sound of artillery was deafening. The blaster bolts and energy-cannon rounds formed such a thick cloud that Nuri had to seek shelter against the building even though he was certain the blasts could not kill him. It was too heavy a barrage for him to keep his feet.

They must truly despise each other, he thought.

He'd witnessed the animosity of battle before. Certainly, none of the colonists he'd killed as a Called soldier had been happy to see him. But the pounding each side had taken and then continued to dish out in equal measure suggested that the two races had been enemies for a long, long time. It did not seem to be a matter of territory or resources, although Nuri admitted to himself that he could have been wrong on that count. The battle had the feel of two clashing ideologies that had been at odds with each other for as long as their species had existed.

Shuffling down the street with modest cover from the building, Nuri worked himself away from the battle's epicenter. He could see light streaming out from a large, open structure ahead and knew it was the hangar Colt had promised without needing to see any ships. Nothing stood in the way of him hijacking a fighter now. Even if soldiers guarded the vessels, he knew they would be few with so much happening outside the building. Besides, even before he was Hidria, he would have been able to take out a minor guard detail on his own.

The hard part will be learning how to fly one of these ships, he thought.

Again, though, he was confident he would figure it out without much trouble. Now that he was Hidria, nothing seemed impossible.

But how will I get to Prime? he wondered.

Colt hadn't given him any specific directions on where to go nor explained where he was in the universe. And even with a reference point to gauge how far he needed to travel to return to the distant mountaintop, he would still be missing the coordinates for Prime.

If you are destined to see the Divine Infinite, Colt told him, *you will be guided to Him.*

Nuri knew better than to argue with her. She would either turn his logic on its head or shoot it down completely. Besides, his perception of Colt as a malevolent being who existed only to complicate his journey had been turned on its head already. He trusted her now as his greatest asset. Even greater than his Duri Master, he supposed, whose voice had all but disappeared from his consciousness in the new reality.

As he suspected, only a handful of locals had been stationed in the hangar. He made quick work of them with his blaster and climbed into the nearest fighter, which was about five times the size of the vessels that the Called used for space combat but was still smaller than any other ship in the massive structure. Unlike the Duri fighters where the cockpit was accessed by ladder and the opening of a glass canopy, the alien vessel required scaling a precariously angled ramp that shot almost directly upward into the ship, then opening a circular hatch by pressing a bright blue button. Once inside, he had to climb an unevenly spaced ladder and walk a long, narrow corridor to access the controls.

There were two stations in the cockpit (which was more of a bridge than a single-fighter control pod) and he looked each one over carefully before deciding the console on his left controlled the weapons and the one on the right controlled propulsion. The arachnids didn't require seats and were taller than he was even when resting on their legs, so he had to move an empty canister from the rear of the ship to reach the buttons and levers. Once he accessed the console, however, he had little difficulty activating the ship's drive and gently depressing the propulsion to exit the hangar.

"Where to?" he asked the empty cockpit as the hatch closed automatically and the ramp retracted. He feared briefly that he wouldn't be able to breathe the concentrated atmosphere the aliens required once the life-support systems kicked on, then remembered that he'd breathed easily enough on the surface. The same would likely hold true on the ship.

Reflex, he thought. Breath was the first thing warriors usually thought about when they boarded the ship of an alien species. Not all aliens subsisted on oxygen (in fact, most of them did not), and one couldn't be too careful when sealing themselves in a foreign atmosphere. But even before the warzone, air hadn't been much of an issue for Nuri during the trials, and if dozens of blaster bolts couldn't kill him at point blank, then he didn't think something as insignificant as breath could destroy him. Hidria were too strong for that.

The Duri say Hidria can even travel through space without masks. Is that true?

Colt appeared before him as he carefully turned the ship so its back was directed toward the battle and then activated the thrusters to begin his angled ascent.

"Yes," she told him. "Your physical body is breaking away as we speak. Soon enough, it will not exist as you know it and the transformation will be complete. You will be ready to know the true nature of the Divine Infinite."

"So, I'm *not* ready yet?" he asked. "Even though I'm already Hidria?"

Colt nodded and turned to face the massive viewport looking out toward the stars. "Yes," she said. "Even though you are Hidria. Your mind is still muddled with the teachings of the Duri Order."

He kicked the throttle and shot out from the city, leaving the bloody battle in his wake. A few automatic turrets managed anti-spacecraft volleys of energy pulses designed to ground him, but he managed to avoid the shots with a few careful course corrections. The local ships were too busy engaging the enemy at their gates to worry about ones fleeing their atmosphere.

"Are you saying that the Duri are wrong?" he asked carefully. "That they shouldn't exist?"

"No," Colt said firmly. "The Duri have done plenty of good and much of what they teach is true to the spirit of the Divine Infinite. But they are men, and as with any religion of Man, subject to limitations. They have killed millions of innocent people across the galaxy because they believe genocide to be the wish of Omega, but the Divine Infinite creates all life. Why would He want life eradicated if He took the time to create it?"

"You said there is no such thing as time." To that, she had no reply.

Nuri consulted the charts that appeared in thin air before him and tried to locate a habitable planet to plot his course. He noticed a clearing outside the city where several thousand aliens had congregated in an open field, but none of them were armed.

The civilians, he thought. *They evacuated the civilians.*

It was an oddly noble and touching measure, though one which any army would surely employ to protect the defenseless while their homes were at the heart of vicious crossfire.

"This is the same circular question you asked me before the trials," he said. For the time being, he set a course for the orbit of a nearby planet which seemed to have liquid water so he could reevaluate his situation outside the combat zone, then stepped out from behind the console and approached Colt at the viewport. "That was *you,*" he said. "I understand now. It's always been you."

She stared back, drifting over to intercept him before he reached the window. She gently cupped his cheeks in her cold hands and leaned up to kiss his chin.

"You are the girl from the village. The river girl. The one the Duri killed because I couldn't kill you myself."

She still didn't answer, but she didn't need to. His mind felt suddenly expansive, more efficient, and yet completely empty even though he still possessed his knowledge and memories. It was like his brain had evolved from registering a single letter on a datapad to every word ever written. He could piece together ideas and concepts which never would have occurred to him previously, and at last understood the nature of his kidnapping and imprisonment on the distant mountaintop. How he had been force-fed Duri doctrine to be molded into the ultimate killing machine. How the Duri had subverted the Divine Order of things to their own will rather than God's.

"I see everything now," he gasped, eyes widening. He touched his cheeks and was momentarily horrified to feel flaps of scorched flesh where the alien blasters had burnt away his face. "It's like before. When you took me through the universe," he said. "Everything revealed."

"A great unveiling," Colt agreed. "An apocalypse."

Nuri fell to his knees before her and buried his head in her midsection. She wrapped her arms around him and drew him closer. He closed his eyes and sighed heavily, trying to keep pace with the trillions of subtle connections his brain made each second and dealing with the subsequent guilt from having all his sins laid out for him to pore over with the elevated context of a far superior being.

"I'm a sinner," he whispered. "I'm not Hidria. I'm not *worthy* to be Hidria." He hung his head in shame and stared at his hands. All his flesh had burnt away. He could see muscles, bone, and cartilage flexing when he clenched his fists. It seemed an appropriate affliction now that the rest of his soul had been laid bare for reckoning as well. "I can't go to Prime. I'm not worthy of knowing the true nature of the Divine Infinite." He looked up into Colt's glow with desperation, tears welling in his eyes. "I belong in Tscharia," he said.

She stared back at him without any change of expression.

And then the invading armada locked onto the ship and fired, blowing a hole through the port hull and knocking the vessel off course.

Nuri was thrown against the starboard wall so hard that he would have been killed instantly if he hadn't already begun the physical transformation to Hidria. Colt simply disappeared.

The ship was hit twice more, each blow inflicting significantly less damage than the initial blast since his trajectory had changed and they likely couldn't establish a reliable target lock, and then the bridge fell eerily silent as he spiraled out of control into deep space.

They must think I'm dead, he realized.

Under any other circumstances, they would have been correct. He could see two hull breaches at the back of the ship. The shields had kicked on enough to keep him from being sucked out into infinity, but the invaders would have known it was only a brief respite before the oxygen leaked out (if the aliens did, in fact, breathe oxygen, for the invaders had no way of knowing it was a human on board and not an arachnid) and left him for dead.

God, help me, Nuri prayed as he spun with his eyes closed.

Alarms screamed throughout the ship. He opened his eyes briefly when a new light registered through the lids. A large, golden-brown planet approached quickly through the viewport.

Another planet in this system, he realized. He thought back to his initial scans of the solar system. He'd been searching for an orbit where he could plot his next step toward reaching Prime. There hadn't been any other habitable planets in the database, but he recognized the one on the ship's collision course. He didn't know its name, but he knew it was a desert planet with temperatures well north of three hundred degrees Fahrenheit.

Nuri took a deep breath and closed his eyes again. *Surrender,* he thought.

He felt Colt's cold lips on his ear. "It begins," she whispered.

Even his evolving mind didn't understand what she meant.

"All will be revealed in time."

Time?

The intensity of the alarms grew in volume and pitch with each mile they drew closer to the planet. He heard a loud crack once and guessed by the ship's change in trajectory that the back half had torn off, and then the vessel skimmed the atmosphere and the nose began to burn away.

It begins, Colt said, no longer in the spaceship but burrowed deep inside his brain.

He suspected now that she had a foothold where his Duri conscience had once resided, she would never leave him again.

16

"**This will be your** last mission before the trials," the Duri Master assured Nuri.

The two men were seated on a boulder overlooking the village, shivering in a breeze which had suddenly turned brisk as autumn rolled over the mountain with its Trojan-horse beauty. Sometime in the week prior, the leaves of the surrounding trees had also formed a kaleidoscope of purples, pinks, greens, reds, and blues, though Nuri hadn't noticed either transformation until they were complete. Somehow, it seemed better to him that way. More natural, he supposed. He took a deep breath and watched the villagers complete their daily chores in the dusk half-light.

"I'm ready," he replied after a time.

The Master nodded then frowned, folding the deep-set scars crisscrossing his cheeks into new, peculiar formations. "I know you are. If I didn't believe it, you wouldn't be going."

"No man can know when the Called is ready to become Hidria," Nuri said, paraphrasing a passage of Duri doctrine from the renowned theologian, Xyang Polanos. "The decision is made by the Divine Infinite and manifests in the heart of the pupil."

The Duri Master's frown slowly morphed into an equally intricate smile as his scars realigned. "Very good," he beamed. "You've grown a great deal in your faith since your first cleansing."

Nuri nodded, his brow furrowed in deep thought. "When I was young, I didn't truly believe," he said. "I was lost in a perpetual fugue of anger and doubt, but God has revealed my path. I must be Hidria to follow His will." He dropped from the boulder and steadied himself against the white bark of a Dzatka Tree, whose leaves had turned an icy blue to greet the new season. "I've read every Duri text about the trials and talked to as many of the failed Called as I've been able to contact, but is there anything else *you* can tell me about the ritual?" He turned to look at his Master with the same unflinching stoicism that had dominated his expression since he was seventeen. "Do you have any specific advice?"

His Duri Master continued to stare down at the valley, slowly tapping his sandaled right foot against the boulder in rhythm with his shallow breaths. "The Duri do not perform the same rituals that you do as the Called. We have a different set of trials and evaluations to verify that our faith is sound."

"Still," Nuri pressed, selecting a branch from the ground and waving it distractedly. "You must have *some* insight into the trials. Please, tell me what you went through even if it will be different from what I experience. The spirit should be the same."

The Duri Master dropped from the boulder and began descending the mountain toward the cottage. The comforts of home were but a little way down and the smoke rising from the chimney was nearly irresistible on a brisk evening. "A man's experience in the trials is his and his alone. It should be left between the man and God. Besides, anything you could have learned about the trials you've already learned, and it might be that *none* of it helps once you are in the temple."

"What about Colt?" Nuri asked, trailing him down the mountain. "Did you see her during the trials?"

The Duri Master stopped abruptly and gazed off into the star-filled sky as though something had caught his attention, but Nuri found nothing noteworthy. "That's between God and me," he said quietly. Each word seemed to cause him a great deal of physical pain. In fact, Nuri was taken aback by just how *old* his Master appeared in that moment. More than anything else he'd read or heard from those who'd attempted the trials and failed, that single look of fear and exquisite agony made Nuri question his preparedness for the ritual.

"I understand," he said. "Forgive my intrusion."

"Curiosity is dangerous," the Duri Master replied. His stern demeanor had reformed as quickly as it had vacated. Nuri wondered idly if it had something to do with the myriad expressions possible in the intricate weave of scars by the tensing of a single muscle. "Knowledge can destroy. Sometimes, the Divine Infinite decrees that it is best for us *not* to know a thing. In this particular case, I'd wager it is better for you *not* to know the extent of the trials until you test the boundaries for yourself."

Nuri bowed solemnly with his hands crossed behind his back in a show of respect, then turned and headed back up the mountain.

"Where are you going?" the Duri Master asked. There was no reproach in his voice. Ever since Nuri had proven beyond the shadow of a doubt that he was loyal to the Duri calling, the corporal discipline which had dominated his adolescence had slackened. Now, his Duri Master trusted him to wander the mountain on his own. Nuri was ever mindful that it had not always been that way.

"With your permission, I would like to meditate on tomorrow's mission," he answered. "I'd also like to pray for strength during the trials. I believe I'll need more than just faith to prove myself worthy of the Hidria namesake."

The Duri Master sighed and resumed his descent toward the cottage. "There is more to being Hidria than the prestige of the title, but faith *is* all that you need to prove yourself worthy of God's favor."

"Favor and solemn responsibility are two very different things."

"I suppose you should ask yourself, then, what the purpose of the trials will be for you, and what you are hoping to find in the face of the Divine Omega that you cannot find within yourself."

With that, the Duri Master crept beneath the shadows of boulders and the tangle of tree branches, leaving Nuri to stew in stunned silence. Even considering his own doubts through the years and his exposure to controversial theologies from the colonies he'd cleansed in that time, it was hard to digest borderline heresy from the lips of a trusted purveyor of the Sacred Word face to face. Duri Masters were supposed to be above talk of the value of personhood.

He's quoting The Divine Incendiary, *Nuri realized. I had no idea there was still so much doubt in his heart.*

He hadn't thought much about the controversial text in a while, and it was certainly a book that no self-respecting Duri Master would openly quote before another man of faith. At best, such a slip was liable to cause a heated argument. At worst, torture, mutilation, and death. Still, there was a reason *The Divine Incendiary* had been banned from all databases in Duri-controlled regions of the galaxy. It rang with a little too much truth for the tribunal's liking. Anyone found consulting the text even for historical or anthropological reasons received an automatic death sentence once they were brought before the council on Secondus: the political epicenter of the Duri religion.

I wonder why he chose to quote that passage now, Nuri thought. *Maybe he doesn't think that I know* The Divine Incendiary *well enough to recognize its verses. Or maybe he's testing to see if I will alert the tribunal, which would in turn implicate me by confirming that I can identify specific passages from the forbidden book. Of course, if he turned it around on me, I could truthfully testify that he was the one who exposed me to the verses in the first place.*

Discussing the theology of the book was one thing, but it was outright heresy for a Duri Master to quote passages from the tainted scriptures which had recently been dubbed *The Red Gospels.* He knew his Duri Master must have had *some* motive beyond just casual dismissal, otherwise he wouldn't have taken such a significant, and potentially fatal, risk.

Frowning, Nuri continued climbing until he reached the mountain's peak, then quickly began to descend the other side. He didn't bother pausing to enjoy the spectacular view of the plains or the sea stretching far off in the distance. He'd beheld the aesthetic magnificence of the land plenty in the years since he'd been taken from his family, but his focus was no longer drawn to the physical world around him. He'd devoted himself entirely to realities beyond his perception, and he was eager to glimpse the pure universe where God's existence wasn't a theoretical issue but an incontrovertible truth.

I have already been there, he thought. *I've seen it in my dreams.*

But I must be careful.

The Duri strictly warned against dream interpretation or placing too much emphasis on the subconscious and illusory. It was the Devil's Trap, they said. Yet deep down, Nuri strongly believed that he'd experienced the *Hidriala*: the sacred call from the Divine Infinite to seek Him in the trials.

It could be the Evil One trying to draw me back to unbelief, as he did when I nearly defected.

There were times when he still couldn't believe he'd been the one to lead the mission on the heretic moon colony years before, or that he'd made the right decision in the end through good fortune more than purity. It was almost as though God had reached down and drawn the skepticism directly from his soul.

"You don't believe that, do you?" a voice asked from the shadowed woods ahead of him.

Nuri froze and tried to place the speaker without appearing too alarmed. Deep down, though, he was terrified, both because he'd been caught unawares despite his warrior training and because the voice seemed privy to his innermost thoughts.

It could be coincidence.

No matter how hard he focused, however, the early shades of night were too thick for him to register anything out of the ordinary. His heightened senses didn't detect a single breath to pinpoint the intruder's position.

"A man cannot hide from the All Knowing, and one who hides from his brothers emulates the Evil One," Nuri responded, reflexively quoting yet another Duri saying he'd picked up in some text or another. He could no longer remember which one. Although he'd memorized much during his years of study, sometimes the phrases blended together. It had grown difficult, therefore, to identify a text with any accuracy.

Except, of course, for *The Divine Incendiary.*

"What if I'm *not* a man?"

Relieved that the creature did not appear to bear him any malice but curious nonetheless, Nuri continued his descent to the valley opposite the village. "The same is true for women."

"What if I'm not hiding?"

"Then reveal yourself to me so that I know you are trustworthy."

"Don't the Called hide on every one of their cleansing missions? Or how do you surprise heretics?"

Frowning, Nuri angled toward the voice. It had moved from the patch of trees on his left to a cave mouth on his right. "Combat exists outside the Duri *Catechism* so long as it is a just cause, and I can think of no greater testament to the Divine Infinite than offering blood sacrifices on which to build His kingdom."

A cold, blue light glowed from the cave, stopping Nuri in his tracks yet again.

"Is that how you believe kingdoms are built? On the blood of innocents?"

"They are not innocents," Nuri argued. "They are sinners. Nonbelievers."

"What if they know nothing of God?"

"Then they have the option to convert, or else they must be cleansed in His name."

"I don't recall any passage in scripture that references this bloody undertaking."

"Then perhaps you haven't read the correct scriptures."

Slowly, a face formed from the bright light within the cave. "You're angry." A familiar face, too. Smiling at him. Mocking him.

"You speak heresy. If anyone were to hear you questioning the work of the Called, you would be executed."

The girl from the river laughed with a playful light in her eyes. "What weapon can kill me?"

"He who has the favor of The First and Last does not need material weapon to vanquish his enemies."

"Is every word you speak from the scriptures? When did your thoughts become so pragmatic? You've strangled your own creativity. Nothing of your Self remains."

Nuri ducked into the cave and glared at her. Confronting the apparition was especially irritating given the timing of her arrival. In the morning, he would run his last mission before he undertook the most important trial of his life. "Why waste breath on small talk when I could use the words of the Almighty Himself?"

Again, the apparition laughed. "A noble thought, yet those are not the words of the Almighty."

"They are the divine revelations spoken to His prophets. Therefore, they are His words."

She did not argue. Instead, the light gathered from all corners of the cave and assembled into physical form.

"You look the same," Nuri told her.

"I can take any form I wish. This is only how I looked when you last saw me."

He studied her closely, crossing to the other side of the cave with his hands clasped behind his back respectfully. "Did you die the day I killed the old man in the village?"

"No."

On impulse, he reached out and touched her shoulder. He expected his hand to pass through heavy air, but she was just as solid as the cave walls.

"Are you *still* alive?" he asked, dreading the answer. If she'd survived and still looked as young as she had the day he'd slain the pig farmer in her stead, that meant that she was using a form of dark magic, which could only be learned through direct communication with the Evil One and his Watchmen. On the other hand, if she was dead, then he was speaking to a ghost, and it was also a sin to concern oneself with the afterlife. No matter what, engaging the entity put his soul in considerable distress. It was the last thing he needed before the trials.

"No."

Nuri drew back and shuddered. He'd known, of course, that there was something supernatural about her ever since she'd appeared to him in his room while the jackals cried and his Duri Master drank and read from the forbidden book. Back then, though, he'd willfully denied her nature because he was so intrigued by the mystery of her existence. Also, if he was honest with himself, because she was as forbidden as *The Divine Incendiary*, which made her constitution all the more alluring.

"How did you die?"

She moved gracefully towards him. He retreated another step. "Your Duri Master had me killed. They found me on the forbidden mountain while you were purged of the pig farmer's death and they crucified me for leading you away from Omega."

Nuri swallowed and averted his eyes. He felt like he was about to retch, and he didn't want to show how profound an impact her presence had on him. "Why are you here, then? Retribution?"

Her fingertips tapped lightly against his shoulder-blade, sending ripples of numbness down his back before falling away. She glided to the cave entrance and looked out over the mountain. "I'm here because you need me."

"I don't need *you*," he snapped. "I need to be *rid* of you. Your presence here is an insult to Holy God."

"Only Holy God can decide what is an insult to Him and what is merely the childish offense taken by men to having their beliefs questioned. God is God. He cannot be offended. The very cognitive processes you would use to speak against Him are of His making."

He scowled and tried to step around her, wanting to get as far from her as possible though he knew deep down she would have her say whether he wanted her to or not. "That goes against everything we know about Him from the Old Book. You're an agent of Tscharia. A distraction. You've come here to turn me from the path that God laid out for me as Hidria."

He carefully negotiated an abrupt drop down the mountain with his legs braced on the rocks.

"Do you know anything about the Hidria?" she asked, drifting easily down the slope beside him.

"I know plenty about them. I've devoted my life to studying them so that I can answer the Call and become Hidria myself."

"How have you studied them?"

"Through Duri texts and the holy scriptures."

"But those are the words of men. Humans. Hidria are not human. They are another level of being altogether. They inhabit a different reality and therefore cannot possibly be human. Every molecule in their bodies exists under completely separate physical laws than they would in your reality."

"My reality?" he scoffed. "You say that like it's mine alone and not the shared space of hundreds of trillions of beings."

"How do you know that this *isn't* your reality alone? If God can create infinite universes and infinite realities, doesn't it stand to reason that He could possibly have created this reality for you and you alone? Every birth, death, and breath for trillions of years to prepare for *you?*"

"You wouldn't be arguing against my beliefs and wellbeing if this were my reality and subject to my desires."

"Not *your* desires," the girl countered. "God's."

Nuri sighed and braced himself against a tree branch. They had reached the final stretch of forest before the waterfalls where he often sat to reflect deep into the night.

"You're trying to confuse me. To make me question my beliefs."

"That's what your Duri Masters *believe* I am here to do, but they don't understand my true nature any more than they understand God."

"The dead are no concern of the living."

"Again, these are the edicts of men trying to guess the will of the Omega and not His own words."

"It says so in the scriptures."

"As I told you, the scriptures were written by men."

"Under divine influence!"

"But subject to the errors of interpretation universal among men. Humans are sinners by nature. Each person's capacity for divine comprehension is severely limited by the finite synapses and finite frames of reference stored within their brains."

The waterfalls and mountain river glowed beneath the mountain peak. Nuri trudged his way to a fallen tree at the edge of the water and sat down, gazing up to the trillions of stars in the dusk sky while the roar of the waterfall cleared his head. The girl sat down beside him and stared into the water, deep in thought.

"I don't believe you are here solely to question my faith. I have no interest in arguing dogma with a corpse."

The girl turned to him and smiled, her white teeth sparkling beside the water in the moonlight. "I admire how far you've come in your faith since the last time I saw you, even if it is misguided. And it *is* misguided. The Duri Masters do not know as much as they think they know or else they would be the ones who became Hidria."

"That's false logic. They train the Called so that *we* can become Hidria, and the Called who pass the trials *do* become Hidria, so their teachings are correct."

"How do you know the Called who disappear after the ritual become Hidria? Have you ever seen a Hidria before? Are there any testimonies of those who've passed the trials in all your Duri texts?"

Nuri leaned forward and ran his fingers through the cold water. He didn't respond. Everyone knew the Hidria were never heard from again once they passed through the trials. The Duri attributed mass cleansings to them here and there, perhaps to nurture belief in their existence, but their movements in and out of the human dimension were so sporadic and unverifiable that no one could truly be sure.

"Could it be, then, that the Hidria do not become the same warriors of Divine Justice that the Duri claim them to be?"

"I suppose it's a matter of faith," Nuri replied. "*I* believe that the Called become Hidria."

"Because that's what the Duri scriptures tell you. Along with thousands upon thousands of nonsensical proverbs which achieve little more than muddling the truth."

"And what do you define as truth?" he asked, genuinely curious.

The girl smiled at him. "If your human mind could comprehend it, then God would have already revealed it to you. I can't explain the fundamental truth of life in words. You have to see it for yourself."

"Through the trials."

She nodded slowly. "Yes. The trials are one way to see it."

"Then that means that the trials *are* sacred, and those who don't return have truly been granted a divine revelation from Omega."

The girl shrugged noncommittally and dipped her toes in the water. When the liquid touched her luminescent skin, a pleasant, cinnamon-tinged aroma drifted across the wind to Nuri. He inhaled deeply, ignoring for the moment the Duri warnings against sensuous pleasures, and closed his eyes.

"Those who experience the fullness of the trials see Prime," she answered, watching him carefully. "They are the ones you call Hidria."

"And what becomes of them?"

She rose from the fallen tree and stepped into the shallows. "If God wanted you to know that, He would have revealed it to you already."

Nuri snorted. "That's not an answer and it doesn't make any sense. If you believe that we can only learn a thing by God zapping the information directly to our brains rather than through study and observation, then what would be the point of living or experiencing anything at all? God might as well have skipped creating the universe in that case."

The girl ignored his response and began to walk a circle through the water, her eyes locked on the thundering waterfalls spraying just beyond her reach. She seemed captivated by the natural beauty of it, and that struck Nuri as especially peculiar since she was a dead thing who could seemingly come and go as she pleased and visit anywhere in the universe.

"What was the target of your last cleansing mission?" she asked.

He watched her wade in the moonlight with the spray arcing up behind her. He'd never seen anything so beautiful, and it had nothing to do with attraction. It was simply the best representation of God in the universe he could imagine in that moment.

"A space station," he said, clearing his throat. "It housed a news agency that incited rebellion against the Duri order."

"How did they incite rebellion?" she asked innocently as her eyes blazed through him.

"They were investigating the cleansings and speaking heresy against God."

She eased her body into the water until only her head was showing. "What have they said against God?"

Nuri stood and stepped into the shallows himself, terrified for a moment that she was about to disappear. "They claimed that the Duri are warmongers and a scourge to the galaxy."

"Then it sounds like they insulted the Duri. Not God."

Nuri stepped a little further into the shallows, determined not to take the bait she'd lain for him.

"So, you killed all of them for dissent?" she continued.

"It wasn't up to me," Nuri replied, kneeling into the water with a hitch in his breath as the cold pressed against his skin. "God mandates what must be done to unbelievers."

"Not God," she pointed out. "The Duri tribunal."

"Which receives its revelations from God."

She waded beside him and frowned. "I don't think you truly believe that. You're too smart not to recognize the difference. If there was a perfect law from God, it would not be subject to the politics of the Duri tribunal, nor would it change over time based on progressive ideology. The Divine Infinite sees all things at once—past, present, and future—and therefore would know which edicts were necessary to decree for all generations, assuming any existed. He would not allow them to be idly cast aside by the Duri simply for political gains or due to the socio-economic climate of the galaxy."

Nuri turned abruptly for the riverbank, exhaling in frustration. "You're trying to shake my beliefs just as you did when I was younger. Forcing me to question myself and my Duri Master. You're an agent of the Evil One. I won't listen to your blasphemy anymore."

He stomped angrily away, ringing out his shirtsleeves as he walked, until suddenly she stood before him again. "Leave me, witch," he snarled. "You're a queen of lies. Go back to Tscharia."

"The Divine Infinite is not concerned with the arbitrary laws of a corrupt religious order. The trials were not created by the Duri Masters. They merely stumbled upon them."

"Then God *meant* for them to find the trials. As you say, He is the Divine Infinite. The Simultaneous Ubiquity. He would *know* that the Duri would find the trials and *allow* the transfiguration of their holy, purified warriors. If they were not worthy, He would have orchestrated history to ensure they never found the trials. In fact, He never would have allowed the Duri order to exist in the first place. He created them. He created *all* of us. The Called and Hidria. If what you say is true, God would be culpable for any mistakes made by the Duri."

For a moment, her eyes lit up so brightly that Nuri had to shield himself from the vision. When she spoke, her voice brimmed with excitement. He couldn't understand why. "If you follow that logic to its conclusion, then God also created all sin and even the Evil One, yet that doesn't implicate Him in all sins throughout the realities. He doesn't espouse sin any more than the Duri profess to tolerate it."

Nuri eyed her skeptically. He understood her point to an extent but believed that it undermined all the previous points she'd made, as well. If God created sin, then He was responsible for *all* sin, and that made both of their arguments moot. It made God evil by nature, and Nuri couldn't wrap his head around something so radically heretical.

However, the girl persisted. "Don't you see now that you cannot possibly understand this paradox as a human? How Omega can know something is evil or will eventually lead to evil and *still* create it? Still allow it to follow its path?"

Nuri frowned and rubbed at his eyes. "You're right," he said. "I don't understand it. I *can't*. You're deliberately confusing me so I'll fail the trials. So I won't be able to destroy you and all of your agents in Tscharia."

The girl reached out and touched his palm. "Hidria are great warriors, but they destroy men who claim they know God and speak for Him, not just emissaries of Tscharia. Hidria are warriors against murder and injustice."

"Exactly!" Nuri exclaimed.

She shook her head and let his hand fall. "You still don't understand. The *Duri* are the men who claim to know God's mind, and that is impossible for any human. No human can know the Divine Infinite. That is the point. Your brains are not built for it."

Gripping her cold shoulders, Nuri looked her in the eye and nodded. "Exactly," he said softly. "I will not be human after the trials, though. I will be transformed. I will be Hidria."

As he spoke, her form began to dissipate into blue-white smoke. Her features distorted in the autumn wind. "If you learn that there is no such thing as distraction, only the evil and confused heart of man, then you might become Hidria. But cleansing another colony of innocents tomorrow won't bring anyone closer to God save your victims, and you are actively carving out a hovel in Tscharia with each precious life you take."

Before he could counter the argument, she disappeared beneath his fingertips, swept away by the wind over the valley to shower the people below.

Nuri stared at the physical space she'd occupied, outraged by her audacity yet more outraged because her points made just enough sense to rattle his foundation for belief, and that was a very dangerous animal so near the trials.

What if I fail now? he wondered.

Her voice echoed through his head unbidden. *Then it will be because you're not worthy to be called Hidria, not because I dared to challenge Duri doctrine and it sparked a healthy seed of doubt in you.*

Distraught and confused, he returned to the riverbank and listened to the roar of the waterfalls until the first whisper of dawn touched over the water. By the hour he reached the cottage he shared with his Duri Master, it was time to depart for his final mission as a member of the Called. One way or another, it *would* be the last.

And throughout the cleansing, the girl's words echoed through his head.

"If you learn that there is no such thing as distraction, only the evil and confused heart of man, then you might become Hidria."

The thought haunted him into the morning and every moment thereafter.

17

Nuri rolled onto his side and stared up at the stars through the massive hole at the rear of the alien ship. He wasn't certain how long he'd been pinned beneath the control panel. Long enough for flames to swarm the entire vessel and promptly die on the surface of the desert planet as the oxygen dissipated. He supposed that sufficiently answered his question about the onboard life-support systems and whether he could have breathed prior to his physical transformation, but it didn't seem all that important anymore.

I'm alive, he thought with considerable relief. *I'm still alive.*

Are you surprised? Colt asked.

He craned his neck to see if she'd reappeared now that he was grounded but her physical form was nowhere to be found.

"No," he whispered, and winced at the sound of his own voice. He may not have felt any pain from the violent impact, but his throat had still been damaged. He had difficulty forcing out even that solitary word of negation.

You are here, Colt said cryptically.

I know that I'm somewhere. But where is 'here'?

He waited a while for a response before deciding she had left to attend more pressing issues. He couldn't imagine what they might be, but as with the life-support question, the answer no longer seemed a matter of great import.

Easing his leg out from under a collapsed steel pillar, he pulled himself to a seated position and surveyed his surroundings. The ship had taken a beating running the atmosphere. In fact, he estimated that the transition from space to the planet's skyline had done more damage to the integrity of the vessel than the crash itself. If Nuri hadn't secured himself in a service tube adjacent to the bridge and buckled in for impact, his body would have been pulverized.

And then what would have become of me? he wondered.

Colt had already established that he couldn't be killed outright by conventional weapons while he was transforming from human to Hidria, but if his body was completely destroyed, how would he be able to carry out his mission? If he couldn't even move his lips to speak, he thought, then he may as well have been dead for all the good it would do him in the trials. And now that his eyes had been opened to the nature of the Duri Order, he knew there was no way he could resume his life as a Called soldier if he failed.

You could not fail now and return to your old life even if you wanted to, Colt reminded him. *It's too late to turn back. You will either complete the transformation to become Hidria or you will die outright.*

And go to Tscharia?

It's not for me to say where your soul is bound when your time comes. A lesson the Duri Masters would do well to learn themselves.

He pulled his badly broken arm from the service tube wreckage, kicked aside the hatch (which was only held in place by the grace of God and a few mangled wires), and emerged in the upside-down bridge. All things considered, the interior had held together better than he'd expected, especially since the ship's primary power cells had gone offline sometime during its rapid descent through the atmosphere. It was no small wonder that the shields had held together long enough to prevent the entire vessel from burning into oblivion before it reached the sand.

Climbing carefully through the mountain of hull and computer debris that had dislodged in the crash, he worked his way toward the bright blue sky until he found a hole in the side of the vessel wide enough to squeeze through, then pulled himself into the sunlight and dropped from the ship. He didn't bother aiming for a proper landing spot to ensure he didn't impale himself on the wreckage. His newfound invincibility had already spoiled him.

Don't become too comfortable with it, Colt warned. *Complacency makes you careless. There are still ways for you to be destroyed.*

His back smacked against the hull and launched him forward. He landed with a jarring thud in the endless blanket of sand.

How? he asked. He shuddered to think what creative, macabre devices were necessary to end his life now that his body could take such a beating. Although he knew bullets wouldn't kill him, total dismemberment would surely render him inert since his body simply wouldn't be able to execute his brain's commands. And while it wasn't the same thing as death, being stuck in the desert for eons with only his brain and no functional movement sounded even less appealing than Tscharia. It was its own form of Tscharia, in fact. At least in Tscharia he would have company.

Your understanding of suffering is skewed by your lingering human perceptions, Colt gently scolded. She appeared beside him once again and helped him to his feet. "Those in Tscharia are not alone, that's true enough. But the suffering of their companions makes the experience even worse because they are helpless to intervene on their behalf."

Nuri spat out sand and futilely wiped his charred, bloody forehead with the dangling sleeve of his ruined suit. "Sinners condemned to Tscharia don't strike me as the sort to suffer much over the fate of others."

Colt turned away and looked out over the rolling dunes. "You shouldn't speak of things you don't understand," she continued. "You once again presume to speak for those whose mind you do not know. Empathy and compassion are important steps to understanding the condition of your fellow people, but their judgment is not perfect. Only the judgment of the Divine Infinite is perfect, and He does not judge in the same manner as you would with your limited human understanding of the universe."

She took his hand and led him onward. In the heat of the midday sun, her touch was so cold against his charred skin that it made him shiver even through the thick layer of numbness which had overtaken his nerves. He didn't speak, though. He'd at last begun to understand that arguments were useless while the apparition was explaining the manifold aspects of God.

"Besides," she continued, "the greatest suffering of Tscharia is its total separation from Omega and the prospect of rebirth when the Divine Infinite rejoins with His Alpha. All universes will be transformed at that moment. Perhaps even Tscharia itself."

"Why would God transform the souls in Tscharia? Wouldn't that make it pointless to create a separate universe in the first place?"

Colt shrugged, a startlingly human gesture, and led him forward. "I didn't say it was a certainty. Unlike your teachers, I don't attempt to guess the mind of God. I am only stating it is a possibility that, in His infinite wisdom and compassion, He would spare His creation out of love."

They began to climb a dune that crested higher than the vertical spaceship. "Love," Nuri croaked lamely.

"Love," Colt nodded.

He shook his head. "It sounds too simplistic and sentimental to be Divine."

"Perhaps," she replied, releasing him momentarily to get a handhold on the cascading sand. "But how can He not love all of His creation? Could love exist if it were not part of God?"

"Evil exists. Is that, too, a part of God?" Nuri leapt up the dune, savoring the ease of passage during what would have been an arduous endeavor had he not begun the transformation. By the time he was halfway to the top, however, the thrill of metamorphosis had begun to fade. He glanced back towards the spaceship wreckage and realized just how much of his skin and armor had sloughed off on the way up. The sight further sobered him.

"So where are we heading now?" he asked. It seemed strange that Colt had assumed physical form to journey through the oppressive desert heat. The physical exertion alone weakened her more than he would have expected for a sacred emanation.

They call her the Sonic Prayer, he thought idly. *The Earthless.*

"We are going where you have always been destined to go," she managed through graceful panting. "To find God."

Nuri reached out to help but she either didn't notice his outstretched hand or chose to ignore it.

"This doesn't look like the place to find Him," he remarked skeptically as he crested the dune on his own, searching the endless desert for obvious signs of divine influence.

"Again," she sighed as she reached the overlook beside him, "you presume to know the heart and mind of God. Where would you expect to find Him? Without His guidance, you never would have gotten here in the first place."

He shrugged. "The Duri say you can find Him anywhere."

"Exactly!" Colt suddenly exclaimed. The force of her exhalation nearly sent him tumbling back toward the wreckage. "You can find Him *everywhere* because He is *everything.*"

"There," Nuri said, pointing to a distant speck on the horizon. "What is that?"

Colt smirked and took his hand. "We're going to find out."

She led him down the other side of the dune into the desert flatlands. Neither of them spoke until the dark speck gradually distinguished itself from the unchanging landscape.

"Odd," Nuri remarked once he was close enough to identify the object.

Odd didn't quite cover finding a giant, neon sign proclaiming PRIME in capital blue letters with bright pink outlines on an uninhabited desert world. An arrow at the top angled forward and slightly to the right, directing travelers the way adverts did in the wilderness of Earth colonies.

"Is this the first planet?" he asked, awestruck.

"There's no way of knowing."

"The sign says this is Prime."

"No," Colt corrected. "The sign indicates that Prime is up ahead. It's only a reminder that we are on the right path. And anyway, Prime isn't necessarily a planet."

"That's not what the Duri Masters say."

Colt gave him a hard look and he reluctantly nodded.

"It exists, though. Whether it's a planet or not," he said.

"On what basis have you made that determination? A glowing sign in the middle of a desert? For all you know, that could be debris from a spaceship..."

"Unlikely."

"...or a trap set by the Evil One to make you believe you are closer to the Apocalypse than you truly are."

Nuri bowed his head in thought. He noticed the skin on his shins and feet had completely melted away. He was a walking skinless man, with muscles and throbbing veins and blood squelching in each step he took. "It seems like a lot of trouble to go to for the sake of diversion. Or rather, *distraction*."

"The Evil One will go to any length to confuse and vilify the true followers of the Divine Infinite: the justice-bringers called *Hidria*."

Nuri considered her assessment for a while, but still wasn't convinced the sign was anything more than what it professed to be: an indication that Prime was up ahead, attainable to anyone willing to brave the insufferable desert cleansing to prepare themselves for the presence of Lord God. "You wouldn't have brought me here if this wasn't Prime," he said. "Or at least the *gateway* to Prime."

Colt turned and furrowed her brow. "*I* didn't bring us here," she said. "*You* brought us here. You, and Omega. I simply follow wherever you go. We both must trust your internal compass to find your Apocalypse Point. It is *your* great unveiling."

"You told me we had arrived at our destination," he protested.

"I told you we'd arrived at *a* destination," Colt corrected. "It's between you and God where His nature is revealed."

Once again, Nuri fell silent. Despite the continuing transformation of his brain and body, he couldn't shake the feeling that Colt was deliberately confusing him, leading his thoughts into circular patterns to make him question every aspect of his reality rather than find any clarity. Surely, his body had changed and his mind had expanded, yet somehow he'd never felt further from his objective than he did right then. To top it off, he'd lost faith in the one part of his life that had provided him with comfort and identity. He no longer believed the teachings of the Duri Order, or the claim that they were God's descendants in the galaxy with the authority to speak His will and decimate worlds based on arbitrary and constantly amended doctrine.

They keep it that way so they are never confronted with rebellion, Nuri decided.

Even as the thought entered his head, he realized with his newfound clarity that, in the end, the Duri could not escape Divine justice. Eventually, the colonies on the outer rim of Earth's expansion wheel would tire of living in fear and devise a method of communication that would ultimately lead to unification against their communal oppression.

Or maybe the Crown government will finally acknowledge that the religious order has gotten far too big for its britches, he thought. *Whether or not that happens before a great war between the two political powers, only God can know.*

"There," Colt said, jarring Nuri from his thoughts. "We're close."

He followed her gaze to a massive stone structure ahead of them. The landscape was too uniform for him to approximate how long it would take to reach it. Either way, he guessed the building was at least as tall as the highest skyscrapers in Juriaq, and just as wide. The black stones looked older than time, perhaps from another reality altogether. He saw no signs of footprints in the sand leading up to it, but they were still a way off. He figured any recent markings might have been covered by a sandstorm. Of course, it was also possible that no one had ever visited the site in the first place.

When he didn't see any clear entrance or windows, he began to worry.

"What *is* it?" he asked, momentarily captivated by the contrast of Colt's vibrancy against the clear blue sky and bright sand.

"It's a temple," she answered. "*The* temple. It existed long before humanity's creation."

"How can that be?" he asked.

She stopped walking and placed her hands on his shoulders. "Humans are very young," she told him as though she were explaining the nature of Santa Claus to a child. "Billions of species of sentient life came and went before the first man and woman ever walked Earth."

"So, aliens built this temple?"

She shrugged noncommittally. "Aliens built many temples before humanity, but I do not mean to imply that this one was built with corporeal hands. I'm not saying that it was *built* at all."

Nuri sighed and started walking again. "It's true what the Duri say about you."

She raised her eyebrows.

"You don't provide answers. Only questions."

She emitted a low sound which might have been a groan or a sigh and turned her gaze back to the stone temple. "It depends on your interpretation."

"Case in point."

She smiled and he laughed in turn with maniacal exhilaration. By then, he could *feel* the temple reaching out to them and the prospect of being so close to the ultimate answer for every question in the universe was finally beginning to register. He could barely hold onto his sanity in the face of such utter knowing.

"This would have been a lot easier if the ship had crashed closer to the temple," he remarked, more from the crazed amiability that had overcome him than in the interest of lodging a true complaint. His body no longer felt exhaustion, after all, even as more and more of his armor and skin dropped off behind him. It didn't truly matter how far they traveled now.

"It wasn't *meant* to be easy," she said. "That's why they're called trials."

"Fair enough," he replied with sudden solemnity. He pulled a long strip of skin from his stomach, exposing his ribcage down to his abdomen. "I wouldn't say it's *been* easy, though. I've given up everything to get to this point. My entire family was killed so I'd one day experience this sacred awakening. I've forsaken every aspect of myself to be here, and even if I am granted the knowledge of God and the universes, I will not be able to choose ignorance again. This journey will be the end of me one way or the other."

Colt nodded and bowed her head. "You're correct, and there's no clearer evidence of your shedding of self than the skin you've left in your wake. We crashed precisely where we did for a reason. You must be purified by the desert just as Omega Incarnate was purified on Earth for forty days thousands of years ago. You must leave all aspects of your old self behind and be reborn before you are revealed."

"Then the temple must not be a fixed point. It must be relative to my spiritual perception. I can't see God or the temple until my soul is deemed worthy."

"It's not a question of worthiness. As you said, it's a question of perception."

"Interesting," Nuri muttered. He was trying to take in every aspect of the astonishing world as well as the peculiar dissolution of his physical body, but the simultaneous experience of hyper-reality in proximity to the first temple and his perception of both the transformation and Colt as surreal events was tearing his soul in opposite directions. One path led to doubt and incomprehension, the other to wonder and complete surrender.

"That is the essence of sin," Colt continued. "It is the limit of human perception and comprehension. Literally, sin means 'missing the mark' or 'falling short,' meaning sin is a lack of understanding of God and the universe."

"So, then, you can argue that *all* humans are sinning *all* the time, since their understanding perpetually falls short of the perfect context?"

"In a way, I suppose. But in that sense, you're sinning right now by limiting the issue to absolutes. 'All or nothing' is not an imperative driving God's view of creation. None of us can know His mind."

They both fell silent for a while. Nuri focused on his footsteps and the unsettling lack of Time which hung heavily over the planet.

"Will my whole body decompose?" he asked. He thought seeing his heart wilt and cease to beat before his eyes might be the very thing that pushed him over the edge of insanity for good. He was teetering on the brink as it was.

Perhaps this is what the failed Called experience when they return from the trials, he thought. Except he knew it couldn't be. Colt had told him there was no turning back now that he had begun the transformation. *How can that be true if there's still a chance I will not experience the Divine Revelation?* He frowned and another toxic thought emerged. *What if my personal apocalypse means I will simply cease to exist in this world or Tscharia or any other reality?*

"Again, your idea of an apocalypse is too deeply rooted in faulty human understanding. An apocalypse is a great unveiling. I can think of no greater apocalypse, personal or otherwise, than entering the center point of the universe at the first temple and seeing everything through the eyes of God."

"Have you experienced this unveiling?" he asked. "Is that why you exist in an ethereal realm as well as a physical one?"

Colt nodded. "I am in between. Like the Hidria, but different. I am an emanation."

Nuri frowned again with what little remained of his face and bowed his head. The longer and deeper his body steeped in the transformation, the more he recognized connections that had formed subtly throughout his life. Every waking moment had been a precursor to something else, and every moment was likewise a consequence. It was a dizzying form of hindsight; the ultimate perspective and regret for a life which could have been fundamentally altered by even the smallest occurrence. To point, he was able to trace all his brainwashing at the hands of the Duri to one specific moment on Dublokee when he'd narrowly avoided a Psyanec Cobra bite prior to the arrival of the Called soldiers. The bite would have required his entire family to vacate the planet immediately for medical attention. In the short term, he had avoided a possibly fatal blow. Yet, if he *hadn't* instinctively lurched to his right just before the cobra struck, his whole family might have survived and he never would have been kidnapped.

Which means I also would never have made it here, he thought. *I would never have been given the chance to know Omega. The Divine Infinite. The Highest.*

Did that make his parents and brother martyrs for *his* holy cause, then? Were their deaths worth the highest level of consciousness and communion with the Creator God?

"There's no way to tell how their lives would have played out," Colt offered, sensing his thoughts. She read him easily now. He supposed it had something to do with his transfiguration from a physical being to another form of entity altogether, though he didn't dare venture a guess yet as to what, exactly, he *was*. It was too close to guessing God's mind, and he made a solemn vow on the spot not to contemplate the past or future any more than absolutely necessary. Regardless, it seemed Colt had tapped into a shared consciousness between them. Perhaps *all* similar creatures were linked that way. The idea opened up a whole new concept of knowledge and communication he'd never dreamed of realizing.

"Your parents may have been attacked by Maesalae pirates if they'd taken you to get medical attention, and perhaps you would *all* have died in that scenario," Colt added.

"But won't I know for certain what would have happened once I know God?" he asked hopefully.

"It doesn't work that way. You cannot process all the possible outcomes of every event in your life. Even if you *did* know the answer, it would torture you one way or the other. Peace can never be found in the past. At best, it is a wicked place inhabited by ghosts of melancholy."

Nuri sighed and fell back into his thoughts again, trying to concatenate all her teachings into one linear truth. He was beginning to understand that it didn't work that way either, though.

Nothing here is ever what it seems.

They continued in silence until the building was a mountain before them with no beginning and no end. An ominous storm had settled over their heads in the meantime.

"How will we get in?" he asked, staring at the massive stone walls. "Is the door on the other side?"

Colt turned to him, her shape gradually fading back into the blue-white luminescence of her ethereal form. "We're here."

18

Though he had logged plenty of hours training with steel swords and wooden staffs since arriving on the mountaintop, Nuri never handled an actual laser blade until the morning he departed for his eleventh colony cleansing, when his Duri Master approached him with the new weapon in tow.

"Use this on the mission today," the scar-faced clergyman said. "I'm told your whole squadron will have them. Truthfully, you've been ready for the blade a while now."

Nuri bowed and accepted the coveted weapon graciously, suppressing his excitement and subsequent dread the best he could. He couldn't wait to test out a truly lethal hand-to-hand implement after using strictly blasters and steel-forged weaponry in battle to that point, but it also reminded him of the somber task at hand. Specifically, how the only way he would be able to test his skill with the blade would be to carve up the flesh of innocent colonists who had rejected the proposed Duri theocracy in their solar system. The initial shock of taking lives had dulled to the point where Nuri hardly felt sick in the heat of the moment anymore, and he supposed that desensitization constituted progress even if it was in a direction he didn't care to venture. Yet, no matter how comfortable he'd grown with the act, the memories still haunted him each night after he doffed his armor and blaster rifle, as did the girl from the river who visited whenever the Duri Master indulged in *The Divine Incendiary*'s midnight mania.

"Do you know why Called warriors must use laser swords during cleansings instead of blasters and air strikes?"

Nuri bowed noncommittally. He knew the answer, of course, but he also knew his Duri Master well enough to sense when he wanted to hear himself talk, particularly when it came to the beliefs of his religious order.

The scar-faced theologian gently retrieved the blade from Nuri's outstretched hand and ignited the beam in the musty cottage stillness. Nuri found himself wishing that he would set the timbers aflame with his apparent carelessness, thereby releasing him from the day's burden, but he had no such luck.

"Spiritual purification is most readily attained through an intimate act," the man explained. "When you cleanse someone of sin while looking into their eyes and smelling their fear, the catharsis goes both ways. You receive just as much of a spiritual boon being a vessel for the Divine's purifying wrath as those being purified. With a blade like this, you have the opportunity to *live* the transformation up close. Blaster bolts from snipers are no more intimate than targeted strikes from drop shuttles. They do not require close contact, nor the reaffirmation of faith against the temptation for weakness and undeserved pity. With this, you must make the choice to purge over and over." He waved the weapon back and forth through the air, forcing Nuri to slyly retreat to the rear wall of the wooden structure. "This is why the Divine Infinite deigned to become man Himself and experience spiritual purification firsthand by the whip, nail, and lance."

Nuri bowed dutifully, knowing it was what the Duri Master expected. He couldn't help eyeing the disfigurements that this particular teaching had wrought upon his superior's face, though. Through careful observation of the clergymen and their psychological constitution, he'd found that the actualization of doctrine was, at times, an atypical symptom of lunacy. Some compulsions which would otherwise be categorized as strange and sinister among lay people were deemed sacred the moment a clergyman donned his ritual robes, and Nuri's Duri Master was no better or worse than the others. Case in point, he truly believed self-mutilation was an expression of devotion to the Creator God. He truly believed that spiritual catharsis was best attained through suffering, when suffering brought its own forms of pleasure, especially when used to demonstrate holiness. The subject was transformed into a masochist through the act. It was astonishing.

Although Nuri knew well the basis for the cleansings and self-flagellations among the clergy, he'd never fully grasped the implications until he saw the sharply hooked grooves across the Duri Master's cheeks by the white-blue glow of the laser blade on a crisp mountain morning. He shuddered to think what grisly marks littered the flesh of the man's back. The practice repulsed him. If Creator God considered His creation so valuable that murder was a mortal sin (excluding, of course, the "justified" cleansings of heretics), and that any violence toward believers was wrong, then how was self-injury any different? Was it not still harming His creation?

As with most other traditions of the Duri Order, the commoditization of suffering didn't make sense to Nuri, but he'd learned not to question it openly. Better to acquiesce without thought than to risk angering the Beginning and End. At least if anyone ever challenged him on the practice, he could claim he was merely adhering to established doctrine and the commands of his spiritual counselor. He may not have been as keen on self-flagellation as his Duri Master, but each Called soldier had a requisite amount of suffering they had to endure to understand God's sacrifice. That, at least, he understood to a degree. And when Nuri wasn't strong enough to inflict the damage himself, his Duri Master was always eager to assist.

"Thank you, Master," Nuri whispered.

The Duri Master bowed and clasped his hands behind his back. "Now, go and prepare yourself. I'll meet you at the hangar in one hour to see you off." He left with a shuffle of robes and the smell of dried sweat.

Nuri examined the hilt of the weapon for a few moments, then reverently placed it on his straw cot and began assembling his ceremonial armor for the cleansing.

Later, after the ship's departure from a cave on the forbidden mountain, he sat among his Called brethren and prayed in silence. Try as he might, he couldn't stop thinking about the blade strapped to his hip, nor the peculiar absence of the blaster rifle on his back. The Called still carried Colt VX-413 blaster pistols (named for the ancient Earth weapon rather than the cosmic entity, though Nuri suspected the Duri had carefully chosen the sidearm in place of the standard VP series used by the Human fleet and surely would have considered the title a benefit) in case their blades malfunctioned or were lost in the fray, but the bulk of the killing would be performed with the intimate weapon.

And will you feel the heat searing their flesh through your armor? Will you smell their blood and taste their horror when your blade severs heart and nerve and sinew? Will you feel their souls leave their bodies at your hand?

Nuri clenched his fists and closed his eyes.

Lord of All, be my blade and my resolve.

In the quiet of the drop shuttle, he wondered how many others among his squadron faced similar internal strife. Though he dared not shift his gaze, he could see a handful of armored Called soldiers on the opposite bench through his faceplate. Not one of them examined the new weapon clipped to their utility belts. Each sat with his or her hands folded over armored laps in deep prayer. Though the

Called were expected to spiritually prepare themselves in this way for any cleansing, he supposed the stillness among them was evidence enough that they were immersed in deep, troubled meditation, likely due to the new challenges awaiting them.

The intimate kill.

Beyond the battlefield significance of their modified arsenal, of course, the change held a deeper significance within the faith. The adoption of the sacred blade was the final step before one among them was declared ready for the trials. It was anyone's guess who had earned the Divine's favor, but Nuri doubted he would be selected. He still had significant room for growth in his faith, if not his training. He could handle a blaster and a blade as well as any of his brethren, but every so often, he was still plagued by the doubts that had tainted his youth.

Weakness, he scolded. *Distraction.*

Both were fatal on the battlefield and the stakes would only be raised on the colony once he was limited to the laser blade. There could be no room for distraction, hesitation, or preference when he was placed on even footing with the heretics, and it would be apparent to them the moment that the terrifying red armor emerged from the canyons on the dusty planet's surface that it was a battle to the death. After all, every colonist knew what the arrival of the Called meant for their people. None would be left alive. Not unless they found another recruit.

"Forty seconds," the new commander yelled.

Nuri stood in unison with the rest of the Called and turned toward the exit hatches on either side of the shuttle.

Lord of All, he prayed as he performed a final check on his suit's internal systems, *be my blade and my resolve.*

The unease among his brethren was more pronounced now that they were forced to arm themselves for the surface. Few of them looked confident gripping the laser blade, and the others seemed to go out of their way to avoid glancing down at the weapon to make sure their fingers were ready to press the activation switch. Thanks to the winding canyons on the planet's surface and the heavy, blinding wind, they would drop nearer the settlement's perimeter this time around rather than landing miles off course and trekking across the rugged terrain. It was a welcome luxury, but it also necessitated that every system and weapon was ready to go before they exited the shuttle. Had the stubborn soldiers avoiding the slightest acknowledgement of their blades truly been unfazed by the switch from blasters, they would have dutifully checked the power cells on the weapon to ensure it functioned properly when they engaged the enemy.

"Ten seconds!" the commander shouted.

The hatches slid open. Violent wind swept through the confined shuttle, causing the magnetic locks on Nuri's boots to activate. It took a moment for his muscles to adjust to the sudden shift in control from his body to the spacesuit, but he adapted quickly and assumed his place in line.

This wasn't his first cleansing.

"Drop!" the commander ordered.

The Called soldiers threw themselves out from the shuttle in practiced synchronicity with Nuri third to fall.

Lord of All, be my blade and my resolve.

The wind smacked into his suit as soon as he exited the shuttle. After the initial disorientation from the change of direction subsided, he activated the inertial compensators in his suit and triggered maneuvering thrusters to steer toward his drop target.

"Six seconds to impact," his suit informed him.

He'd expected a shorter drop based on how close the surface of the planet had appeared from the shuttle, but he'd neglected to account for the gale-force winds resisting his descent which forced him to alter course several times.

"Two seconds..." the suit belatedly alerted him.

The artificial voice didn't have a chance to finish before impact, but Nuri hadn't needed the reminder anyway. He'd been through this all before.

But not the killing, he thought as he rolled into contact and allowed his suit's equalizers to cushion the rest of his fall. *Not like this.*

"Reassemble," the commander's voice sliced into the eerie helmet silence. Once the sounds of the hurricane were blocked out, the haphazard trajectories of the windswept vegetation and the overall violence of the surface was a peculiar contrast to the peaceful atmosphere within Nuri's combat suit.

Distraction, he cursed inwardly.

On this mission more than any other, he couldn't afford to let his thoughts stray to his physical environment. The corporeal universe was not a godly one. Beauty and substance were both illusions, and if he allowed himself to be stirred by the terrible majesty of the colonial planet, he wouldn't react appropriately when confronted with the death-stares of the heretics slain by his laser blade.

Will you hear them scream?

His grip tightened on the weapon's hilt and he forced the girl's voice away again. How could she reach him so far across the galaxy, he wondered?

It's not important.

He stepped into the third position of the single-file line and his squadron promptly began their march through the winding canyons. None among them acknowledged the weapons on their hips, not even to make sure the environment hadn't caused any unforeseen malfunctions. The oversight in tactical procedure troubled Nuri, but like the others, he said nothing.

"One hundred meters," the commander's voice boomed over his suit's comm link. "You know what to do."

They reached the end of the canyon where the ground opened out into a wide plain. One by one, the soldiers fanned out until their line stretched one hundred meters. Nuri was the third Called soldier in from the right.

"Activate weapons," the commander said.

He thumbed the switch on the hilt of his blade, careful to give his squad-mates a wide berth to avoid injuring them with friendly fire.

Will you feel the heat of their blood?

His jaw clenched and his stomach churned.

Will you hear their screams?

"They have sentries," the commander warned.

Nuri glanced at the watchtowers on either side of the settlement's entrance and found the blue light of sniper scopes strafing across the line of Called soldiers. Evidently, the sentinels themselves were awaiting orders or simply unsure how to proceed. Fighting the Called was a hopeless endeavor, of course, and those who laid down their weapons to accept their fates were considered amply purified in the eyes of God, but many colonists saw the Duri as ruthless tyrants and would sooner fight to the death than acquiesce. The shock of seeing the armored death-dealers on their planet must have thrown the people into frenzy from the top down.

It will be like slaughtering pigs in a pen, Nuri thought. The comparison reminded him of the pig farmer he'd slain in the mountain village, however, momentarily diverting his focus.

Will you hear their screams?

"Steady," the commander said.

Lord of All, be my blade and my resolve.

"Don't let them see you flinch."

The sniper scopes suddenly disappeared. Nuri immediately braced himself to track the incoming bullets from his faceplate's holo-display.

"They're coming," a female voice whispered over the comm line.

Nuri shuddered at the sound. Only the commander had spoken over that frequency since they'd departed the warship orbiting the planet. Truthfully, he hadn't expected to hear anyone besides their leader at any point in the mission. The cleansing was straightforward enough aside from the wrinkle of using a brand-new weapon on the killing floor, but it was that very wrinkle which negated the need for open communication during the mission. When employing blaster rifles and air strikes, it was necessary to check in with the rest of the squadron to ensure everyone had cleared the area before a blast or else to request covering fire while advancing your position. In hand-to-hand combat, all bets were off. The comm links were no more help than an extra day's worth of oxygen. Whoever was left standing in the heaps of corpses when it was over would be extracted and returned to their designated training planet.

Is it because her voice reminds you of me?

Before he could process the loaded suggestion, the first wave of bullets crashed into their line and his thoughts were silenced by the steady impacts in his chest and helmet plating. The suit was built to withstand a barrage of the conventional ammunition colonists purchased on the black market, but it was still difficult to concentrate with the incessant jolts as the rounds found purchase.

Lord of All, be my blade and my resolve, he prayed.

It took a great deal of will and concentration not to break into a sprint or at least increase his pace to rid himself of the maddening, concussive *pings* as soon as possible, but that was not the way of the Called. The cleansings endeavored as much to grow the legend of the supernaturally endowed warriors and discourage colonists from rebellion as they did to actually purify the offending heretics. Perception, therefore, was always paramount on the off chance that security nodes captured the massacre and transmitted before the settlement was destroyed, or in case a few targets survived somehow and carried the tale to other worlds. If he were to break formation and rush the city gates, it would lead to lashings from his Duri Master at the very least and public execution at the worst. Although Nuri had overcome most of his battle-nerves through the years, he still needed to remind himself of the consequences for recklessness each time he dropped in heretic country.

"Ready blades," the commander said.

The Called soldiers raised their weapons in unison and held them at the ready. The gates were still a long way off, but a defense force had assembled beneath the watchtowers for a charge. As Nuri watched, three-dozen armed men and women shrieked at the top of their lungs and rushed toward the line of Called soldiers.

"No matter what happens, hold formation," the commander told them. "You are not individual soldiers. You are the Called."

Nuri suppressed a shudder. He struggled to likewise contain the adrenaline-rush triggered by watching dozens of enraged heretics charging toward him with weapons blazing, determined to kill him and all other Called soldiers where they stood, but his vital-signs assured him that his attempts at self-control were unsuccessful. He was ready for the kill. His battle instincts were kicking on full blast, and no matter how much he tried to convince himself otherwise, he craved the rush. He enjoyed the power he felt when he extinguished the life of a rebellious offender of the faith, although he'd never looked a victim in the eye and watched as terror overtook them and their life-force floated into the ether on its way to Tscharia.

Will you feel their souls leave their bodies?

He supposed it was that same powerful satisfaction that drove the Duri Masters' need for expansion after years of ordering the deaths of all opposing them in the fragile colonies. They had to feed their addiction.

It's no longer about spreading the word of God to them, the alien voice inside his head persisted. *It's about power. It's about comfort. It's about control.*

Nuri clenched his jaw and tightened his grip on the hilt of the laser blade. The heretic horde was twenty meters away and closing. In a matter of seconds, he would be forced to take a life up close again, something he hadn't done since slaying the pig farmer in the village.

Will you falter?

The readings on his faceplate began to prioritize targets and track the movements of each colonist so it could alert him to imminent danger.

Is this how you serve your god?

"Calm and swift," the commander said.

Lord of all, be my blade and my resolve.

A bearded hulk of a man in a patchwork atmosphere-suit charged with a seemingly endless stream of bullets preceding him. Each slug pinged off Nuri's armor without incident, but the red alarm-glare appeared in the upper right corner of the holo-display on his faceplate. He couldn't take much more abuse without system malfunctions spreading in his suit, especially at such close range. The armor was built to withstand a lot of damage, but two hundred bullets—archaic or otherwise—tended to take their toll.

And I haven't even killed one of them yet.

Considering many of his brethren were in the same boat, he thought there was a decent probability that the excursion might be just as ill-fated as the disaster with the apostate commander.

I can't worry about that now.

The heretic's eyes were wide and bloodshot, his lips cracked beneath a lunatic smile and second-hand rebreather, but with one dodge and a swift upward thrust, Nuri opened his innards to the harsh winds howling through the canyon. It was easier taking the first life with the blade than he'd thought it would be, but he also hadn't truly stared into the man's eyes as the blade found purchase and gutted him. The poor soul's intestines plopped onto the sand before he even had a chance to curse Nuri's name, as victims of Duri retribution so often did. By then, Nuri had already moved on to the next target that his suit designated for him. The woman it deemed the greatest immediate threat to him and the rest of his squadron.

Pieces of living creation reduced to a hierarchy of threat, and a little bit of the Divine killed with each fallen being.

Nuri winced as the woman caught him with a barrage of assault rifle bullets just above the collarbone, but he'd already severed the weapon in two by the time the pain registered and then crashed into her shoulder-first, driving her beneath a stumbling mass of enraged locals. She quickly slipped towards the back of the line, out of his reach, but didn't return to the city. Nuri lost sight of her as the first wave of pain in his shoulder hit.

Can you taste their fear?

He frowned and calmly dodged another strafing rifle as he surveyed the damage through a system check.

This is all wrong.

The shock absorbers on his suit were beginning to fail, and that was troubling. He shouldn't have felt the impact at all beyond a light tap. In most cases, primitive bullets were supposed to be as insignificant to a Called soldier's armor as insects hitting the viewport of a shuttle.

They must have modified the rounds.

Even with such a persistent stream of gunfire, the Called line should have held better than it was.

Are we going to lose this battle? he wondered.

"Pick it up!" the commander screamed over the comm.

Nuri sliced cleanly through the two nearest colonists, still carefully avoiding eye contact lest he lose his composure or resolve, then moved on toward the city gates.

There will be children inside, the taunting voice reminded him.

He held his breath as one of the colonists attacked from behind and dragged him to the ground. Two others joined the effort, pinning him to the surface while the first scrambled to activate the release switch on Nuri's helmet. If they managed to break the seal, he was a dead man. Even if he somehow managed to survive the toxic wind and the mission was a resounding success, it would show in his suit's automated report that he'd been exposed to the atmosphere during the battle, and that represented abject failure in the eyes of the Duri Masters. Without any other punishment, the inevitable exclusion from his chance at the trials carried enough shame to be considered a fate worse than death.

Lord of all, be my blade and my resolve.

A fourth colonist joined the party, then a fifth knelt on his shoulders so he couldn't raise his arms. Nuri could no longer see anything but the tainted sky and the mess of limbs struggling to keep him down. He felt the twist and tug of the original attacker's probing fingers and knew it would only be a matter of moments before he located the emergency release button and his life was forfeit. Panic predictably took hold and he cried out, thrashing against the smothering weight of five heretics and managing nothing but an increase of internal temperature. What surprised him was the emergence of a separate peace beneath that heavy layer of shock and panic. A sense of relief. A sense of going home.

Can you taste your fear? Do you feel your soul leaving your body?

At last, common sense reasserted itself and Nuri took a deep breath. His suit had an electric shock built in as a last defense in case the situation escalated to a worst-case scenario.

Like this one.

All he had to do was trigger the charge with a single word.

"Purge," he said with a faltering voice.

A tremendous pulse surged from his armor plating accompanied by a brilliant, electric-blue light. The four colonists who had pinned him beneath their collective weight were thrown against the city gates while the fifth collapsed dead on the spot, his hands still searching for the elusive release on Nuri's helmet. The man's cheek pressed against Nuri's faceplate, eyes wide and bloodshot from the shock of death. His flesh sizzled, and even with the barrier between his heated corpse and Nuri's nose, the stench of burnt hair and skin filtered into the atmosphere of his suit.

Do you smell his death? the voice asked. *Do you feel the weight of his life?*

Nuri stared into the dead man's eye with mounting horror. He *could* see the soul leaving its body, he decided. It slackened jaw muscles. It vacated the whites of the eyes. It froze the expression in perpetual un-being.

This is how we all will be.

And then another Called soldier kicked the corpse off him.

"Get up!" the commander screamed.

Nuri leapt to his feet and rejoined the battle. The heretic line had broken while he was down. Their careless use of ammunition out of heroic fear had depleted their reserves and the rest of the colonists had retreated into the settlement.

The rest, therefore, was easy. Everything except the nightmares.

19

The world around them shifted. Suddenly, Nuri stood at the end of a long stone corridor with his laser blade in one hand and a severed head in the other.

The Evil One, he realized, glancing down to see his muscles, bones, and pulsing veins were cloaked in the same blue-white glow he'd so often beheld in Colt's natural form. His skin was slowly reappearing, too. It wrapped over his innards in opaque layers to overwrite the naked horror he'd become.

Everything is the same, he thought. The stone walls had the exact luminescence as when Colt first thrust him into the trials. *It's all repeating.*

The idea of reliving the grim realities of the vision quest threw him into despair. He could barely force his legs to move beneath him.

It is not the same, Colt clarified as he started down the hall toward the shadowed figure that awaited him. A Watchman, no doubt. Perhaps the same one who'd blocked his way at the start. *The events may not have changed, but your perception is different.*

Free of the distractions that would pull me from the truth, he agreed. *Free of illusion. Free of obfuscation. I have found total clarity.*

I am no longer human.

I am Hidria.

He held out the laser sword and tossed the severed head of the Evil One down the hallway.

"An offering," he said. "A bargain." He paused to reset himself. "Where will you take me?" he asked.

The hooded figure bent slowly to retrieve the head of the Evil One, carefully brushing blood and dust from the dead thing's horns. "By the end of this day, you will know the face of the Devil," the Watchman spat. "Not tricks. Not illusions. You will know what it means to have your soul ripped from your body before your eyes. You will see the agony of Tscharia."

Nuri stopped walking just as the corridor widened into a square. He nodded. "I've already seen my soul ripped from my body. It is happening right now." He held out his arms to display the blue-white glow emanating from his veins as new layers of skin continued to envelop him. "And I will never see Tscharia. Not as a corpse. I am Hidria now, and I cannot be unmade."

The Watchman squinted with rage. "We *kill* Hidria," he growled. He circled Nuri where the hallways intersected and motioned down a corridor bathed in darkness. Suddenly, Nuri was surrounded by a horde of the red-masked Watchmen. At least one blocked each hallway, and unlike the first time he'd encountered the wraith, there were no doors nearby he could use for escape.

"You no longer need to fear for your life," Colt said, appearing beside him in her physical form gripping a laser sword with an ornate hilt curved in the face of a pale horse. "You are *Hidria* now. You *are* fear." She pressed her back against his and ignited the weapon with an electric hiss that made his still-growing skin prickle from head to toe.

"I am Death," he said calmly, drawing back his blade.

The Watchmen cast their red masks aside ceremoniously, a gesture of extreme hatred among their kind considering the disfigurement and menace of their naked faces. All nine attacked at once.

Nuri and Colt reacted in turn and parried each blow from the Durakian steel employed by the guardians of the undead realm, not landing any kill strikes but repelling the first wave of attacks without overly exerting themselves. He could hear Colt's robe swish through the air with movements so graceful and abrupt that the Watchmen opposing her quickly withdrew to regroup.

"Can they kill us?" Nuri asked over his shoulder. He ducked beneath a swinging blade and kicked the legs out from one of the Watchmen, stabbing toward his throat but missing the mark when another wraith opened the new flesh surrounding the ribs beneath his left armpit.

He threw his head back in agony and cried out, rolling away from the raining blows that followed. He didn't have much time. The Watchmen wanted to finish him while he was on the ground. Pain was a black, rotting worm that dove between his ribs and spread its poison up into the base of his neck. It pulled greedily at his new knowledge and identity as though it existed solely to suck his life-force and convictions.

And it probably does, he thought.

He managed to kick off the wall separating two passageways just before three blades converged where his head had been, then used the adjustment in momentum to catapult to his feet with a backwards flip that nearly sent him crashing into Colt. Her peripheral senses alone prevented a catastrophic impact. She drove forward just before his feet connected with her, impaling one of the Watchmen against the stone wall and swirling around to decapitate another before he could parry the blow.

Colt inhaled deeply and crouched down. Her physical form began to disappear again, but she looked him dead in the eyes. "This is your battle," she said with more than a little regret. "I cannot intervene any further."

Nuri wanted to know why, wanted to plead with her that he was wounded and wouldn't be able to fight seven of the Devil's swordsmen on his own, but she was gone before the words formed on his lips and he had to duck beneath a vicious hack from a Durakian blade a moment later.

"Your witch is gone," the first Watchman snarled. "You'll bleed out long before we get a chance to take you to the corpse fields of Tscharia. But don't worry. Plenty of horrors await you in the Godless universe."

"No," he growled, twirling his blade derisively.

They all attacked at once. He parried, ducked, dodged, rolled, leapt, and hacked, but all he managed to do was survive without thinking through a sequence of moves. He could only react.

"What good is this?" he screamed, hoping Colt would hear him somewhere in the ancient temple and fly to his aid. He jumped and landed a kick square in the jaw of one of the wraiths while blocking a two-handed hack aimed at his throat but landed hard on the floor, barely managing to slide beneath a lethal jab. "I thought the Hidria were Peacekeepers. Like God!" he shouted again. "Why must I fight?"

Colt's emanation wavered to life over the shoulder of another Watchman, who unknowingly used the distraction to his advantage by striking Nuri just below the eye with the hilt of his black blade.

"No one said you *need* to fight. You can always surrender."

Nuri tasted acid in his mouth instead of the coppery blood he was accustomed to. The distraction proved costly yet again as another Watchman stabbed him through the leg before he could swing his laser blade to deflect the blow.

He wanted to scream but held his tongue, knowing his agony would only give the keepers of the corpse fields greater satisfaction in victory. Instead, he staggered to his feet and sought refuge against the wall, where the Watchman that Colt had slain was still pinned down with melted stone settling into his gaping wound.

"What is the point of this?" he demanded as he hacked savagely at the seven advancing Watchmen. It was a graceless press. He threw all his weight into each blow, expending unnecessary energy but also managing to catch one of the creatures off guard. He separated from the parry and swung around to tear the wraith in two just above the waist.

Six, he thought with satisfaction.

Then he saw the black emptiness where the blade had skewered him below the knee and his stomach turned sour. The blue-white skin that shrouded Colt had consumed him now, but the spots where he'd been touched by the blades of the Watchmen were black with rot. *And they'll never return to normal,* he realized. *No matter what form I take, their mark will always be there. I'm tainted.*

"We *all* are," Colt said.

The six remaining Watchmen removed their cloaks simultaneously and grinned a challenge beneath their yellow, soulless eyes.

Nuri growled and started swinging wildly before they had a chance to coordinate an attack. Fighting for survival was a whole new experience compared to the remorseless slaughters he'd grown accustomed to as one of the Called.

I'm failing, he thought. *I should have more control of my actions and emotions. Violence against God's creation is an affront to His Holy Name.*

"Violence is sometimes necessary," Colt countered, watching as he stabbed a Watchman through the stomach and flipped sideways over the next. The wounded wraith didn't drop but he favored his left side where the laser sword had pierced him, and Nuri mercilessly struck at the advantage. "It's the same paradox I mentioned earlier."

"You said destruction of any part of God's creation was destruction of God Himself," Nuri grunted, blocking two blades at once and driving both demons back with a roar. "*All* violence is evil, then. It is *all* sin. Even against servants of the Evil One." As if to accentuate the point, he drew the blade over his shoulder and whistled it down at the exposed back of a reeling Watchman. He used all the force he could muster in close quarters while staying mindful of the other wraiths.

"That is not wholly true," Colt said. One of the Watchmen hissed and swung his blade through her, but it had no effect on her emanation. Just as she wasn't able to physically intervene against the creature while straddling the two cosmic realities she inhabited, they couldn't touch her, either. "We cannot know God's mind. It is entirely possible that He created certain elements and adversaries to *strengthen* our faith. To force us to contemplate the deepest recesses of our being and respond to His call to return home."

"He *created* Tscharia knowing that some of His creation required eternal separation from Him. Suffering for predetermined sins they had no choice but to make." Nuri bent backward as a blade stabbed for his head, then completed a backflip to avoid another that sought to undercut him at the same time. He felt the landing all the way through his bones, and that worried him. It meant he was still vulnerable so long as he was in his physical form, and he didn't yet know how to jump in and out of realities the way Colt seemingly did. After everything he'd endured to become Hidria, though, he refused to allow himself to die so near the final Divine Revelation. His own personal apocalypse.

"A paradox, surely," Colt agreed. "One we cannot understand with our limited perception, except to say that Omega has committed to loving us enough to imagine free will, and we are the ones responsible for corrupting it, not He. Yet even Hidria do not know *everything* about God." She wove her way between the five remaining Watchmen—four a moment later, when Nuri at last hacked diagonally through the chest of the one he'd stabbed in the arm—and stood directly in front of him, blocking his view of the wraiths. "There are reasons to fight, though," she said. "Such as limiting the suffering of others by wiping out the disease at the root of their misery."

A black blade split through her body and cut into Nuri's abdomen before he could dodge the point. He cried out and fell to his knees, holding his stomach as black blood spilled onto the floor.

"Even now," Colt continued unabated. "You can end your suffering through violence, and it would be a just end for your foes."

"Self-defense," he muttered, struggling to his feet and hopping back just in time to avoid a slice with the black blade that would have ended his life. "That's what you mean. Self-defense is permissible." He scoffed bitterly as he parried successive blows from two of the wraiths, who it seemed could no longer see or hear Colt. "Then Omega has no better justice system than the courts of Man."

Colt shook her head sadly while Nuri shouted and went on the offensive yet again, clutching his stomach as blood dribbled onto the stone floor. "You still don't understand. It's *not* self-defense. It's sacrificing some of your purity and goodness for the good of others. It doesn't matter what form it takes so long as the one performing the sacrifice has a broader perspective of the action's ramifications. That is why only Hidria are capable of purveying Justice and Truth in the galaxy. Not solely because their form gives them superior combat intuition and abilities, but because humans and humanoids are not possessed of souls capable of understanding the essence of the universe."

As she moved toward him again, Nuri backed away, sensing another surprise attack from the Watchmen while she distracted.

"What *is* the sacrifice, then?" he demanded. He limped dramatically. He knew he couldn't last much longer against the four of them. He simply didn't have the strength, and the Watchmen were formidable foes, indeed. Their prowess was the scourge of peoples throughout the galaxy for a reason, although Nuri supposed the Called had committed far more atrocities in their short history than the Watchmen in that same period of time.

"The sacrifice is of your selfhood. You must be willing to die for those you do not know, even for those who have let the Evil One twist their hearts and minds."

Nuri caught a swift jab from the nearest Watchman and spun off nimbly enough to bury his laser blade in the creature's back. The hideous wraith collapsed to the floor with black bubbles frothing from his mouth, gasping for breath.

"You must be different than them," Colt continued, gesturing toward the dying Watchman and the three that remained. "You must only kill those things which will cause substantial suffering to the galaxy, not those who seek to offend the Divine Infinite with words, ceremonies, or preferences. They are all innocent in His eyes because it is their human lack of comprehension that prevents them from knowing God and seeing the Truth of His ubiquitous, omniscient presence. They cannot know the nature of Omega because they are utterly incapable of doing so. Why, then, should they be punished?"

Now that he understood the fundamental flaws of the Duri order, Nuri didn't believe people *should* be punished for dissidence, even if it came in the form of direct mockery of the Holy of Holies. But he was also tiring of the charade and specifically the performative nature of Colt's lectures. He was beyond weary of the trials and couldn't understand why she chose to prolong his suffering and prevent him from gazing on the face of his Creator at last. The supplemental data, he thought, could be covered once his identity had been ascertained.

"Hidria kill with compassion, empathy, and humility based on their broader understanding of creation."

He danced away from two charging Watchmen and blocked the ensuing strike from the third.

"Do you understand now?" Colt pressed. "Do you see how it isn't *self*-defense? Do you see how trivial the perceived sins of Man are in the context of infinity? Do you see the responsibility you've been given?"

"Yes," Nuri grunted, shouldering one of the three Watchmen backward and spinning into a kick so powerful that he felt the creature's bones crack beneath his foot. Just as he raised his blade to finish the stunned demon, however, Colt sprang into action. Before he could process her movements, she twisted his arms behind his back and held his humming laser blade a centimeter from his throat.

"No," she said. "You *don't* understand. You are still like the Duri, trying to rid yourself of an inconvenient distraction." She withdrew the blade and stared solemnly into his soul. "*They* will show you what it means to sacrifice, though. They will show you the true meaning of misery so that you know how to recognize it and prevent it from infesting Omega before we all reach the endpoint and are reborn."

He began to mouth a protest, but she opened his chest with the laser blade before the words formed on his lips and threw him to the floor.

Gasping, he lurched against the wall, trying desperately to stay a step ahead of the Watchmen while his life fled through his stomach and chest.

"You destroyed me," he choked. "Why?"

One of the Watchmen grinned cruelly, then struck him hard with the hilt of his black blade, sending jolts of pain and broken synapses through Nuri's body.

"I told you," the first Watchman laughed, lifting his head by the hair and spitting in his eyes. "Before the day was over, you would see Tscharia."

Colt's form wavered and disappeared. He drifted into unconsciousness soon after. The last thought he had before the Watchmen dragged him roughly down the hall, cutting little triangles out of his back as they went, was that the Duri Masters had been right all along. The danger of the trials was falling victim to Colt's blade. He'd worried over it in the beginning and known not to trust her, but he'd let himself be diverted from the true nature of his mission.

Has it all been a lie?

20

On the morning of the trials, Nuri walked along the riverbank alone. It was a ritual he'd performed hundreds of times since he'd arrived on the mountaintop, but this walk was different, and not just because it began a full hour after he normally completed his route and returned to the cabin to start his lessons. It was different because he suspected it would be the last time he ever looked upon the surface of the river. There was no room for personal indulgence or reminiscence after one had answered the Lord's summons. If he succeeded in the trials, therefore, he would have no reason to visit the planet where he'd trained in the ways of the Called. The greater galaxy would be his proving ground and his sole occupation. Likewise, if he failed the trials and survived, he would be relocated to one of the Duri military facilities on a staging world and aggressively expand the reach of the Duri Order until he outlived his usefulness, or until an enemy blaster outlived it for him. Either way, his training was complete as of that morning. His life as he knew it was over.

One final visit.

In another hour, he would enter the sacred temple on the forbidden mountain. A host of attendants in ceremonial garb would escort him from the main chamber to a crypt in the deepest recesses of the mountain where he would lay across a cold, stone altar. A series of sterilizing fluids and opiates would be inserted intravenously at strategic points in his forearms and brainstem. After that, his vision quest would begin in earnest beneath the watchful eye of his Duri Master. A bittersweet watch, to put it mildly. It was to be their last spiritual journey together before Nuri was transformed and a new recruit was brought in for the Duri Master to break.

And then I will be Hidria, he thought.

And what if you fail?

He frowned and crouched beside the flowing water to hear its taunts more clearly, but he was not deterred. In the years that the river girl's voice had dwelled within him, he'd grown accustomed to the challenges arising from the depths of the cold water. His walks were undertaken as much to center his conscience towards her objectivity as it was to purify it, and hers was the only voice of dissent in his life. Her ideas mostly made him uncomfortable, occasionally angered him, and almost always directly contrasted with his deepest-held beliefs, but they were refreshing in their own way. Though he never would have admitted as much to the Duri Masters lest they deemed him weak of faith and prone to undue acts of mercy to the unworthy, he considered it important to have some experience with the humanizing aspects of the heretics if he were to fully understand them. His Duri Master had always warned about the dangers of viewing the cleansing victims as anything more than direct threats to the Divine Infinite, but Nuri thought he would be a blind soldier indeed if he didn't recognize the strengths and weaknesses of his enemy, and he saw no merit to blindness in combat. Understanding may have creaked open the door to doubt in more than one Called soldier through the years, but Nuri didn't see how it could be avoided if he wanted to survive.

The Duri Masters do not understand the way you do. They do not look their victims in the eye as they perish, and when they do, it's after the souls of the heretics have begun their journey to the Omega Point.

Nuri shook his head. *No,* he said firmly. *Not to the Omega Point. After they've begun their journey to Tscharia.*

The condemnation had once been nothing more than reflex while his mind was still in the process of molding to the Duri teachings, but now he truly believed the sentiment behind them. All enemies of Holy God were bound for Tscharia, and all enemies of the Duri were enemies of Holy God.

"And how do you distinguish between friend and enemy? Where is the space for innocence in between? Shouldn't there be a spectrum even in the strictest of religious laws?"

"There is no in-between. There is no spectrum and there never will be. If you are not for us, you're against us."

The girl sat beside him on the riverbank and touched her naked toes against the surface of the water. "What has become of you? You once questioned the Duri teachings. You rebelled against their hypocrisy. By any definition, you were against them. Should you have been killed outright for your unbelief?"

Anger stirred beneath the perpetual stoicism he affected when his face was exposed, but he'd come to expect the emotion whenever he engaged the girl, who was no longer truly a girl. Sometime during his own journey from an angst-ridden boy to a devout servant, she'd transformed into something else entirely. A woman, surely, but more than that as well. She no longer even approximated a human entity in physical dimensions. She was a specter.

Nuri said nothing.

"How do you gauge the threat level of a child in these heretic colonies to the will of God?" she asked.

He exhaled slowly and stared into the water. "Nothing can threaten the Divine Infinite, least of all a child."

"Then what is the purpose of the cleansings? If no one can threaten God, then what to God is the dissent of a flea? What are you killing for if not the Divine Infinite, who requires no help from creatures like yourself?"

Again, Nuri said nothing. He had learned better than to address every provocation she threw in his direction. Therein lay the path to his Duri Master's crisis of faith through *The Divine Incendiary*, he knew, a failing which was more and more difficult to turn a blind eye toward as his adherence to Duri law grew stricter. Someday, he would no doubt be forced to reveal his Master's weakness if the sin persisted, but he hoped he would be beyond the reach of such trivial matters by then.

No sin is trivial in the eyes of God, he thought.

Somewhere far beyond the veneer of radical ideology slathered over his conscience, the rebellious Nurisarma wondered how that could be true since all men and women were sinners by nature.

Are we all bound for Tscharia, then?

Where is the redemption in that?

"How can men decide what offends God? How can men deem the minutiae of colonial law a direct threat to the omnipresent influence of the Divine Infinite? If the existence of conflicting ideologies so offended His delicate ego, would He not eradicate the threats Himself?"

"He *does* eradicate those who offend His Holy Name."

"*He* doesn't," the specter insisted. "*Men* do."

"His Called warriors," Nuri agreed. "Men and women charged with the sacred task of purifying the galaxy so it may be reborn."

The specter rose from the riverbank and stepped into the water again with her back turned. She waded deeper as he watched her go. "This will be the last time you see me this way, so please listen and understand. The Divine Infinite cannot be threatened nor offended by beings like you. These are constructs of Man." She glanced once over her shoulder. The electric blue glow of her pupils made him shudder, which was no small feat given his training. "If you believe in an entity capable of creating all things in all realities, then you cannot possibly believe such a being would be susceptible to the spears and bullets these so-called 'heretic' colonists hurl at you. It is *your* ego and *your* doctrine which prevents the unification of the galaxy. Man cannot purify any space or any soul, only the Divine Incarnate, but communion is another matter."

Nuri said nothing. She waded deeper into the water until only her glowing eyes showed above the surface. In another moment, she would be nearer the shore of the forbidden mountain than his seat on the riverbank and her words would be swallowed by distance.

"You can only be purified through utter transformation, and you can only be transformed through knowledge of God and the universe. Remember during your trite ceremony that you cannot accomplish anything but through surrender, and if you do, you may find your path regardless of the meddling ego of Man."

Trite?

Nuri rose and angrily cast a stone into the shallows. "Your heresy goes too far," he growled, emboldened by the solemnity of the trials and his own pride at being chosen for the vision quest to find God at the heart of reality.

She smirked maddeningly and floated back in his direction. "I ask again, what to God is heresy? Who decides what constitutes a threat to the Divine? Would you kill me for mere words spoken with a human tongue? Wouldn't destroying a creature into whom God Himself breathed life run counter to His interests?"

"You speak beautiful nonsense. Leave now before I'm forced to turn you in to the tribunal. There is no truth in your poison."

"Only because your understanding of God and religion is limited to absolutes. Like the Duri, you've falsely intertwined religious institution and politicking with reality, and that leaves no room for the interstitial space where knowledge of the Beginning and End dwells. What to the Divine Incarnate is the method of worship and thanksgiving? Is it worth killing over?"

She floated toward the forbidden mountain again. Her form began to dissipate before his eyes.

"What, to God, are the Duri?"

He waded into the shallows himself, desperate to catch her before she disappeared so he wouldn't be left with the sickening rot of doubt pooling in his heart, but he couldn't bring himself to speak. Once again, she had left him devoid of argument.

"The Duri are human, and like all humans, they cannot know God. We are all corrupted by a lack of His perfect context." Her form was little more than a whisper on the wind, a slight discoloration in the morning sunbeams, but her voice was as strong as ever. "To survive the trials, to know God, you must not be human."

Hidria, he thought. *I must be Hidria.*

By the time he opened his mouth again, she was gone.

Nuri said nothing. Instead, he returned to the cottage in silence and prepared himself for the death of his old life.

21

For a while, he simply floated through space.

He had the sensation of being dropped down a long flight of stairs, passing out of the turquoise luminescence of the ancient temple into a pit of darkness which gradually changed from black to red to orange, and then his consciousness, his sense of self, expanded over nebulae in the heart of deep space. He felt his brain flex again. His skull struggled to keep pace with the rapid growth but fell miserably short. From beyond himself, he watched his head burst open from the strain and expose the pulsing gray matter beneath. The pain was extreme but the clarity that accompanied the expansion was equally formidable.

Has it all been a lie? he asked, again hoping that Colt would respond.

But he was alone in the endless vacuum, doomed to spend eternity in a state of simultaneous expansion and separation.

Not eternity, he realized, focusing on the pull of his body. A force moving towards something greater. *Until we all reach Omega.*

He wasn't exactly sure what that meant but he knew it was true. He felt it at the very core of his being. He was no longer bogged down by the constraints of human comprehension or the necessity for an explanation of the impossibility of eternity, of an entity with no beginning and no end. For the first time in his life, he truly realized a critical component of knowledge was not necessarily the retrieval of facts but the mysteries and questions themselves. Every aspect of creation would always be a mystery to some extent regardless of data and context. Yet another paradox of the Divine, he supposed. He could experience the perfect context of the Almighty and *still* not know everything there was to know about reality.

That must be why there are so many interpretations of the scriptures, Nuri thought.

He felt the pleasant tug of his new form toward the Omega Point, where everything past and present would be reborn at the end of the universe. He'd always felt that pull at his heart, sending shivers down his spine in small moments when he reflected on the existence of a Divine Infinite, but the sensation had never been as strange or invigorating as it was right then. It was the total reconciliation of intuition with genuine knowledge. For millennia, the expansion of the universe had been considered the indefinite precursor to the slow death of all planets, but now he knew the truth.

The Second Coming, he reflected, then felt the enormity of the phrase which stretched far beyond even his advanced mental capacity as a reborn Hidria.

Colt's face wavered before him in the blackness of space, then exploded into dust. "And you will soon see why His return will change all things," she said. "You'll see how far His Word has reached, to every corner of every universe and everywhere in between, yet still misinterpreted over and over into bloodshed, oppression, and all manner of evil." She shimmered in the starlight and danced through a gas cloud.

The Great Colt appeared before him once again, but her face was now a rotting skull with maggots crawling through her eyes and mouth.

This is how we all must appear in the eyes of God, he thought.

It was a whole new universe open to his mind, and he needed only to endure this peculiar cosmic suffering to attain it. A trial more terrible than any battlefield or enemy dungeon imagined in the most perverse minds of the troubled galaxies. A sonic prayer emanating from his cries of agony, and hoping that the God of the universe would not turn a blind eye (or rather, ear) to him in his time of need.

"Then show me," he said.

Her maggot-filled mouth curled into the wicked grin of the first Watchman, and then he was suddenly stretched out in an X on two intersecting pillars with nails pinning his wrists and feet. His shoulders slouched forward, slowly breaking him with his own weight, and his forehead was opened with pincers.

Crucifixion, he realized, crying out in agony when his weight began to violently drag him toward the foot of the pillar-cross and his appendages slipped further into the nails.

He was on a dead planet emanating a dull-orange heat haze, surrounded by thousands upon thousands of aliens of all conceivable constitutions. Each one was in the throes of crucifixion. The flatlands between two short, barren mountains were filled with their screams.

"The Great Sacrifice," Colt proclaimed. She stood at his feet between the three remaining Watchmen, who were now resplendent in full ceremonial armor with the red, wooden masks that identified them as the Devil's Honor Guard. They were larger in stature in their own realm and—against all odds—far more terrifying. Nuri was further dismayed to see that the other six Red Masks that Colt and he had slain in the ancient temple were still alive, tending to the hapless souls condemned to suffer excruciating deaths for all eternity.

Which meant he could only be one place in all the universes. The one place distinctly separate from God.

"Tscharia," the first Watchman grinned, jerking a spear from the stomach of an insect-like alien in the row across from Nuri. He examined the tip of the blade theatrically, attempting to fill Nuri's heart with dread and thereby summon the screams in his heart. The screams and hopelessness that fed the damned and the stewards of the corpse fields, in other words. Nuri was already filled to the brim with agony and terror, however, even though he finally understood the necessity of the macabre spectacle.

The other two Watchmen from the temple stood on either side of the cross and stripped him naked, brandishing whips they'd left in the acid trenches beneath each crucifix and flicking them at his leg to make him squirm deeper into the nails. His weight drew him further and further down.

"You are not Hidria," the first Watchman mocked. "Hidria cannot be killed so easily." He laughed maniacally and the other two started whipping him with the hooked, acidic tips on cue.

"AAAAAGGGGGHHHH!" he screamed, gasping for breath.

The pain was white-hot electricity in his brain mixed with the feeling of black infection. Tscharia's atmosphere dug into his soul through his bodily wounds with its poison. He wouldn't last long.

"This is what He endured," Colt said calmly as the Watchmen took turns whipping him. "This is the final piece of His perfect context. This is the ultimate lesson He teaches about empathy."

The Watchmen whipped with greater intensity. Under any other circumstances, Nuri would have been either dead or unconscious, but Tscharia did not allow for such conveniences among its prisoners, nor would his body go into shock and numb his pain receptors while they were torturing him. He would simply have to endure.

"He came to Earth and told us that the greatest directive of Omega is empathy. To love your neighbor as yourself. And then He demonstrated the *greatest* empathy, to lower Himself to a corporeal form and experience a despicable death at the hands of those limited by their opinions on the mind of God. To free us. To save us. To teach us the same empathy, and that we do not know better than the Divine Infinite."

The Watchmen took their black blades and made small incisions in his stomach, then flung acid over his skin. Nuri screamed and began to weep.

"All of these creatures," Colt continued, unperturbed, "are the Divine Incarnate. He has lowered Himself to the forms of each of these alien species and redeemed them through His blood the same way that He did on Earth. Through that sacrifice, He has achieved the ultimate empathy. The ultimate context. The ultimate knowledge of every brand of fear and agony."

The first Watchman lifted a massive axe from the ground and regarded it distractedly before his attention was pulled away by commotion a few rows over. Nuri glanced in that direction and saw a few blurs of movement followed by what appeared to be weapons fire, but he was in too much agony to care.

"Now, you have empathized with Him," Colt said. She had crossed the aisle to his feet and wiped the blood from his shins with her robe. "Now you have the context of what He *endured* for the sake of His people, not what He *inflicted* the way that the Duri do. He willingly fell into the depths of Tscharia and redeemed all, and He will return to do the same when the universe reaches the Omega Point."

The first Watchman heaved the mighty axe over his shoulder and brought it down onto Nuri's thigh, separating his right leg and causing him to slip further still. He could no longer breathe. His lungs were collapsing.

"The Duri have not experienced this sacrifice. Their doctrine is motivated by their own conceptions of right and wrong and increasing their strength, not by the message of the Divine Infinite."

The first Watchman groaned in delight and brought the axe crashing down again, this time severing Nuri's left leg at the thigh. Without legs to support him, his body dropped and collapsed his lungs completely. His back was broken. The stumps below his waist spurted blood all over the ground, even covering Colt. She didn't flinch, though, and the Watchmen savagely lapped up his blood.

"Do you understand now?" Colt asked, stooping to grab a spear from the filthy ground.

You killed me, he thought at her, knowing he didn't have the breath in his lungs to articulate it aloud.

"As we all killed *Him*," she replied, gesturing toward the trillions of Messiahs in the corpse fields. "You understand His sacrifice, then, as much as is possible." She reared back with the point of the spear pressed against his ribcage. "The fundamental truth of the Hidria transformation is that you cannot be reborn unless you first die."

He lifted his head to look her in the eye and held her stare as she drove the spear forward into his chest.

"So, yes. I've killed you."

He was distantly aware of the Watchmen leaving his side as the commotion intensified several aisles over, and then his consciousness was sucked out of his body and he was rocketing through space again.

You are no longer human, Colt told him as he retracted all the way back to the Alpha Point on the desert planet. The first temple, built by God Himself to teach those who answered His Call. *You are Hidria*.

He closed his eyes against the fury of deep space and relished the lack of pain in his body.

I am Hidria, he declared.

And then, he was standing in the ancient temple again where he'd started, holding his own severed head in one hand and his laser sword in the other. Instead of the

Watchman at the intersection of hallways, though, Colt awaited him with a warm smile.

"You are here at last," she said. "You've completed the trials."

Her presence was startling. He'd seen her physical form before, but he realized then that it hadn't been her true incarnation. Now when he looked at her, he felt his vitality. No living being had ever been so *present* with him, and it made him tremble.

She stepped forward to meet him and gently took the head and blade from his hands, setting them on the stone floor and guiding him down one of the corridors.

"Now, you are ready to gaze upon the face of the Divine Infinite."

22

For a long while, they walked the labyrinthine corridors in darkness. Nuri said nothing. The experience of Tscharia had shaken him to the core and all human worries had been stripped from his consciousness as his old body melted away. He was awed by the new, complete form that had replaced him and could focus on little else but processing the sight of his new being. It was nearly unrecognizable. Where there wasn't scarring from the black blades of the Watchmen, his skin bore the same blue-white luminescence as Colt's, making him wonder if his eyes also glowed with the same unnatural, pupil-less vibrancy as her stare. Otherwise, his only concern was following his spirit guide through the darkness.

He would never know how long they traveled the snaking corridors, which often bent back on themselves the way that they had come and thereby destroyed any mundane sense of progress Nuri felt along the way, but he was comfortable in that unknowing. Perhaps the destruction of expectation was a lesson in itself, he thought. A dose of humility directly to his soul before he learned the Truth at the heart of everything.

As if the rest of the trials have not been humbling enough.

In truth, he couldn't remember a point in his life when he'd felt as insignificant as he did now that he'd been exposed to the complexities of his faith and the failings of his religion.

Is that the aim of all this?

He realized he might never know for sure and took solace in that ignorance. There were some things, he supposed, which fell outside the scope of Hidria understanding, and if that were true, it was probably that way for a reason. Even a transubstantiated being couldn't know all.

Only while humanity dwells within you, a voice told him. *If you were wholly transformed, you wouldn't have these questions. You would either know the answer or you wouldn't wonder because you would know it wasn't important.* He suspected Colt was addressing him as she observed his inner dialogue from the sidelines, but he was too distracted by the transformation to ruminate too deeply on the source of the unsolicited response anyway. It could have been God for all he knew and he wouldn't have recognized it in the moment.

And what if it is?

His fascination stopped short at the thought. All at once, the air became heavier. A high-pitched ring sounded off the close walls of the corridor. His skin prickled and a dizzying electricity sizzled in his veins. Colt, however, didn't seem to notice.

"Is *He* here?" Nuri asked after a beat. He felt the same shudder of Divine recognition he'd experienced in his old life only with a thousand times the potency. His mind was nearly crushed by the breath of creation filling the corridor. It was nauseating.

Colt glanced back at him and the totality of her being only heightened his wonder. "He is everywhere. Always." He gaped at her, waiting for her to expound for greater clarity, but she evidently had said all she wished to say on the matter.

Maybe I'm supposed to know without asking, he thought. *Maybe that's part of the final test. Seeing if I can block out all distractions to recognize the true voice and presence of God amid a sea of fantastic circumstances.*

With that, Nuri lapsed back into silence for a long time. He'd already been humbled by Colt's calm acceptance of the long journey through the temple and felt foolish for wondering about the location of the presence of God when— as Hidria—he should have been fully aware of the Divine's ubiquity. He knew the idea of it, of course, but confronting the reality of an omnipresent entity was another matter entirely. It was like the difference between knowing your human form would inevitably die one day and actually feeling a laser-blade slitting your throat. His soul had fallen into a state of hyper-reality. Hyper-awareness.

As they continued walking, the doors around them—all of which had remained closed to that point—finally revealed the realities contained within them. It was an unnerving change, most of all because he fully expected the environments to come crashing through now that they lacked a true barrier, unhinging the doors and unleashing cosmic chaos upon the corridor in the process. In some cases, no doors blocked the other worlds from spilling out at all, and those portals troubled him the most. The frames were little more than borders on moving pictures of universes Nuri had never dreamed existed.

And where do they all lead?

He studied each opening as they passed. It was disorienting to view such radically variant landscapes no more than ten feet from each other on either side of the hallway. Endless deserts on his left directly contrasted blizzards blown through the doorway on his right. Jungles rife with vibrant vegetation and bustling wildlife were paired with dusty plains and the coarse skin of giant monsters from another universe. Some doorways were submerged with a wall of deep ocean water and absurd aquatic creatures holding against an invisible barrier as though they didn't see the doorway at all.

They don't see it, he realized. *Even in the places where there are no doors to hold them, they can't see into the temple.*

Colt glanced back and followed his gaze to the open doors.

"This is how our emanations appear at any given point in a designated galaxy."

He frowned but continued to examine the doorways. "What do you mean by designated galaxy?" he asked.

Colt motioned to the nearest opening. "All Hidria are charged with protecting a specific galaxy. It helps us to keep total context within the constraints of our higher consciousness. Only God can oversee all galaxies and universes at once. We have been transformed—elevated—but there is still only one perfect being. Even now, after the transformation, you are still a sinner. Even now, you are limited by your flawed sensory perceptions."

"Are these doorways how you've tracked my progress through the trials?" he asked.

"Yes," she nodded. "But my true form remained here, waiting for you. When we pass through the doorways, we are merely emanations. To physically intervene, we still have to travel to the desired planet."

"You mean in a ship?"

Again, she nodded. "Just as the Divine Infinite traveled to Earth through the vessel of a human male, we must journey to our destination by corporeal means. Again, it's the only way to fully understand the ramifications of our intervention. By experiencing the scale of the universe, we understand the magnitude of our footprints upon it."

Nuri nodded, continuing to study the alternating worlds contained within each door frame. With each new galaxy they passed, he found himself imagining what lifeforms existed in their massive, spiraling arms and what it would be like to live as one of them. He was able to piece the histories together with remarkable clarity using his reborn consciousness, passing several years' worth of study among the native populaces in the time it took to cross one opening.

And then, at last, they reached a nondescript, wooden doorway at the end of the corridor.

"We've arrived," Colt told him. She stepped forward and tapped her index finger against the rough surface. "A human will die as soon as this door opened," she said, staring at him with eyelids narrowed to slits to drive home the implication. "Human minds cannot comprehend the fullness of reality on the other side. They would lose their sanity for a few moments and then their heart would stop completely." She moved behind him and placed her hands on his shoulder, standing on her toes to lean her chin against him. "It is the face of God," she whispered. Her lips grazed his earlobe and made him shudder.

All at once, the weight of the impending revelation came crashing down on him. His knees buckled and he fell prostrate before the door. "No," he groaned. "I don't want to see. I'm unworthy." He gulped back a moan. "I'm terrified."

But even as he protested, the door creaked open.

"Please!" he cried out, shielding his eyes with his forearms. He was suddenly convinced that he *wasn't* truly Hidria, that too much of his human doubts and ignorance remained to sufficiently process the vision of all things he was about to experience. It would be the end of him. He was certain of it. And on top of that, he would have defiled the perfect purity of God by laying his pitiful eyes upon Him.

He expected a furious blast of wind through the doorway followed by the melting of his physical form and banishment to Tscharia for daring to offend the sight of God. Instead, a silence enveloped the temple, powerful enough that it felt like his eardrums had inverted or else he'd gone completely deaf.

Keeping his arms locked in front of his eyes, he shouted to Colt, "What's happening?" He hoped his desperation would inspire pity and abort the catharsis before it was too late. It was a futile exercise, though. His words didn't penetrate the atmosphere. In fact, they didn't even register inside his head. There was nothing but silence everywhere.

Is this death? he wondered.

It seemed a startling absence coupled with the fullness of everything, and he wasn't certain what the conflicting realities meant for him. Still, he didn't dare open his eyes. He'd decided his only chance for survival was to avert his gaze from the face of Omega and hope his reverence spared him from judgment.

Omega judges all things gently and with perfect context, Colt's thoughts suddenly surfaced within him, not as a separate voice but as a part of himself. They were his own thoughts. Not merely occupying his mind but communing with it. *He is not a malevolent being or nothing would be left in your universe. If He were the god of the Old Book, every minor slight would have spurred His wrath to the point of complete decimation.*

Nuri crawled on his hands and knees toward the doorway, hoping to close the portal into the realm of God before it consumed him.

Now, Colt continued. *We open our eyes.*

No! he screamed inside his head, focusing all his mental energy into that solitary negation.

But Colt opened his eyes before he could will himself away from the door again.

No! Please!

Suddenly, he was in the middle of space staring into the enormity of everything with all universes surrounding him.

Please...

For a moment, the sensation was akin to what he'd felt when Colt transported him through the space between realities, and he realized that she must have been preparing him for this eventuality all along, with subtle glimpses of the Divine Infinite to flex his perceptions into the correct focus.

The trouble isn't finding the planet Prime, she explained. *It is in changing yourself so that you can perceive what exists there.*

He tried to calm himself against a swirling tide of voices and dark matter. Then, the spiritual rapture occurred. His personal Apocalypse. The Great Unveiling of Omega.

He is here, Colt gasped with an exhilaration unlike anything Nuri had ever heard. If he'd managed a word or thought in that instant, though, he would have sounded the same. Perhaps even more awed.

Small.

Helpless.

An explosion of light engulfed his thoughts, flooding images of all peoples and all histories and all suffering and all ecstasy in one spasmodic tremor of reality that shattered him into a trillion pieces and then rebuilt him in one breath. His mind and body were aflame, rotating in furious circles of sentience that drove him into a greater insanity than any human creature had known before him. The true nature of God. A history of all things back to the creation of Time and all universes in the Big Bang.

I SEE!

He hadn't known what to expect when and if he reached the Divine Infinite, but he'd imagined Omega as either a giant entity, a face as large as galaxies, or an eye gazing out on creation. This was different. It was all those things, and everything else, too. Even with his adapted Hidria mind, he couldn't process the information well enough to *begin* to articulate all he saw.

All of Creation. All of Time. Everything. Weaving in and out of his brain in complex algorithms he wouldn't satisfactorily decipher in a billion lifetimes.

Every aspect of his being was transformed. His perspective on every detail of his life and the lives of those around him.

You know what you must do, a voice thundered through his head, filling his exposed soul.

The light rapidly receded. Reality began to settle back into focus. The images rearranged themselves into comprehensible flashes until all he could see was Colt's face.

The Duri, she said as the ancient temple began to reform around him. *You must atone for your sins.*

I know now, he replied. *And I know why you are here.*

She smiled at him. They were alone in the ancient temple before the wooden door again, but the sense of that Other presence was still heavy and electric in the air.

"We are one," she said, taking his hand and pointing to the door.

Nuri nodded and rubbed his temples. His brain ached terribly but even that sensation was beginning to recede. All pain drained away again. When he looked down at his physical form, he saw that the faint blue-white glow had returned beneath his layers of skin.

"We are the first Hidria for a thousand generations, since long before the Duri began to use the trials," Colt proclaimed.

He knew it was true, of course, now that he'd been granted insight into the history of the Hidria and their sacred charge.

"All others have perished, but you will return. *We* will return."

The door began to open behind her and Colt's face morphed into a skull with writhing maggots filling her eye-sockets. She opened her mouth wide to devour him, and then the door flung open and the temple faded away.

23

"He's stirring," one of the Duri Master's attendants reported.

Disappointed, the Duri Master sighed and rubbed the crisscrossed scars on his cheeks in frustration. "Get the physician, then. We may need to treat wounds that won't appear until he's fully emerged from the vision."

"Yes, sir," the attendant bowed, then returned to the altar where Nuri's unconscious body was hooked to dozens of computers and IVs.

"You failed," the Duri Master muttered quietly enough so that the attendants wouldn't hear him. "Pride dwells in the tongue of the dead man." The words of *The Divine Incendiary* seemed to fit the situation since he'd been confident Nuri would pass the trials. Certain of it. Outwardly, at least. Nuri had been the most promising pupil in generations. One thing the Duri Master had learned about Nuri, though, was that his true thoughts were difficult to read. He suspected he'd carried many secrets in the years the two had shared a cottage on the mountain overlooking the village. Ones which would undoubtedly call his loyalty to the Duri Order into question.

It's too late to uncover them now, he thought. *But not many who enter the trials become Hidria. Almost none, for all that we know. He was doomed to fail before he started and it's a result of my poor example.*

Emerging from the sacred observation room, the Duri Master approached Nuri's body slowly. The convulsions would come soon enough, he knew, signaling his return from the trials and communion with the human reality. It was truly sad that Nuri had failed, he thought again. He'd had high hopes for the boy they'd taken from the pleasure planet Dublokee when he was young. After all, if Nuri had joined the Hidria, he would have been an invaluable political and spiritual asset to the Duri Master. He had no doubt Nuri would advocate for him to the Divine Infinite when his time came, no matter his fanatical research into *The Divine Incendiary* prior to its prohibition. God would forgive him that sin, for all men were born sinners and died sinners.

That's The Divine Incendiary *talking*, he realized, and quickly pushed the thought away. Sinners were to be abolished entirely, not forgiven. If he were ever to admit his transgressions, he would suffer the same consequences as those the Called cleansed on the rebellious planets.

As it should be, he thought dutifully, wary of the Divine Overseer who assuredly monitored his every thought to catalogue each sin. Once he reached his quota of acceptable transgressions, he knew the Called or Hidria would be sent to kill him. Judging by the way he'd lived much of the last decade, he figured they would be coming soon enough. He couldn't afford any additional outrages.

His mind was distracted by these worries as he reached the first step of the altar, hardly noticing the open, glowing eyes of the body lying before him. He was distantly aware of the doctor and a few attendants rushing through the chamber to reach the body and try to ease it back to consciousness before it went into cataclysmic shock. This was not of any concern to the Duri Master, however, since Nuri's life had already lost its purpose. Countless resources had been invested in him over nearly two decades, yet the order had nothing to show for it. He would be sent to the ranks of the main Called army and serve his term on the battlefield to atone for his sins, but he would die namelessly just like all other Called soldiers. If he was lucky, Omega would await him at the end of his toil, but it was more likely that he was bound for Tscharia. Grunts curried no favor with the Divine Infinite. They existed solely to keep blood off the hands of the Duri Masters who commanded them.

What wasted potential, he frowned.

It was a pity. Such a terrible tragedy. He couldn't imagine informing the tribunal of his Duri sect, who would undoubtedly blame him for wasting such a prodigious talent as Nuri by approving him for the trials before he was truly ready.

Forgive me, Lord, he prayed as he began the involved task of disconnecting the IVs linking Nuri's body to the trials through the Sacred Conduit: an opiate which was only available on one moon in all the explored galaxy. *It wasn't my fault.*

He reached to unclasp the mouthpiece regulating Nuri's oral reception of the sacred conduit, but a cold hand sprang up and stopped him short, gripping his wrist so hard that he felt the bones snap before he processed what was happening and who was responsible.

"Nuri!" he gasped. His eyes were wide with shock and confusion. After that, the pain was too sudden and severe to voice, so he merely gaped.

In one blur of movement, Nuri swung the Duri Master around by his wrist, twisting him until bones jutted out from his skin into a point.

"I am not Nuri," the entity on the altar declared. His voice was now two voices, the Duri Master noticed remotely. The familiar, male voice of Nuri and a female voice. "I am not human."

Then the glowing, blue-white creature that looked like (but was clearly not) Nuri drew the Duri Master in close so they both faced the onrushing doctor and his attendants. The creature tore the breathing apparatus from its mouth and a flood of cold breath prickled hairs on the Duri Master's neck.

"I am Hidria," the voices whispered.

The Duri Master's eyes widened in terror and recognition, and then the transformed creature jerked the protruding spikes of bone upward into his throat and out the other side. Blood splashed across the altar, drenching the holy relics that had been placed around it to remind the Called of their solemn occupation.

Hidria.

The Duri Master died instantly. His soul vacated his body before he even hit the floor and the Hidria watched it go with distant curiosity. It was the first time that the reborn entity had witnessed the departure of spiritual essence at the moment of death, and it saw merit in cataloguing the experience to understand the ramifications of its actions. And then, standing, the Nuri/Colt creature flexed its fingers and knocked the doctor and his attendants unconscious in a swirl of blue-white movement that was imperceptible to their human eyes. It dropped them ungently but ensured they survived.

The room was clear in a matter of seconds. The entrance to the ceremonial chamber stood wide open and unguarded, assuring safe passage through the facility up to the shuttle hangars. There was little need to heavily defend the altar room where the trials were initiated since all hostile forces would be detected well above the planet's surface and, failing that, long before they touched down on the forbidden mountain. In the event of an attack, the security forces in the upper levels of the military outpost would have more than enough time to assemble a defensive strike-team and bring down the heretics before they desecrated the holy site. The Called presence on the mountain was therefore formidable, but they were wholly unaccustomed to monitoring the altar room or scouring their own ranks for attacks. Such heresy was unfathomable to the Duri Masters once a warrior was deemed fit for the trials. To be chosen for unique service to the Divine Infinite only to spit in the face of the Creator was the ultimate blasphemy in the eyes of the Duri, and none schooled in the teachings of the sacred faith would dare risk such abject damnation. Nuri himself had trembled at the very thought of raising his hand to a Duri Master or a fellow Called soldier once upon a time, but that had been well before the transformation. Well before he'd gazed into the essence of God.

When it was finished, the Hidria retrieved its clothing and weapons from the preparation room, then scanned the datapad of the nearest attendant for directions to the main hangar from the ceremonial chamber. It knew where it was to go next without receiving explicit instructions, but now that it had returned to Nuri's physical body, it would need to physically journey to the destination or else it would be nothing more than an emanation in the galaxy.

The moons of Jupiter, it thought, still wrestling with the dual identities contained within its soul. *Purification. The Order's reach has grown far for them to risk an attack so near to Earth.*

A long way from the Duri corner of the galaxy, to be certain, but a place where the tribunal clearly believed they could make a grand demonstration of their might to the Crown government. If successful, a colossal war would break out between the fleet and the Duri, one which humanity could scarcely afford with their hold on the colonies tenuous as it was. Called soldiers had already been dispatched to the site, it seemed. They would take the solar system outpost by outpost until they reached Earth, starting with Pluto and the outer dwarfs.

But Hidria would be waiting when they got there, and it would only kill the wicked.

Hidria, it echoed.

Before long, it hijacked the transport shuttle Nuri had ridden to so many cleansing missions and set a course for Earth's Solar System.

I am not human, it thought one last time before drifting into meditative trance.

Colt.

The FTL drive roared to life.

We are Colt.

ABOUT THE AUTHOR

Joseph Williams is an author of science fiction, dark fantasy, and horror who lives in Farmington Hills, Michigan. He has previously released four short story collections and five novels.

Also by Joseph Williams

Novels

The Hunt
Bunyan Undead
Furnace
Pit
Stasik I: Origins
Stasik II: Parin
Stasik III: Harvest
Hallelujah: Exegesis of a Father's Suicide Note
Analytical: Death and Other Absurdities

Short Story Collections

Detroit Macabre
Swinging from Stars
Timbers of Fennario
Justify the Thrill

Essays

Ode: A Journal from Suicide Watch

www.ingramcontent.com/pod-product-compliance
Lightning Source LLC
Chambersburg PA
CBHW051417170626
46809CB00006B/2193